TANK

SEAL TEAM ALPHA

ZOE DAWSON

BLUE
MOON
CREATIVE
LLC

COPYRIGHT

ACKNOWLEDGMENTS

I'd like to thank my beta readers and editor for helping with this book. As always, you guys are the best.

To all the K9 handlers and their amazing warrior partners out there who do so much, endure so much...this one is for you.

Change is never easy, you fight to hold on, and you fight to let go.

Unknown

1

"Don't fucking tell me what to do." Tank stepped into the street thug using his considerable brawn, intimidation on him like biker leather. "My brothers and I aren't interested in your gang, your drugs, your freaking lifestyle. So take a hike. He couldn't even look at his brother's bruised and bloody face or his anger would get the better of him. If you ever touch Jordan again, even look at him sideways, I'm coming for you and you can kiss your ass goodbye. Comprende, pendejo? There'll be no quarter. No me jodas."

No me jodas. "Don't _fuck_ with me." He repeated in English. The memory from when he'd walked the mean streets of East LA as a tough kid boosted his adrenaline and grounded him. His adult life as a Navy SEAL wasn't much different. Protecting. Fighting. Demanding control.

Thorn "Tank" Hunt looked at himself in the mirror as he fumbled with the tie of the impeccable tuxedo. "Yeah, you're such a freaking badass," he said and laughed. Chitchatting with a bunch of wealthy donors while eating finger foods and drinking bubbly champagne wasn't really his style. He'd much rather wear his uniform to this shindig, even if the collar was stiff. His dress blues were like body armor. He wouldn't drop his guard for anything...or anyone. He wasn't named Tank for nothin'.

He was doing this for Dr. Alyssa St. James's charity, Military Working Dog Foundation. He and Echo, his MWD had been working with her ever since his younger brother Jordan, who worked at her vet clinic, had asked Tank to meet her two months ago. He'd dumped his iced coffee all down the front of her neutral blouse because he was too busy eyeing a sweet thing who had walked through the coffee house door.

They'd gotten off on the wrong foot, but it was evident from the first meeting attraction was flowing both ways.

Hell...the cause was worthwhile. After knowing her for two months and being part of the Dog and SEAL Show for her charity, it was clear to him this go-getter powerhouse was determined to reach her goal for this year. In addition to the fraternization issue, him being enlisted navy and her being an army reservist officer, there was the fact that Tank didn't want his apple cart upended. He swore softly. She was upending him every time they were in the vicinity of each other. Who was he kidding? She was constantly on his mind.

He didn't want any one woman on his mind, especially not one who had commitment and picket fence written all over her delectable body. But, there was also a driven quality about her he admired to go with her buttoned up and no-nonsense personality.

"Masquerade ball...hoo-yah," he mumbled, sighing as he tied on the ornate black mask. He was used to covering his face, but the one he wore for missions was definitely more ninja badass. He rubbed his chin, then lifted it. She'd asked him to shave. Ha! No way. The beard stayed whether she liked it or not.

He left the bathroom and slipped his feet into his boots. She wouldn't like them, but with the plain Jane way she dressed, she couldn't talk. They helped to balance out the namby-pamby mask.

Downstairs, he grabbed his keys and pulled open the door. Rebecca Dassault or as he knew her, Becca, stood there ready to knock. She was dressed as usual in shades of pink and looked like a little powder puff to his two hundred and forty pound, six four frame. They were friends with benefits and that was all. He'd met her at one of the SEAL bars where women hung out to snag a gunslinger. He'd had an on again, off again relationship with her, but since he'd met Alyssa, it had been more off. His excuse was that he was busy, and they hadn't found the right time to hook up. He wasn't going to read anything into it. No way, no how.

"Babe?"

"I was wondering if you wanted to hang out, but I can see you're busy." She gave him a slow once over and he smiled.

"Yeah, gotta take a rain check on that. I've got to go to this charity party for Military Working Dogs." He had to give her credit. She was cool as a cucumber and had never pushed him when he was busy. It's the only reason she'd lasted so long. Showing affection for him or trying to cling made him run in the other direction.

"Oh, that's a good cause. That's the only way anyone would get you to wear a tux and that mask."

"I know," he growled, stepping back as he closed and locked the door.

He headed for his vehicle in the driveway, and she said to his retreating back, "Call me later. I'll still be up."

He waved in a noncommittal way, still trying to tamp down the urge to crowd the buttoned-up Doc into a dark corner and getting up close and personal with her.

The drive over to The US Grant Hotel, located near the Gaslamp Quarter touted as the "Historic Heart of San Diego" with its Victorian architecture, was slow this time of night. He'd been here often with Becca as the lively neighborhood was a draw for the younger crowd with its clubs, dive bars, and cocktail lounges. With Balboa Park, the San Diego Zoo, Horton Park, museums, plenty of places to eat, and a smattering of theaters and cultural centers, it was a huge tourist attraction.

He left his truck with the valet and walked up the pavement to the front doors of the imposing structure. Entering the expansive lobby, he mingled with guests and other arriving patrons. Several women glanced his way, but he was distracted thinking about seeing the Doc again. He passed through the expansive lobby with its seating arrangements, decorative Doric columns, and bright crystal and gold chandelier. As a poor kid growing up in squalor, this place made him edgy. It was no different than being in his gear slogging through the jungle or kicking up sand in some hostile desert. SEALs didn't know the meaning of 'being out of their element.'

But to hell with how he was feeling. He was here to do a job for Alyssa and he wouldn't let her down. He saw a huge red, white, and blue banner that said Military Working Dog Foundation and followed it to the ballroom where the low hum in the room rumbled as he approached. Outside the door were Harlequin jugglers, stilt walkers in regal reds and glittering golds, and fire-eaters. He stepped inside, producing his invitation for the woman at the door.

Although, with this getup and the mask, how she could think he was going anywhere else was beyond him.

Her eyes lingered on his face, briefly meeting his eyes and then sliding down to his mouth and along his jaw. "Go right in, sir."

"Thank you," he murmured, immediately scanning the room. He was just getting the lay of the land, scoping out the finger foods and the champagne, he told himself. He wasn't looking for anything...or any*one* in particular. He liked his life just as it was. Keep the status quo because routine, like training, was grounding, but pesky change seemed inevitable. He had his family—his brothers and the brotherhood were all he needed. Females only complicated things. And they were bossy when they had a hold of a man's heartstrings. He'd prefer them to have a hold of his dick with either those wonderfully soft hands, those beautiful, skillful mouths or gloving him in tight, wet heat. He knew exactly what to do with a woman's anatomy. Sex was so damn easy.

His eyes snagged on a woman in the crowd. Part of it was the stunning outfit she wore, but the other part was the way she held herself. It seemed so familiar. The high waistline hugged her ribcage, the gold bodice accentuated her breasts, and the tiny sleeves caressed her lean shoulders. The mask on her face was gold, sparkling and filigreed, and the shoes gold, strappy and embellished with pearls. But the crowning glory were the butterfly wings in a graceful arch from her back. Her dark hair was piled up on her head, with one curl cascading down the side of her neck. The mask accentuated the lower half of her face, the delicate cheekbones, the sensual mouth and determined jaw. Then she turned her head and his breath backed up in his throat, his jaw went slack, and all he could do was stare helplessly.

The plain Jane caterpillar had morphed into the ethereal Butterfly Queen.

He pulled at his tie and it unraveled. Unbuttoning the tab at his collar, he felt like he couldn't breathe.

She had him by the dick right now, and he didn't like it one damn bit.

"You've been transformed, Alyssa," her closest friend, Holly Moore, said with a smile as she sipped champagne. Holly and Alyssa had grown up together in San Antonio. They had gone to vet school together. Holly had chosen a teaching position at the University of California Veterinary Medical Center and Alyssa had opened up her practice.

"This is all you and you know it. I was planning a different outfit."

"One that was unimaginative, Lissie."

Holly had come to the clinic a couple of hours before they were to close and several before the ball. "So, tell me what you're wearing," she'd said as she set her chin on her hand, her curly blonde hair framing a pixie face. "I bet it's brown, drab, and frumpy."

"Wear?" Alyssa said as if she hadn't been quite sure what Holly was talking about.

"Yeah, tonight..." When Alyssa looked at her blankly, she'd said, "The masquerade ball? Hello. Is this thing on?"

"Oh, the ball. I've got a dress and shoes. Aren't those what's required?"

Holly had snagged her wrist. "You are something else. You work so hard and this charity means everything to you. Don't you want to make an impression? Show the patrons how important it is to you?"

"Of course. Do I need to dress up to do that?"

"Are you kidding? Yes! You do!"

Holly had taken off the stethoscope and stripped Alyssa of her lab coat. She'd slipped behind her and started pushing on her back. Alyssa had dug in her heels. "You can't be serious. I can't leave to shop."

Her receptionist Lisa had smiled. "Oh, yes you can. Your schedule is free."

Jordan had smiled too. "We've got you covered, Doc. Go raise a ton of money."

Alyssa sniffed, remembering the encounter and feeling out of place in her glamorous outfit. "You know something? Being a girl has never gotten me anywhere." It was true. Everything she'd achieved had been about downplaying her femininity. It was what it took to make it in a man's world. In a man's profession.

"No, I suppose not. That would be your big, beautiful brain."

"Exactly. I don't go in for all this...girly stuff."

"That's your dad talking. He always wanted you to be like your brother, and you've done your best, other than changing your gender, to fulfill that wish."

Robbie, her brother had died a long time ago, but he was still here, still between her and her dad.

Holly kept talking, unaware of Alyssa's quiet contemplation. She was hell-bent on making her point. "But your eyes lit up when you saw those shoes. You're girly, admit..."

Her words trailed off and she stared into space. Alyssa snapped her fingers. "What's happening?"

"Where has that man been all my life? Wow and wow again. Gorgeous."

Alyssa turned her head, and her big, beautiful brain completely shut down in the wake of...Thorn Hunt.

It was like she'd released a bull into a china shop—destruction everywhere, especially in her resolve to keep her hands off him. He didn't fit in here, yet he looked completely at ease like one of the millionaires mucking up the Crystal Ballroom, all 007 sexy, but with a thick, dangerous edge. Except 007 had never been that big, that imposing. It made her crazy at how big he was. No man had ever sent a shiver down her spine every time she saw him. In the mask he exuded masculinity, his almost mohawk rebelliously tousled. Her mouth tightened at the sight of his beard. He'd blatantly ignored her instructions to shave, and that only added another layer of devastation.

He filled out the tuxedo with a rough grace that was all Tank, and her mouth tightened again at the sight of those panty-melting, black-buckled and silver-studded boots, with silver wing tip toes no less. They were just barely civilized, like him. She could easily imagine him with that soft smirk on his lips thinking he'd show her.

Then there was the mask. If she was being honest with herself, she'd never expected he'd wear it. It could only be described as elegantly masculine, but instead of looking ridiculous on such a daunting man, it gave him a raw, mysterious power, the lower half of his face dark and intriguing, so handsome it should be deemed criminal, a brooding Lucifer brushed by dark, invisible wings.

If she was the bright Butterfly Queen, he was the Dark Shadow King.

"Tank," she whispered, and Holly dragged her eyes away from him.

Alyssa and Tank stared at each other like dangerous explosives that were about to blow.

"As in a lady-killer machine?"

"As in Navy SEAL call name."

"Oh my God, he's a hero, too?"

"He's my dog handler. I've mentioned him. Brace yourself. He's part of the bachelor auction along with four of his teammates."

"Yeah, you mentioned him, but he deserves much more than a mention. Did you say four more like him?" Her eyes glazed over. "I wonder what my credit limit is. I have a dog that needs to be handled, stat."

"Holly."

"But I guess I'm much too late to this show."

She dragged her eyes away from him and met Holly's eyes. "What is that supposed to mean?"

"Ha! Like you're not standing there imagining what it would be like to put your hands on him."

Alyssa's mouth went dry. Holly was not only correct, but the longing for him twisted her belly into knots, sexual frustration something she was accustomed to since she rarely gave into her strong desires. But this time...it was much, much worse. Almost uncontrollable. "He's in the Navy. I'm in the Army. I'm an officer and he's enlisted. There are fraternization rules, Holly. I'm not free to touch a hair on his head."

Holly squeezed her shoulder. "But you're reserve. That's different."

Alyssa laughed softly. "I'm sure the inside of a brig doesn't distinguish between reserve and active duty, Holly."

"Being jailed for love. Hmmm, I'd say he's worth the risk."

"What risk?" Tank's deep, melodic voice broke into their conversation.

"Nothing," Holly said brightly. "Holly Moore," she said reaching out her hand. His eyes behind the mask were intense as usual. They flicked away from Alyssa to center on

Holly and her outstretched hand. Before he could say a word, Holly said, "Thorn Hunt, Navy SEAL. Right? I've been filled in." He engulfed Holly's small hand and she sighed. Alyssa nudged her, and she let go of him. "It was a pleasure to meet you," she murmured. "I need to go find some more...champagne."

His presence moved through her like a hot, aching wind. "I was expecting you to show up in full battle gear instead of as a gentleman," Alyssa said.

"No one is going to mistake me for a gentleman," he said.

Her awareness of him was so natural, so *inconvenient*. Almost a year of this was more than she could take. Maybe she should find herself another Navy SEAL MWD handler. But then she would have to explain to Jordan why she didn't want his brother.

She closed her eyes. *Want his brother...* A buzz at that thought sent the sexual energy humming in her nerve endings into an off-the-charts jacked up mode.

"No. You're not a gentleman," she said. She gave him a tight smile and snapped, "Follow me."

"Through the gates of hell," he rumbled as she walked toward the small room off the ballroom the hotel had set aside for her use.

As soon as they were inside, she reached for his collar. "At least you should look like one."

He grabbed her hands, the warm, calloused feel of his skin a shock to her system, and at the feel of him, a satisfaction that radiated into every pore in her body. "I didn't say you could touch me, pretty butterfly." He leaned in, the heat of him raging against all her exposed skin. "Ask me for permission first," he said, with a touch of moodiness on his sculpted mouth. "Unless this is an order and you're pulling rank. Are you pulling rank, General?"

Her breath hitched at the challenge issued not only from him, but to her control. Chaos looked out from his deep, dark brown eyes. Surrender was never something she had given in to. But wasn't it true that surrender could only happen at the end of a battle? He had no idea how to be soft and gentle. Tank was all metal and gears, all power and thrust. She knew why SEALs were of a particular breed because surrender wasn't in their genetic makeup. Tank didn't know how to back down either.

She had taken an oath. She was breaking it now and every day in her thoughts. But short of allowing her role model for her program to go out there looking like a disreputable rake, she was duty-bound to challenge him.

"It is an order, mister. And it's Lieutenant Colonel St. James, not General."

"I was making a...*general*ization," he said, that smirk in place. She moistened her lips and his eyes followed the movement. "Then give me an order. Say, 'Petty Officer Hunt, I order you to allow me to touch you.'"

The intake of air was involuntary, and his smirk widened into a smile that cut through her like a saber. Damn him and his confrontational nature. "Petty Officer Hunt, I order you to allow me to touch you."

He let her go, dropping his big hands away from hers. "Carry on, ma'am."

He stepped closer, way too close, way too personal. She reached for the button of his collar, the skin of his throat against the back of her fingers warm and smooth. She wanted to lean in, to breathe in the scent of him, press her mouth to that hollow and kiss his skin, taste him, the power of him making her knees weak and her fingers tremble.

"Do you want me at attention or at ease?" he whispered, the sound and the heat of his breath vibrating and wisping over her skin as if he'd physically touched her.

"At ease," she whispered, trying not to sound as breathless as she knew she did. He set his hands behind his back, which was, as far as she was concerned, a relief. She did up the collar, then reached for the tie. With the beard shadowing his jaw, the rebel chaos of his hair, the thickness of his eyelashes evident in the openings of the mask, his face so close, kissing seemed inevitable. Her nipples were hard beneath the dress, her core aching. Months of the most intense attraction of her life and she couldn't follow through with anything. Not with this man.

There were so many reasons. He was an enlisted member, and while it was true that she was a reservist in the Army, they were still under the same Uniform Code of Military Justice edicts. Getting physically, emotionally, or romantically involved with him could pose a serious violation. He was intense, earthy, and raw—so opposite to her grounded, calculating, and studious personality. He was a womanizer. He was reckless and had the kind of job that kept him gone most of the time. It would be the same song and dance as it had been with Stephen. Her marriage fell apart because they grew apart.

She'd pledged to her career. Her own expectations for her achievements were important. So, right away there was a problem here. Being deployed so much put a strain on a relationship. If only she could just have sex with him, maybe it would take the edge off, but could she risk her whole future on a physical desire? She looked into his face, into those eyes that seemed to see to the bottom of her soul. There was so much more to him than his intensity. There were layers, but he was guarded. She wasn't sure she had the skill or the energy to peel them back or if he'd even be willing to allow her to get any further. So it was best that she take her frustration and stuff it into a compartment like she always did.

The tie now done up, she knew she should step back.

But that moment, her necklace chose to come loose, and it dropped from her neck. With a quick flick of his wrist, he caught it

TANK DIDN'T WANT to let her go back out to the ballroom. He couldn't seem to break this spell she had over him, and it made him chafe and swear inside his head.

The necklace was warm from her skin and he raised his eyes to hers. Her mouth was parted, her hands, feeling the piece slip, were already on her throat even as he'd saved it from tumbling to the floor.

"The safety clasp must not have been fastened," she said.

He wanted intimacy with her, knew that it was against the rules and against what he thought he wanted in his life. Meaningless sex was all he'd allowed himself, and it kept his life uncomplicated, filled his needs, and never engaged his heart.

Alyssa was a threat. He instinctually knew that. But he still wanted to be inside her in every way possible.

Instead of placing the necklace in her hands, he stepped back and indicated the mirror that was on the wall close to the door. She looked at him for a minute, but when he thought she was going to speak, she moved and stood before the mirror.

He stood at her back and slipped the jeweled collar around her neck without touching her. But the necklace was made to fit against her throat, and the small, hidden catch felt tiny against his big fingers, requiring him to press against the nape of her neck.

A light fan of hair at the base of her hairstyle brushed his finger. It felt warm, her skin cool. He looked up into the mirror.

She was gazing at the reflection, at the necklace, at him.

He meant to take his hands away. He let go of the catch, raised his hands too quickly. A lock of her hair fell free of the loose pinning. The necklace sparkled at her throat. She and the stones were like light, with darkness all around: himself darkness...and tumbling...tumbling...

He shouldn't have touched her, should have given her back the stones and let her fasten it back around her slender throat.

The overhead lights found deep highlights in the lock of hair. She lifted her hand as if to tuck the curl back into place, but before she could, he touched it. He gazed down at his hand, fanning the curl between his fingers, resting his fist against the slope of her bare shoulder. It was as if his actions didn't belong to him—and yet they did: he felt every texture, every delicate strand of hair, every light breath she took.

He slid his knuckles in a feathery brush up her throat, past the necklace, to a place beneath her ear that was soft with a sensation he had never in his life known before.

He stood silent, touching her. It was beyond him, beyond him; he couldn't turn away as his will failed him.

It felt so good to have her, even this much of her beneath his fingers. She looked at him in the mirror, her eyes wide and deep green. There was regret there. And longing. There were no mixed signals with Alyssa. He knew she was off limits, and not just because of their UCMJ issues. He could only want her on a temporary basis. The only family he needed was his brothers. But standing here with her, he wondered how it would be to expand that family by one.

They had danced around this for weeks. Her vulnerability at this moment seemed enormous to him, her stillness beneath his hand an act of infinite trust.

With his hands, he could do so much damage and destruction. But she reminded him there was another side to him. A side that was gentle, but strong, a side that had needs that required filling. She reminded him that he was a man beneath the uniform he wore.

Lust flooded him. What he wanted...God, what he wanted...

He thought of all the women in his past, and they just paled in comparison to the vibrancy and beauty of Alyssa, and he had never been alive until the instant he'd met her.

He spread his hands, his thumbs brushing the skin beneath her earlobes, his fingertips resting on her temples, just tasting her cheeks. Still, she only stared at him in the mirror. Such fine eyes she had, the deep green of a saturated jungle, the lashes so long that he felt the sweep of them against his fingers.

He stood there touching her, imagined her hair gripped in his fist, her body, the voluptuous scent, the sounds. His own throat tightened with a suppressed moan. He wanted only to hold her, to gather her up and cradle her against him—and he wanted to overpower her. There was a terrible violence inside him. All he knew, all he had experienced and mastered in his life, was destruction. Will and determination kept him in check, but his resolve had failed him.

But he knew his heart would be his downfall, especially when it came to the off-limits Alyssa. With that thought came fear, for his heart could be the sword that cut him the deepest.

It was only self-preservation, dire need for protection, that finally impelled him to open his hands and let her go and walk briskly from the room.

2

Petty Officer and Corpsman Ocean "Blue" Beckett entered the ballroom, pulling at the lacy cuffs beneath the gold brocade jacket, taking it in stride that he was dressed like a medieval nobleman. His shoulders ached from the previous day's workout where they had pushed themselves beyond the limit. Something they did as a team every month. Sweating and heaving big heavy weights was a guy thing, and just because he spent most of his time on the team between combat and medicine didn't mean he couldn't keep up. Out in the field, his skills could be the difference between life and death. But medicine to him had been a breeze—both his Navy course when he'd initially enlisted and the advanced school after completing Basic Underwater Demolition/SEALS, or BUD/S. He did everything the guys did but got the additional medical training as well.

He saw Tank leaving a small room looking...edgy. Oh, boy. He knew that look. Something was testing his friend's control. When Doc came out after him looking shell shocked, he had his answer. He made his way through the crowd. "Let's get us some of this fancy champagne," he said, slinging his arm around Tank's massive shoulders.

"I need something a little stronger than that," Tank growled, and he steered them over to the bar. "You look like a pansy." Tank was a typical SEAL with one difference. His control was too obsessive. As a connoisseur of control, Blue was aware that the tighter a guy held onto it, the closer he came to losing it.

Blue laughed and said, "I'm much more grounded in my masculinity and can pull off this getup. I see you went for the staid and boring. A tux. Man, you have no imagination."

"I don't need an imagination. It can get you into trouble." He eyed the Doc.

"Hoo-yah, I hear you." He followed Tank's line of vision. "She causes chaos."

Tank looked at him. "She's a pain in my ass."

But Blue did believe that if there was no struggle, there was no progress. The problem with Tank was the progress part. "Okay, same thing, different label." He handed him a whiskey and got the attendant to pour him a club soda.

Tank threw back the alcohol, his eyes watering a bit, then shrugged and rolled his eyes. "You going to guru me?"

Control was about a deep-seated fear. Get to that fear and control was less important. Understanding that fear led to the ability to let go. Tank just had to find out what that fear was. There was nothing Blue could do to help him there. That was a private path he had to follow. "I can. It's fun to watch you all look at me like I'm from a different planet, but then later on come up to me and tell me how spot on I was. My messages might at first be cryptic, but the journey of figuring it out is up to you. You have the code to break it. But all I have to say is: We think holding on makes us strong, but sometimes it is letting go."

Tank looked at Doc again and sighed. "Letting go wouldn't be a good idea. Someone could get hurt. Also, I'm stronger than that."

Blue sighed, too. "Still, a journey gives us knowledge." Growing up in Hawaii, Blue understood the ways of the ocean. In his oneness with the sea, he understood a lot of the cycle of life. Especially when it came to control. No one could control the ocean—not surfers, of which he was one, not the fishermen, not even its inhabitants.

Tank had to consider the fish. A fish swam in a chaotic sea that it couldn't possibly control—much as they all did. The fish, unlike them, was under no illusion that it controlled the sea, or other fish in the sea. The fish didn't even try to control where it ended up—it just swam, either going with the flow or dealing with the flow as it came. It ate, hid, and mated, but didn't try to control a thing.

Blue knew better.

He'd been taught better.

"You're not being very cryptic right now."

Blue smiled and took a sip of his club soda. "Be like the fish," he said softly, setting down his glass and heading over to the stage, leaving a confused Tank in his wake. Tank needed to learn that it takes losing control to regain balance. Sometimes things have to fall apart so you have little control over losing control and learn to let go.

ALYSSA STOOD THERE for a few minutes after Tank left. This was bad. Very bad. So very, very bad. She had liked every minute of having his hands on her. Oh, dammit. What was she going to do about this? Talk to him? Get it out in the open and have a conversation about how hot they were for each other?

Would that only make it worse, openly acknowledging this...thing between them?

One thing was for sure, she couldn't hide in here. She would never shirk her duties. She had a function to run, and she needed to focus on that right now.

She exited the small room back into the festivities of the ballroom. Even more people were arriving, looking stunning in their costumes.

A woman touched her arm and Alyssa stared into a red sequined mask. "Paige?"

Paige Wilder smiled, looking stunning in a red dress, her dark hair caught up and cascading down her back. Kid Chaos, her husband, stood behind her at her right shoulder in a red military styled jacket, dark shirt and pants, a filigreed mask on his face. He gave her a broad grin. They had met last summer when Kid had been on vacation in Bolivia. Paige was an NCIS agent. They'd gotten married shortly after returning.

"We're here for support," she said, slipping her arm through Kid's. All of Tank's teammates had been great in helping out with fundraisers. Alyssa was thankful to them for the assistance. "Everything looks amazing. You've outdone yourself here."

"I agree," Dana Cooper said. She and her husband Ruckus complemented each other in royal blue. He was the team's leader and Dana was a humanitarian reporter. Their other teammate, Cowboy, and his fiancée, Kia, also looked amazing, she in a black, strapless, silk tulle gown with silver sequins on it. If Alyssa was the Butterfly Queen, Kia was the Star Queen. She was a hacker for hire and split her time between San Diego and Reddick, Texas. She owned a bar and hotel in her small home town. Her fiancé was dressed like an old-world cowboy with bling on the silver vest. Quite a sexy gunfighter. They'd also met last year, and their wedding was coming up soon.

She pushed her problems with Tank to the back of her mind. "Thank you all for coming."

"Hey, Doc," Hollywood said, looking devastatingly handsome with Scarecrow and Wicked making it hard to breathe with so many gorgeous men in one small space.

"Here are my bachelors," Alyssa said. In addition to Hollywood, there was Wicked and Scarecrow...wait. She smiled and looked around. "Where's Blue?"

"He's here somewhere," Hollywood said. "But who's looking for him, beautiful? Like, wow, Doc, you're a stunner."

She flushed at his words, his beautiful blue eyes going over her with appreciation. She didn't normally fall victim to flattery, but there was something so deliciously irresistible about Hollywood. Wicked nudged him, and he shrugged his shoulders. "Keep it in your pants, Casanova."

He chuckled and winked at her. "What? I'm just giving the lady a compliment."

"Sure you were," Wicked said, rolling his eyes.

"The auction isn't for another hour. So mingle and work your magic, guys. Again, thanks for doing this."

"You're welcome," they said as the music started up.

"Go and dance. Get this party started, people," she said.

As the night wore on, people bid on the silent auction items: gift baskets, wine pull, free vet care for a year, and a private tour of the Navy's Marine Mammal Program. The live auction was a huge success with dinner for two with an admiral cooking the meal, a private tour of Coronado and dinner with the commander. Her military working dog charity would have the support they needed for a long while. But it was the bachelor auction that fetched an enormous amount, especially the five SEALs. She'd itched to bid on Tank, but she couldn't. It wouldn't be a good idea, her being the sponsor and the whole problem with the fraternization policy. It was safer to keep her paddle by her side. But it killed her when a beautiful blonde won him.

Once the auction was over there wasn't much more that she had to do. She went to the bar and got an apple martini and sipped it while she watched the couples in their resplendent costumes dance. She sighed. Another fundraiser down. There were plenty more things to do, like take a look at her website and make sure it was up to date—

"I never took you for a wallflower, my queen."

His warm hand slipped up under her elbow, and she turned to find Hollywood smiling at her. Oh, God. Could she not get away from these enlisted men?

"Could I have this dance?" At her non-response, his confidence never wavered. It was clear he was used to wooing women and he enjoyed every minute of it. "C'mon. I put myself on a stage for you and let women bid on me. One dance."

She wavered. He was so handsome, and that smile. Geez. "Okay, one dance."

That smile widened as he led her out and slipped one arm around her waist, the other clasping her hand. They moved to the music.

She hadn't seen much of Tank since the end of the auction, and she wondered if he'd gone home. The lights dimmed, leaving the room bathed in the twinkle lights strewn above. The song playing was beautiful, lyrical, but there was just something missing in her enjoyment of the waltz. She glanced into the crowd and saw Tank staring at them, his face like granite, his eyes dark with mood. There was an instant, just a flash of time, when their gazes caught and held; then the muscles along his jaw tensed and his mouth hardened as he started to turn to go.

Alyssa stared across the ballroom, a fierce longing clenching around her heart, a longing that splintered and fractured when she saw the tight set of his shoulders. She was a fool, but she couldn't seem to let him go.

She glanced at Hollywood, and it was quite clear he hadn't missed a beat. He released her immediately. "Go," he said softly.

Uncaring of who she bumped into, she fought her way through the swarm on the dance floor, her heart hammering frantically in her chest, urgency pressing in on her. Breaking through the last of the crowd, she dodged a scattering of people who stood watching, finally reaching Tank at the door.

Realizing this was crazy and forbidden, she couldn't seem to help it. Her voice breathy, she said, "Tank."

He stopped and turned, his face set, the lines around his mouth white with tension.

Catching a ragged breath, Alyssa tried to keep her voice from breaking, tried to hang on to some form of control.

"You're not going to leave without giving me at least one dance. That would be what a gentleman would do. And I think we already established you aren't that civilized."

He stared down at her; then he looked away and swallowed hard, his grip almost crushing as he took her hand. Without saying a word, he laced his fingers tightly through hers and led her back onto the dance floor.

Insulated by the crowd, he drew her against him, the weight of his hand against her back pressing her deeper into his embrace. Her forehead nestled against his jaw. Alyssa closed her eyes and cupped the back of his neck, trying to hold in all the emotions rolling through her. Inhaling unevenly, Tank rested his head against hers, his arm tightening around her as they began moving to the music, drawn into the intimacy of their own private space. The sensual, intimate tempo floated around them, the power and eloquence of the lyrics expressing the soul of their own private longing.

She could pretend for this one moment in time that she was free to be with this contrary man, free to enjoy this contact even though it was prohibited for them to take it any further.

Easing into his embrace, she looked at him, her eyes taking in every detail of his face as if she'd never seen him before, her longing a great fountain inside her. She smiled, sure her gaze revealing everything she was feeling. She didn't have a very good poker face.

"You did a great job," he murmured. "It's a success. I'm proud to be working with you on this charity, Alyssa."

Her first name on his lips jarred her. He usually called her Doc, but she couldn't be sorry he'd used her given name. It sounded good in that deep baritone.

"Thank you. It wouldn't have been such a success if it wasn't for you, your amazing Echo, your teammates and their wives and girlfriend."

Moving to the rhythm of the music, he stared down at her, his gaze dark, intense, unwavering, searching. Tightening his hold on her hand, he pressed her knuckles against his mouth, his face the softest she'd ever seen it. Drawing a deep breath, he drew her closer, urging her head against his jaw. Then he tucked their joined hands against his chest, letting the melody and lyrics enclose them in their own cocoon. "You're the driving force behind it, and our guys overseas are reaping the benefits of having you behind them, supplying them and their dogs. It means more than you know. On their behalf, I thank you."

The music segued right into another slow one, and they continued to move through the semidarkness, letting the music move them, oblivious to everything and everyone. Alyssa never wanted it to end. He was a wonderful dancer— it surprised her that such a big man could be so light on his feet. Moving with him was pure pleasure. She loved the physical closeness, the feeling of being enveloped in his strength, the feel of his body moving against hers. Moving toward space at the back of the ballroom, where the shadows made for near-complete darkness, Tank tightened his hold and brushed his mouth against her temple, a trace of amusement in his gruff voice. "Thank God the military made me learn how to dance."

Her smile came right from the core of her. Alyssa lifted her head and looked at him. "Dancing and combat? Hmmm, real life skills."

He gave her an irresistible half grin, white teeth flashing, an intimate sparkle in his eyes. "Stealth requires finesse," he said huskily.

Feeling as if she could float if he let go of her, she held his gaze, smiling up at him. "Okay, twinkle toes."

He slid his hand down her back, molding her hips snugly against him, the grin and the glint intensifying. "What the hell? No one's ever called me that with a straight face."

She laughed and hugged him, hating that this couldn't be real and knowing she was indulging herself.

Tank's half grin took on a special warmth, the sparkle in his eyes softening into a steady gaze that was intimate, intoxicating and very sensual. His voice was soft and gruff when he murmured, "This is damned inconvenient. It was easier when you were giving me a hard time."

Alyssa's smile softened as she gazed up at him, something warm and poignant unfolding in her. "Yes," she murmured. Finally, she said, "Tank—"

His cell chimed, and his wasn't the only one that went off. Every single member of his team received a call at the same time.

He pulled out his phone and his mouth tightened. "I've got to go."

She grasped his arm. "We should really talk—"

"Later, babe. I've got to go now."

She nodded as he and his team members filed out of the door. This was an emergency, which meant something in his world wasn't right. That meant danger, combat, and distance. She had no idea when she would see him again...if ever. Her heart in her throat, she ran as fast as her impractical heels would allow. He was just getting into his truck as she pelted to the curb.

Startled, he froze, and their eyes met. Feeling as if her face had gone numb, she stared helplessly at him. She reached back and untied her mask. There was no hiding from what she was feeling. "Please, please take care and be safe," she whispered. "All of you." Unable to drag her eyes away, she watched him, a swell of intense longing clogging her chest.

He let out a pent-up breath. "I always do." Tank gazed at her, the muscles in his jaw taut with restraint; then he finally managed a small smile. "You take care, too. I'll be back."

He slid into his truck and then he was gone.

It was so hard to let go of him, harder yet to watch him go. An unexpected breeze blew tendrils of hair into her eyes. Pushing them away, Alyssa watched his vehicle disappear around a corner, feeling so at odds with what her head knew and what her heart felt.

A memory surfaced, unpleasant and unwelcome, but she couldn't seem to help the feelings that came with it. So many times, she and Stephen had said goodbye, loving goodbyes, until they weren't, until they were bitter and stony silences.

The memory also brought with it the hurt as love died, the pain of losing her husband as the distance between them stretched out until there was nothing left. The realization coursed through her and sent her reeling. She turned away from the street.

She must be out of her mind. It was impossible. She knew it. And, with him, it would be so much worse. A Navy SEAL was always gone, secretive; a good chunk of him belonged to the brotherhood and the rest to Uncle Sam. But the biggest obstacle to overcome was the fact that falling for him, getting involved with him...her breath caught...loving him would be a violation of the UCMJ with the mildest punishment being a slap on the wrist and the worst incarceration, her life ruined and in tatters.

He'd used the word inconvenient. He had no idea how much he was affecting her. Getting it out in the open would put a nix on it once and for all. She would make that clear to him when he came back. Clear that there could be nothing between them, even when deep down she had a feeling there was everything.

3

WHEN HE GOT to the ready room after picking up Echo, changing out of his tux and into his uniform, it was more subdued than usual. Everyone had assembled around the table with Ruckus talking on the phone in low tones. Tank knew his leader, and the pinched look to his boss's face told the story. Something had gone horribly wrong.

He sat down next to Blue, who was sitting there like he was attending a yoga class. The guy was always calm, cool, and collected. Nothing seemed to faze him, like he had already transcended the human condition. It was almost impossible to get a rise out of the guy. Instead, you got philosophy and insight. Blue was one of the most grounded men he'd ever met.

"What's this about?"

Tank shrugged. "Don't know. But the way Ruckus is acting, it's not going to be good."

His calm blue eyes turned to Tank. "Yeah, we're the dudes that make sure everything does turn out right, man."

"After we wade through a whole lot of bad." Hollywood

threw a ball for Echo and he chased it, bringing it back to him to throw again.

"Just adds more bad to our badass quotient."

Tank chuckled. This situation was dire, there was no doubt about it, but like his situation with Alyssa, SEALs in tough conditions had to be realistic about the danger they were in—but they had to be confident about their ability to handle it. He could handle whatever LT was going to tell them once he finished his phone conversation, and he would handle this...*disorder*...with Alyssa. A challenge was nothing but something to overcome. He knew who he was and what he wanted.

Sitting next to his teammate, he wanted to absorb the energy he projected, but he still churned about her. When she'd been breathless after having chased him out of the hotel, he was sure he was going to get himself into deeper trouble. It had been more than just a woman wishing a man a safe journey. Hell, he'd never expected this to happen.

Dammit. She was making him question everything he believed. It wasn't good right now and damn distracting when his head should be in the game and focused on what-ever had LT looking like he could chew nails. Bedding Alyssa was a complicated mess, and one he should stay away from both in action and in his head. But that wasn't the head he was thinking with right now.

He didn't have to fall hopelessly, crazily in love with her. Hell, he wasn't going to do that. He'd made love with lots of women without falling in love. He was very particular about his lovers. He liked women—loved them at their best and was fascinated by them at their worst—but he didn't need to sleep with everyone he met.

He just needed to fuck Alyssa.

For a long time.

LT slammed the phone down and stood there with his hands on his hips, his chest heaving. The guys looked around at each other. Even Kid's usual smart aleck remarks were silent.

He turned to them, his eyes bleak, shaken. Lieutenant Bowie "Ruckus" Cooper was shaken. That made all of them sit up straighter in their chairs. Some shit had gone down.

"Charlie Squad is KIA."

Shock coursed through Tank. He suspected it was bad news...but this... He sat there with the rest of his team, decimated at losing eight operators. Eight elite, special forces men who they had worked and trained with. Three teams were trained for this mission, and they had drilled together for weeks before Charlie took off with Bravo in reserve, and Team Alpha, Tank's team, would do any mop up needed. The mission to dismantle a minefield to get at the Kirikhan rebels entrenched in an area in the small country of Kirikhanistan in the Soviet Union that might hold their High Value Targets, Boris and Natasha Golovkin. They were wanted in connection with some weapons that had been stolen from Coronado. About half of them had been recovered when Kid Chaos was working with Special Agent Paige Sinclair, now Wilder, in Bolivia months ago. But there were still five ballistic warheads out there that had to be recovered. They were pulling out all the stops to get them.

After the initial shock came the anger, then the determination to make sure the sacrifice his brave teammates had made wouldn't be in vain. The enemy, nothing but international thugs, also needed to discover the cost of going against SEALs. Tank was well aware how the gang mentality worked.

There was a long, strained silence; then Cowboy asked,

"What? The whole squad?" Cowboy's distressed tone mirrored the way each of them were feeling.

Tank stared straight ahead, reality striking home, and a cold feeling sluiced through his gut. Clenching his jaw against the awful sliding sensation in the pit of his stomach, he forced himself to take a deep breath. This was unprecedented in the SEALs. But more importantly, they'd lost damn good men. Each of their faces flashed in his mind and he felt sick all over again.

"They were ambushed and everyone killed. The wounded were executed. Bravo Squad went in after them and only five made it out. Three POWs."

"Who did those fuckers take?"

"Speed, Pitbull, and Fast Lane."

Tank took in the information, filling in each of the captured men's names to ground himself. Pictured each guy in his mind so that he could solidify his resolve. Justin "Speed" Myerson, Errol "Pitbull" Ballentine, and Ford "Fast Lane" Nixon.

"Fast Lane? Dragon's LT," Kid ground out. "It's payback time."

Ruckus's eyes narrowed. His gaze circled the room. "Damn fucking right. There were seven NATO and Army taken as well. We're tasked with taking out the Golovkins, kill or capture, and recovering those warheads, but our main priority is going to be our guys."

Tank was with him one hundred percent, a sick, hollow feeling overriding his fury for a moment, sending out a silent message to the men who were now no doubt terrified and fighting for their lives. Torture whispered across his mind, then his will hardened, his jaw set. *Focus on getting them out of there*, he told himself. His team was going to make that happen.

The faces around the table were set and determined, Wicked's eyes glittering. "We're going in hard and tough and when the smoke clears, we'll be the only ones standing."

"Whatever it takes," Scarecrow said, his voice ominous.

"Hoo-yah," reverberated around the room.

Tank went back to his locker. He pulled out his cell and pressed his contact list. When the call connected, he said, "Jordan, I'm deploying." There was silence on the other end of the line for a long time. "Jordan?"

"Yeah," he said wearily, "I'm here. I just— Damn, I needed to talk to you, but it can wait."

A funny, uncomfortable sensation coursed through Tank, and he straightened, his insides going dead still. "Are you sure?"

"Yeah. This is going to be more than a hurried five-minute discussion when you're going into combat. Call me when you get home."

He was torn here. It was clear Jordan needed him right now and he couldn't be there for him. It was the reality he lived with. It drove home to him how sketchy he was in the support department, made him realize that his brothers deserved more—anyone he cared about deserved more than his absence. He thought fleetingly of Alyssa, trying to tell himself that she wasn't a factor because she was off-limits and temporary at best. Did he want to jeopardize what he had professionally for a good fuck? And she would be good. He had no doubt about it. There was something...untested about her, something ready and willing to emerge. He was the man who could bring that out in her, a passion she didn't even know she possessed.

But his chosen profession, his life's work dictated the rules. "I don't know how long I'll be gone, but you know not to ask."

"I do." He sighed, his voice soft, strained but upbeat. Jordan's optimism was legend in their family. "Go save the world. I'll let Dan know."

"Be good, little brother."

"Stay safe, Thorn. Call us when you can."

"Copy that."

Feeling as if he had a fist jammed in his heart, he hung up and started packing up his gear.

EVEN WITH THE delays that inevitably happened, a day in Dover and two in Germany, Tank had patience because he knew that they were going to get to their destination and would mete out their own brand of justice. Echo was quiet even though the guys were ragging each other. His canine partner was picking up on Tank's iron control of his emotions. He couldn't think about anything except the mission at hand.

His problems at home would have to wait until he could focus on them again. He'd only slipped once when he'd seen a dark-haired woman at Landstuhl, bringing Alyssa immediately to mind. He couldn't once remember thinking about any of the women he bedded unless he was horny as hell. It wasn't that he wasn't hot for Alyssa, he was. There was just other stuff riding him about her.

Hollywood leaned over and asked, "So, what's up with you and the Doc?"

"What do you mean?"

"You crashed my dance, man. Like a bulldozer."

"I'd explain it to you, but I didn't bring my puppets and crayons."

"He was saving the lady from your bullshit, Hollywood," Wicked said, leaning his head back with a slight smile.

With a cocky look on his face, Hollywood laughed. "What? Even my bullshit sparkles." He grinned widely, and Tank knew from seeing the guy in action that he was right on the money.

"Your flexibility amazes me with the way you put your foot in your mouth and your head up your ass," Kid said, deadpan in a voice that was so complimentary, all the guys laughed.

"I'm going to file that between fuck this... and fuck that..." Hollywood said unfazed.

"File this," Tank said and gave him the finger.

Hollywood leaned over and said in a lowered voice, "I get it. You don't want to talk about her. That makes sense since she's an officer, but different branch. That count?"

"I don't know, Hollywood. Just keep it in your pants. She's not some conquest."

Hollywood smirked and sometimes Tank wanted to haul off and wipe it off his face. "Oh, is she yours?"

"No," he said with disgust. He rose and went over to check his gear to get away from the questions. He hadn't been thinking straight at the ball. When he'd seen Hollywood touching her, it set off a chain reaction in him that he'd never experienced before. Breaking bones came to mind.

Ruckus piped up. "Who's spreading the bitchy dust around, ladies?" He looked right at Hollywood. "Is it you, Stinkerbelle?"

"Just had some questions, sir."

"Right. You engage your mouth before engaging your brain?"

"On occasion."

"What's that got you?"

"Some bruises, a black eye, sore jaw, getting laid."

Tank grinned. Hollywood...damn him.

"But the chicks dig scars and glory is forever. Am I right, LT?"

He chuckled. "Lay off."

Tank felt Hollywood boring a hole in his back. Suddenly Blue materialized beside him as if he, too, was checking his gear. He glanced up, those calm blue eyes making Tank cranky. "I don't need your Obi-Wan bullshit right now."

"The force is strong in you, grasshopper."

"Fuck you." Tank chuckled. He couldn't help it. Blue delivered the line with an Asian accent. Only he could pull that off.

"Hollywood can be a dick. Don't let him get to you."

"Handsome, sparkling dick, apparently."

Blue laughed out loud. "Yeah, but the guys are on edge."

Tank studied Blue for a moment. "But not you."

"I thought you didn't want my Obi-Wan bullshit?"

"Sometimes I wonder how you can be so unaffected."

"I'm not unaffected. I'm just surrendering to what is."

"Surrendering?"

"Yes. Surrender is nothing but yielding to rather than opposing the flow of life. Now is all there is. So accepting the present moment is surrendering to now. Inner resistance to what is means saying no, but that doesn't mean you don't take action to change the situation. Doesn't mean we're not going in and doing everything we can to complete the missions. Just means you accept what is. It's totally internal."

"You're giving me a migraine, Blue."

He chuckled. "Dr. Alyssa St. James tests your boundaries, makes you think in a different way. I say that's not such a bad thing."

"If you were in my head, Blue, you would."

"Maybe the thinking would go better if you used the right head."

The flight landed on a strip of land about ten klicks or approximately six and a half miles from the small Afghanistan town where the rebels were entrenched as a fortification and barrier to their stronghold just across the Amu Darya river, dividing Kirikhanistan from Afghanistan. To the west sat Termez, Uzbekistan near the Hairatan border crossing into Afghanistan and not far from there the Friendship Bridge built by the Soviet Union. Termez was a major supply hub for NATO during the war, founded by Alexander the Great and the old part of it destroyed by Genghis Khan.

The air was a chilly fifty degrees and the team didn't come up for air for two and a half days. Tank had only slept nine hours. Most of his time he was unloading gear, making up his rack, sighting in his weapons, and planning every detail of their assault. By the time they were finished it was a small town with tents, latrines, a mess hall and command center surrounded by fencing with regular patrols. The afternoon of the third day slipped into evening. Tomorrow they were going after the Kirikhan rebels.

Ruckus was currently at the combat center and given a briefing on the operation planned prior to their arrival. That's when the shit hit the fan. Tank heard him shouting from where he was exercising Echo. He eavesdropped unabashedly.

In this situation, they were tasked with working with NATO forces and the Green Berets who had their own reasons for going after the Kirikhans. Even before this op got underway, Ruckus had been going toe to toe with the brass about separating his SEALs to work with the Army commandos. LT was having none of that shit, and he told the brass in no uncertain terms that it led to mistakes. They were an elite fighting team, and the team wasn't going to get separated.

The brass insisted, and Cowboy was the guy who got Ruckus to calm down as their LT was bordering on insubordination, but Tank agreed with him. Separation was a mistake.

He went to one knee and fiddled with Echo's harness, checking for chafing, but he was really gathering his composure. His mind thick from no sleep, Tank focused on Echo, a disturbing feeling rolling over in his gut.

Moments later, Ruckus stalked angrily from the tent, swearing up a storm, Cowboy right behind him. His LT knew they were counting on him, and he wouldn't jeopardize his command of Team Alpha by getting thrown in the brig. But they sure knew he was against this cockamamie proposal. And if his LT was against it, Tank was with him.

He hoped that his viewpoint wasn't askew from lack of sleep and tension. After that, he, fed and watered Echo and they entered his bunk, made sure his body armor and helmet were ready for tomorrow, then lay down. Echo curled up next to him. He was wary of how tomorrow would go. They worked better as a team and separating could easily spell disaster. Team Alpha was used to having each other's backs.

Even though he'd vowed she was off-limits both in his thoughts and in every other way that mattered, Tank thought of her. She felt like a touchstone more so in this moment than his brothers or the men he was going to be working with tomorrow. After all, she and all she stood for was what they were fighting for.

With the memory of her burning brightly in that butterfly costume all light and beauty, he offered up silent condolences to the families and loved ones of the men who had died. Their bodies would be landing back home soon.

Finally, he thought about the men who had been taken and what they must be enduring. That gave him resolve. He would never let them down.

Hoo-yah. We're coming for you. Hang on.

His last thoughts before he drifted off were how incredibly soft Alyssa's skin had been as he ran his knuckles down the line of her neck. Had he ever noticed that before?

~

"Get up, you sleepyhead!" Alyssa called out cheerfully, announcing her presence as she walked into her best friend's apartment, which was located right down the hall from her own place. "I brought donuts, so dig in while they're hot and delicious."

Alyssa headed into the kitchen, but no one was there. Figuring Holly was still getting ready for work, Alyssa went ahead and poured herself a cup of coffee and rummaged through the refrigerator for the cream. She and Holly had an open-door policy for the most part, and keys to each other's apartments. Most mornings they met for breakfast before Holly had to head to the university in La Jolla and Alyssa headed off to Coronado where she was filling in for the one of the active duty vets who was on maternity leave. Being on base again made her remember her active service, her love affair with Stephen, something she wanted to forget. She couldn't refuse her commanding officer's request as they went way back to before she'd been commissioned. He had been the one to suggest the Army scholarship that had gotten her through vet school on a full ride.

"Do you have to be so alert every morning? Can't you grumble just once? And donuts, again. I swear you don't put on a pound. Me, I'm getting a rubber tire around my midriff. How am I going to snag a hot Navy SEAL with padding?" Holly grumbled as she entered the kitchen wearing a pair of form-fitting slacks and a pretty navy sweater over a blue striped top. Her blonde hair was a beautiful tousled mess, as if she'd just rolled out of bed instead of showering and grooming.

Alyssa chuckled and eyed her friend's trim waist. "Uh-huh. Bagels tomorrow."

"With cream cheese," Holly said with a laugh.

She grabbed her own cup of coffee and sat down at the table, choosing a powdery, chocolate cream filled donut.

"So you want to talk about it?"

"Huh?"

"Maybe I should say him. You want to talk about him?"

"Who?"

"Here we go again," Holly said, then took a bite. When she'd swallowed, she said. "Hunky Navy SEAL that's gorgeous enough to melt a woman into a gelatinous mess. That's who."

"I work with him, Holly."

"And that lame ass response is supposed to close my mouth. It wasn't me who ran out of the ball like her wings were on fire."

Alyssa toyed with the sprinkles from her donut. "He's being deployed. I wanted to tell him to be safe."

"You wanted to kiss him and more."

Startled, Alyssa sat up straighter. She was absolutely not

going to tell her friend about the vividly erotic dream she'd had last night about Tank. She'd been deep asleep, but the image of Tank's hands and mouth pleasuring her in such steamy, breath-taking detail had seemed so real. Intensely so. She'd felt the heat and strength of his big body stroking in and out of hers, and each hard, fierce thrust had sent her spiraling into the sweetest kind of ecstasy.

She'd woken up panting and moaning as her body clenched deep inside and the last ripples of an orgasm coursed through her body. She'd been shocked and realized that she'd had the equivalent of a wet dream, proof that her body truly was sexually deprived.

"Holly, he's enlisted." Her face warmed at the memory, and she ducked her head to hide the flush on her cheeks before Holly noticed and called her on it.

She polished off her donut and sipped her coffee. "In the Navy and you're Army, reserves. Surely there's some leeway."

She shook her head. "I don't think so. UCMJ applies to all branches of the service."

Holly frowned. "Have you looked into it?"

"No. I told you. We work together." She emphasized the words.

"Have you kissed him?"

She could still remember their encounter in that small room where she'd fixed his tie, could still feel the way he'd used his knuckles on the back of her neck to the slope of her shoulder and how his touch had ignited such a powerful sexual awareness between them. At that moment, she'd wanted to kiss him—the kind of slow, deep kiss infused with a heady rush of sensation. Could have sworn by the heat and desire in his eyes that he was thinking the same thing.

She was certain a kiss would have been so good between them...until he'd stepped away and she came out of her daze. Her lips tingled just thinking about making out with Tank. He'd saved her from herself. Her father would call this...lapse her stupid girl-induced hormone-saturated senses.

Other than the fact that he wasn't much interested in a long-term relationship, she wasn't sure she could keep herself from getting in too deep. But it didn't matter. *Enlisted!*

Tank's lips and his heavily muscled body were a career killer. Her father would be so disappointed in her for throwing her future away and giving in to being female. He believed that women were much too emotional to handle a man's job. He'd told her to get rid of sentiment, toe the line, and keep it platonic. He wasn't happy when she'd married Stephen. She was sure it reminded her father that she was a woman.

Holly rapped her knuckles gently against Alyssa's forehead. "Come back from dirtymindland. I'm guessing you want him to kiss you."

"I haven't kissed him, and he hasn't kissed me. Satisfied, nosey?"

"No. Not really. How can I live vicariously through you if you don't cooperate?" She pushed her plate away and sighed.

"I think you need to stop living through me, honey, and get some real action." Alyssa got up and washed out her coffee cup.

"Okay," Holly said with a smirk, turning toward Alyssa at the sink and crossing her legs. "I'll take you up on that. How about we go out on Friday night?"

"Ah—"

"I wont' take no for an answer. Please, I need some male attention."

Holly's eager and pleading look did her in. She was a

sucker for her friend's pathetic face. "Okay, I'll be your wingman even though I'm in the Army."

Holly gave her a great big smile. "Great. It's a date."

She left Holly's apartment and Alyssa's thoughts strayed to Tank again. Foremost in her mind was his and the team's safety. She had a lot of affection for the bunch of them. But it was Tank's handsome face and big, beautiful body she couldn't get off her mind.

She approached the gate to Coronado. She was waved through. The morning streaked by and as the lunch hour approached, Alyssa was starved. She was heading out the door to the mess as her commanding officer was coming in. "Just the person I was looking for."

"Colonel Johnson? Did we have a meeting?"

"No, this is an impromptu visit. I want to talk to you."

"Sure. I'm just heading to mess. You interested?"

"I should grab a bite. I have a busy afternoon."

As they arrived and then got their food, Alyssa wondered why he would make a special trip to the clinic.

"So, what did you want to talk about?"

"You going to active duty. After I've seen what you've done here, I'm even more impressed. We need you in the Corps and I have the perfect assignment for you."

Alyssa had begun her career as an active duty Captain in the U.S. Army after she graduated from veterinarian school and was commissioned. She spent three active years in the Army Veterinary Corps working military public health and delivering services to military working dogs and other government-owned animals. It's where she met and married Captain Stephen Wilcox. After her divorce, she'd transferred to the reserves and opened her own practice. She'd been juggling both with drill one weekend a month.

"Go active duty? I hadn't—" The thought of getting back

into active duty made her pause, big time. She'd left to get more grounded, focus on veterinary work, build something instead of living a vagabond life. *Lick your wounds after you divorce.*

"I know. It wasn't on your radar and you have your practice. I get all that, but I want you to head up surgery at Lackland."

She gulped and choked on her water. "What?" she wheezed. "Are you serious?"

"It would include a promotion."

Her heart stalled. She would make full colonel before she was in her mid-thirties. That was pretty amazing, but there was only one catch. "Stephen is at Lackland, Jack."

"I know. He would be taking orders from you, though."

That made her smile. "Can I think about this?"

"Sure, you have a bit before Dr. Peterson comes back to work. Want to see pictures of the baby?"

He pulled out his phone, and as he scrolled through the pictures, Alyssa couldn't stop her mind from spinning at the news and the fact that her career would get a huge boost here. It wasn't exactly what she'd planned for, but could she pass it up? She loved the service, the people, the job. The only cons were that she'd be back near San Antonio, and Stephen wouldn't take it in stride that she was not only a rank higher than him, but his boss. That would rankle the hell out of him. But she wasn't sure she really cared about that. Her days of worrying about Stephen Wilcox were over.

This move would also take her away from the temptation of Tank, and that was an even better reason to consider it seriously.

Except she immediately felt resistance to putting distance between them. Time was ticking away for her to have a serious relationship that would lead to marriage, children. She was so busy that it was only in her quiet moments when she felt the lack of those things. Marriage itself wasn't evil. She didn't fear it with the right man. Truthfully, she lived the lifestyle and was well aware distance between a military couple was part of the equation. But she realized also that it would take one dedicated person to be the home base, the touchstone who dealt with everyday details to make it work.

Her path right now was about career, not family. She wondered how anyone dealing with such stressors ever got it right.

TANK WOKE to dust and the cold. He'd slept fully clothed, minus the boots. When he swung off the cot, the high-pitched whistle high overhead hit the compound and exploded somewhere on base. "Well, that was a nice wake the fuck up call," he growled as he laced up his boots and went to muster with the rest of the camp until the all-clear call came. Echo by his side. The SF and NATO guys all came dressed in body armor with their weapons. Wicked said, "Don't sweat it, guys. It's already blown up." They laughed softly amongst ourselves.

After breakfast they got down to business. They trained the rest of the day, and Ruckus and Cowboy attended the tactical-leader debrief. After dinner, Tank tried to call Jordan, but he didn't answer. He instead called Dan. He picked up the phone and his brother's face filled Tank's laptop. He was at work dressed in his navy blue uniform.

They chatted for a bit, then Tank said, "Do you know what's up with Jordan?"

Dan frowned. "Nothing that I know of. He's thinking

about going back to school to become a vet. That sweet Doc of yours is a great influence on him. I know he loves working with her."

"She's not my Doc, Dan."

"Sure she's not. You two should get a room already."

Before Tank could reply, the siren went off in the firehouse. "Gotta go, bro. Stay strong and loose over there and come back alive."

"Got it."

Dan disconnected the call and Tank was still left with an unsettling feeling about his baby brother.

As morning dawned bright and clear, except for the dust the unrelenting wind had kicked up, they met with the Green Berets and NATO troops and piled into the choppers. It was a tight fit, but the short flight went fast. It wasn't long before their point man, Kid, shouted, "One minute out."

When they exited the chopper after touchdown, they deployed right into a thick dust cloud and Tank followed the man in front of him until he went down to one knee as they waited for the choppers to ascend, clearing the way to their objective. The air was heating up but in this part of Afghanistan, it didn't usually hit eighty.

Tank surveyed the troops moving forward. He easily recognized his team members by the way they moved and didn't like the fact that he would be separated from them. Wicked and Scarecrow were to his right, and Kid and Hollywood were to his left. They disappeared. They were all making their way along with the main effort, paralleling Tank's movement. There was something going on with the group, but no one was on comms, and as he looked for the rest of the team, he got uneasy about the disorganization.

When the Green Beret's main breacher didn't show up to the main side of the street, Tank looked at Blue and shrugged. "Screw this. We'll get this done." Tank, Blue and their two Army team members blew and cleared several doors and rooms. Moving steadily into the city, there was little resistance, which only made Tank think something was up. There was no one on the bridge that connected the city across the river. They all filed together while Explosive Ordnance Disposal did their job of clearing mines, then fanned out on the other side, continuing with their breaching and clearing.

He didn't like the eerie calm. Echo was agitated, and he only got that way when there were bad guys just beyond his senses. When something was up with his Malinois, Tank got even more alert. "Blue, Echo's antsy. Watch your six."

"Copy," Blue said, his eyes always scanning. The calm he radiated never missed a beat.

Tank entered an open space that had already been cleared by EOD. He glanced down an alleyway and saw Wicked and Scarecrow with their Army buddies. Then there was a bright light and the deafening sound of an explosion. The ensuing dust cloud enveloped Tank's team members and their Army partners.

Tank and Blue raced down the alleyway when Wicked broke radio silence. "We need a medic." His stomach dropped. Don't let it be Hollywood. But when they got to the scene, Wicked was kneeling over the two downed guys who'd each lost both their legs. Blue immediately went into action, calling for evac.

"Watch out!" Kid screamed into the comm. Everything slowed down. Echo was struggling against the leash and Tank pivoted toward the sound of Kid's voice. A man stepped out into the center of the area, an RPG launcher grasped in his fist. The rebel raised it the same moment Tank released Echo. The dog sprinted across the open space between them and hit the bastard just as he engaged the device. He went down under sixty-five pounds of raging, snapping canine, and Tank watched the shell arc into the air. "Fuck! Take cover!" But his words had just come from his lips when the shell hit. The explosion blew them back.

And everything went dark.

Blue came to, dazed, confused, and disoriented. He could hear the most awful sound...it was an animal in distress. The high-pitched cries hit him in waves of sound, his head throbbing as if someone had punched him hard in the back of the head. People were shouting in the distance, bursts of gunfire, but it was all a blur of noise to him. He struggled up from bodies and blood, his hands slick, choking on dust and the metallic smell of blood mixed with gunpowder heavy in the air. He got to his feet and stumbled. Vaguely he registered that his helmet was gone, his comm hanging in a mangled mess against his chest like some thick, dark spider. He ripped it away and stumbled again, his gait uneven, falling to one knee. Someone needed him. He panted, the dust making it hard to breathe.

He lurched away, his mind telling him to *find the animal, help him...help him*. But he couldn't get his bearings. He had to help—that was all he kept thinking. He shambled along for what seemed like a long time, the noise and shouting receding. He lost everything, motor movement, coordination, thoughts nothing but a jumbled mess in his brain.

He went to his knees and retched, then collapsed to the ground. He heard a shout in a language he recognized, but the words were gibberish to him. It was a woman and she was frantic, but he had no idea why. Then she was there, prodding and nagging him upright, walking him to something wooden beneath his hands. She shoved him up and he fell flat on his face, the lurch beneath him barely registering as everything faded to a silent and all-encompassing black.

4

TANK OPENED HIS EYES, his head ringing like a bell, his body feeling as if it'd turned to metal and someone had hit him with a hammer and everything was vibrating at the same time an electric shock had coursed through. He was flat on his back. His chest hurt, and for a moment he gasped for breath, his lungs feeling as if they were about to rip apart and his legs as unstable as jelly. The high-pitched whimpering and yelping made him sit upright. His head spun, then stabilized. Pain radiated from his shoulder down to his hand when he moved, but it wasn't excruciating, so he ignored it. He was covered in blood, but most of it wasn't his.

Echo!

Panic seized him, and he knew that was a precursor to losing control. He couldn't lose it when Echo was in danger. Pushing everything into the back of his mind, he struggled to his knees, then to his feet. He looked across the expanse of the compound and saw Echo on his side, struggling to get up. The rebel was on his back and unmoving. Tank took off sprinting across the open ground until he reached Echo. He was horribly wounded...shrapnel had sliced across his shoulder, exposing muscle and bone, blood in his fur. His gut twisted in anger and fear. The rebel started to stir, and Tank noticed a device in his hand. A detonator. He stepped on the man's wrist and reached for his weapon. Tank pulled his sidearm and shot him in head twice.

Holstering his weapon, his breathing raspy, he folded down to the ground, tucking the detonator in his pocket. "Easy, boy," he said as Echo tried to get up again. He placed his hand on Echo's side. "Stay," he said, and Echo relaxed. He worked hard to keep his voice calm, to quiet Echo from his thrashing. Stabilizing him for transport was his number one priority. Tank went to work. Pulling out his muzzle, he gently covered Echo's snout, noting how glassy his eyes were, an indication of shock. The yelping down to whimpering now that Tank was close by, he opened his kit and pulled out a hemorrhage bandage to stop the bleeding. Echo cried out, a high-pitched, abrupt yelp as he lifted the Malinois and applied the elastic bandage around the wound, trying to be both gentle and quick.

Men were arriving as gunfire bursts sounded close by but not in his immediate vicinity. First Kid materialized next to him, swore softly, then knelt down and took up a position to protect Tank, then Wicked and Hollywood, both covered in blood, nicks and cuts to their faces, did the same. Making a half circle around him and his injured dog.

"I'm a medic," a guy said rushing over and kneeling down. As he moved closer to Echo, who growled in his delirium and pain, he glanced at Tank.

"It's okay, Echo," Tank said in a soothing tone, and Echo relaxed against him as the medic delved into Tank's kit and started an IV. Then he used one of the provided injectors to administer pain medication. While he was working over Blue, Tank looked up at Ruckus. He pulled the detonator out of his pocket. "You might want to get the EOD guys on this. He was waiting for us." He handed Ruckus the device. He moved off and started talking into his headset.

With Echo ready for transport, Tank covered him with the provided blanket and together, he and the medic lifted him onto the canine litter Tank provided.

All set to head to waiting choppers that had landed in the field just outside the city, Tank stumbled, and Hollywood caught him. His chest started hurting bad, his breathing labored. They worked at removing the body armor and Wicked said, "He's bleeding!"

Tank collapsed down to his knees and Kid called out, "Blue!"

"Where is he?" Ruckus asked, and Tank looked to the area where Blue had been prior to the explosion.

"Over there," Tank pointed, his stomach dropping. In all the commotion, he'd lost track of Blue. Where the hell was he?

One of the medics who had been working on the downed Green Beret guys came rushing over once Ruckus sprinted across the compound and tapped him on the shoulder. He frantically searched each of the bodies, then rose. Tank could see the grim expression on his face. His vision started graying on the fringes and he was really laboring to breathe.

"Pneumothorax," the medic said, and Tank realized he wasn't going to be able to go with Echo. He tried to rise, but they held him down as the medic began to work on him to re-inflate his lung. Blue was missing, and Echo was going to treatment without him. The severity of the wound hit home, Tank realizing that he might never see Echo again. He squeezed his eyes tightly closed, worry about Blue filling him with dread, and the pain of losing his beloved canine partner radiated and coalesced in his chest. He struggled with the tightness in his chest and the burning in his eyes. "Echo," he said softly, then he grabbed the strap on Wicked's body armor. "Find Blue," he said fiercely.

AFTER A BUSY MORNING at the base clinic, Alyssa traveled over to Old Town to her own clinic. She made a mental note to talk with her staff and tell them what a great job they were doing. Stepping inside, she smiled at Lisa at the desk who was checking in customers. She went into the back and grabbed a lab coat. Exiting into the hall, she stopped when she saw Jordan leaning against the wall, his face pale. He was shaking.

She rushed to him and the moment she touched him, his eyes popped open. "Jordan? What's wrong?"

He smiled and said breezily. "Just an upset stomach," but it was so clear to Alyssa that he was lying.

"We're going to my office and you're going to tell me what's going on or do we need to take you to emergency?"

"No!" Jordan said abruptly, then in a softer voice, "No, that's not necessary. I know what's wrong."

"Then we're going to my office." She assisted him down the hall, and once inside, she helped him to a chair and he folded down. She sat on the edge of her desk and let him catch his breath, noting the way he held onto the arm of the chair with one hand in a white-knuckled grip and the other arm across his midriff.

"Water," he said, and she went over to the cooler and poured him some. He dug in his pocket and pulled out some pills. Popping them into his mouth he took the water and swallowed them.

She wasn't one to jump to conclusions. As a medical professional she dealt with facts, but she couldn't tamp down the worry that churned in her. "What is going on?"

He looked up at her and closed his eyes briefly. "I'm sick, Alyssa."

"Oh, my God, Jordan. What is it? Have you been to see a doctor?"

"Yes, I've been." His voice roughened, and he blinked rapidly, his eyes moist. "I had a test and it wasn't good."

She tried to stay calm, but the rush of affection for Tank's brother overshadowed even her medical professional demeanor.

"What is it?"

I have elevated levels of tumor-associated antigens. They need to run more tests."

She covered her mouth, tears welled up in her eyes, a hollow, sinking feeling settling in her abdomen. *Cancer.* Her expression drawn, she shook her head as if that could make the outcome change. "No." She took a deep breath, then knelt down covering his hand. "Oh, Jordan. I'm so sorry."

He nodded, his eyes, even with this news, not as bleak as she would have expected. He was so different from Tank. Unable to help herself, she hugged him, and he hugged her back. She held him for a few minutes. "I'll be with you through this, Jordan." Tears slipped down her cheeks.

When they separated, he gave her a wan smile.

"What's the next step?"

"More tests and more tests."

She absorbed that information, her throat tight. "What can I do?"

"You're already doing it."

She squeezed his hand.

"I hope they find out what the problem is before it's metastasized. I really want to become a vet."

"Oh, God, Jordan. That must hurt so much. I'm so, so sorry." Reaching out, she squeezed his hand again. She hurt for him. He was not only one of the best assistants she'd ever had—competent, kind, so good with both the human and canine patients—she had no doubt he would make an amazing veterinarian. Would he get that chance?

"I'm feeling better. I should get back to work." He went to rise, and his cell chimed. Pulling it out of his pocket, he answered. "This is he. How can I help you?" His face went from puzzled then to alarmed. "Is he all right?" There was another burst of conversation, then Jordan said, "Why can't you tell me...all right, I'll head there now. Thank you."

"What is it?"

"Thorn, he's wounded. He's at the base hospital. I'm sorry. I've got to go."

She leaned into the desk for support, swallowing against the awful feeling of vertigo that washed over her. Tank wounded. *Oh, God. No. Please don't let it be severe. Let him be okay.* "I'm going with you," Alyssa said, fighting to contain the nearly unbearable ache in her throat. "How badly wounded?"

"They wouldn't say."

They left the clinic with Alyssa driving. She worked at staying calm, trying to will away the awful panicked feeling that suddenly pressed down on her. Jordan was too wound up, and he was still getting over that terrible pain from his episode.

The thought of losing Jordan—damn, she felt the tears well up inside her again, hurt. He was more like a little brother to her than her employee. It was clear he had the same affection for her. She was still processing his health news, her emotions raw. Now Tank was hurt. How badly they didn't know. How could she feel this way about him when she'd only met him just months ago? She couldn't deny it. There was no way she could have gone on with her day after hearing about him being wounded. All she wanted to do was get to him, see for herself that he was all right.

They passed easily through the gate with her credentials and were soon at the hospital. Jordan inquired at the front desk, and they ran into his brother Dan once they exited the elevator.

"Dan! Did they tell you anything?"

"I just got here," he said.

They went up to the main desk, and the nurse told them what room his brother was in. As they headed in that direction, Alyssa braced for seeing Tank.

She paused outside his door, closing her eyes and taking a deep breath, trying to put on a composed front. Letting her breath go, she schooled her face into an even expression and entered. Her false calm lasted about thirty seconds. When they entered the room, he was upright, hooked up to an IV. His head turned at the sound and their eyes met; his softened, then shuttered, a rigid set to his jaw. In that moment, nothing mattered. Everything in her relaxed with relief, then ramped up at the sight of him. He looked good, so good, a warrior fresh from battle. Except for the cuts and bruises on his beautiful face and that stark pain in his eyes, he was whole.

"Thorn," Jordan said rushing to the bed, and each of the brothers hugged him hard for several seconds. Tears pricked the back of her eyes, but she held them in check. It was clear that these guys were a tight, cohesive unit. She thirsted to hear their story, wanted to know everything about Tank and his past.

After the preliminary greetings were over, Alyssa felt awkward. This was really a family thing and she was being way too intrusive. She felt jittery after all that adrenaline shot into her system. But she hadn't been able to control her worry when she'd heard Tank was injured. She stepped back, but Tank looked at her and said, "Alyssa."

She stared at him for several seconds, caught in that intense gaze. She hadn't really prepared herself to speak to him after what had happened at the ball. She had strategies for fending off men, ingrained for far too many years, but nothing for near-miss sexual encounters. She had no string of lovers in her past to draw experience from. Her ex-husband was the only man she had ever been seriously involved with, and while Stephen was a solid and intelligent, he wasn't the kind of man Tank was.

His raw sexuality overwhelmed her. She seemed to never be in control—of him or the relationship or herself.

"I drove Jordan. He was worried about you and I didn't think it was a good idea for him to drive himself."

Jordan turned to look at her. "She's great," he murmured. "But this isn't about me. How are you? What happened?"

"Things went south. Blue is missing in action."

He glanced at her when she gasped. The memory of the sweet, smiling man who had only days ago been auctioned off to a roomful of eager women made her heart contract. But this was the life of a SEAL. He put himself in harm's way every day. She didn't want to accept that something terrible could have happened to the handsome man she knew and liked. "The other teammembers?"

"The rest of the guys are all fine. There was an explosion." His deep voice caught, and it took a minute before he went on again. "Echo was severely wounded. I got a mild pneumothorax from the explosion and a gash from my collarbone to shoulder. Twelve stitches.

"Ah, just a small boo boo. It's not even your worst," Dan said with a smile.

"Exactly," Tank said. "I'm only here for one more day and I'm out. They said my lung has fully inflated, but they still gave me leave for two weeks."

He might look good and fine, but he wasn't. Maybe his brothers didn't pick up on it, but Tank was agitated. His mood seemed volatile—a tense stillness that hid a building storm. "It's clear you don't want leave," Alyssa said.

"No, I want to find Blue," he growled, his frustration clear. "If he was captured... We've just got to figure out what happened."

It was clear to Alyssa that Tank was holding everything in. This was much more mentally damaging than he was revealing. Was it a macho attitude or his rigid control?

"Well, now that I know you're okay, I'm on duty. I gotta get back to the firehouse. I'll come and visit tonight."

"Don't worry about it. I'm really fine. Stop by the house when you get off shift."

"Will do." Dan nodded to Jordan and then squeezed Alyssa's shoulder as he passed. "Thanks for coming and for bringing Jordan."

"I should get back to work, too." Jordan glanced at her.

"I can take you back." Alyssa moved back toward the door, but Tank spoke.

"No, I was wondering if you could stay, Doc. I need a favor." He met her eyes and the fierceness of his request was reinforced. She moved closer to the bed, his expression lined with worry.

Dan clapped Jordan on the shoulder. "I can drop him back to the clinic," Dan said, smiling and exchanging looks with his brother. They said their goodbyes and left the room.

"I'm so glad you're okay," she said, coming even closer. Her heart gave a painful little twist when she saw his face contort. His shoulders sagged with a bone-deep weariness. He looked unusually tired and preoccupied as he shifted to face her.

"I'm not exactly okay," he said.

She was shocked that Tank would admit that to her, but it was clear to her that he'd been through some intense trauma. It would lower anyone's guard.

"We fucking need to find Blue and laying here is driving me crazy."

That wasn't a surprise to her. Tank was a man of action, and with his teammate missing, all of them must be frantic. "I'm so sorry about him missing. Do you know what happened?"

Alyssa stared at him, experiencing feelings she had no business feeling. He looked so solitary—so isolated and alone in his thoughts—and so damned exhausted. She would have given anything to have the right to comfort him, to draw his head against her breast and just hold him—to ease the awful pain she saw in his eyes.

"Without going into mission details, one minute he was right next to me when the explosion went off. I got knocked out and when I came to...Echo's cries distracted me. I needed to neutralize the insurgent first and help Echo before he did more damage to himself."

"That must have been awful," she said, her voice uneven. Shaken by her thoughts and the need they aroused, she ached to touch him.

He jerked his head up, his gaze riveting on her, and Alyssa realized that his frustration had jumped their bounds. "You can stop with the platitudes, Doc. I don't need them."

She met his gaze head on.

"I see shit every day over there. I need to find out about Echo. Usually a handler goes with their working dog, but I couldn't breathe, and they had to give me medical attention. He took off and I can't seem to get any information about him." He stared at her for an instant, then looked down and finished in a softer, gruffer voice. "I was hoping you could find out for me since you're an Army Vet."

Feeling as if she was caving in, she tried to get a breath past the thickness in her chest. The thought of that beautiful dog injured was more than she could bear. She took a fortifying breath, trying with all her might not to give her tears free rein. Crying in front of him would only make it worst. "Of course. I can contact Lackland. They would know where he is in the system." She couldn't help but grimace. The person she could call would be Stephen. He would know what was going on with Echo.

It must have shown on her face. "Is that a problem?"

"No. It's just that my contact there is...my ex-husband." Immediately, she felt inadequate. But that was just because Stephen would often blame her for the problems in their marriage. He had said she was too ambitious and too competitive, especially when she would often advance before he did. He claimed that he hadn't left her, but that she had driven him away, that she had crushed their young marriage with the weight of her competitiveness. That was probably true. Alyssa didn't try to deny it. She had attributed it more to the distance between them that serving in the Army dictated, but she had to admit, she had been the one to refuse to leave her post and follow Stephen.

Tank's eyes narrowed, his voice dropping an octave. "You were married?"

She watched him, the wild flutter expanding, her breath suddenly jammed up in her chest. "Yes, for three years. It didn't really end well."

"You'd call your idiot of an ex-husband to help me out?"

"Idiot?"

Tank was true to form. His bluntness almost made her smile.

Exhaling heavily, he stared at her. He finally shook his head, his voice flat, "He must have been to let you go."

"He...left me," The words still stung a bit, but it made her more angry than sad now.

"Stupid fucker," he growled. He held her gaze for a long, charged moment, then looked away, his face taut with strain. Alyssa saw him swallow, and when he spoke, his voice was so gravelly that she could barely hear him. "I would be so grateful if you could do this for me. I know it's asking a lot. I love that dog," he whispered.

Biting her lip against the increasing fullness in her throat, Alyssa nodded. "I know you do. I'll do everything I can for him. I promise."

She pulled out her cell phone and walked away from the bed. Dialing the number for the facility, it was picked up after one ring. "Lieutenant Colonel St. James for Major Wilcox."

"Yes, ma'am. One moment."

"Alyssa?"

"Yes, hello, Stephen. I'm calling on a business matter."

"All right. What is this business matter?"

"I need to know the status of a military working dog, Echo." She gave him the number that was tattooed inside his ear.

"Just a moment."

She waited, glancing at Tank who was watching her and listening to every word.

"He's in critical condition. His wound is debilitating. We're trying to stabilize him for surgery. He's not cooperating. Euthanasia was discussed."

She stiffened and said fiercely, "What? You're not even giving him a chance?"

"I said it was discussed, Alyssa," he snapped. "You get much too emotional about these animals."

Stunned by his uncaring tone, the first flicker of anger pumped through her. There was no way she wasn't going to do everything in her power to save Echo. He'd gone to war, fought bravely. He had a right to every shred of care. He deserved it and she wasn't going to stand by and let this happen. "Don't you do a damn thing until I get there."

"What? You're coming here? We can handle this dog. I'm not incompetent!"

Fortified with a deep energizing rage, she straightened, curling her hand into a fist, holding her phone in a death grip. "I don't give a damn, Stephen," she said, her tone quiet and precise. "If Echo is put down, I will hold you personally responsible."

"Yes, ma'am." There was a trace of bitterness in his voice.

She didn't even bother to hang up, but disconnected the call. Her throat suddenly aching, she looked up at the ceiling, willing away the sudden sting of tears. This was going to be more than trying to protect Echo. San Antonio was her home. Going back there would bring back the memories of not only her childhood, but her brother's death and what it had done to her family. He was only fifteen when he'd collapsed at a basketball game. The doctor said his heart had a defect. Her dad had never been the same. She was

64 ZOE DAWSON

planning on going to San Antonio for Thanksgiving. But now, she couldn't seem to face a prolonged visit. While she was there, she'd call her dad and cancel. Her heart wasn't in it. She wanted to be here for both Tank and Jordan.

Regaining control, she turned around. Tank was moving to the edge of the bed, reaching for his IV like he was going to yank it out. "What the hell do you think you're doing?" she asked.

"I'm going with you."

5

"TANK, YOU HAVEN'T BEEN DISCHARGED."

He was already sliding his feet over the side of the bed. He wasn't going to stay here and let them euthanize Echo. No fucking way. With anger eating away at him, he swore savagely, so damned mad he could barely see straight. He didn't want to acknowledge the fear and how he had spent his life trying to be careful, but Echo had gotten in. The guilt about Blue rode him hard, too. He couldn't do anything for his teammate, but he could do something for his valuable partner who was fighting for his life. If he wasn't careful, this woman would also slip beneath his armor. Then there was the pain, the downright agony of losing Echo forever without seeing him again. It almost broke him in half after that dog had saved their lives. "I don't give a damn. I'm not letting this happen."

"Tank! Please!" She rushed over to the bed and pushed down on his shoulder, grabbing his wrist when he reached for the IV. Her grip was strong as hell. "Wait, don't you dare do that." Her face went white and part of him liked that she cared about him, but the other part was determined to get out of the hospital and on a flight to Texas.

He got in her face, urgency running through him. "Don't tell me what to do, Doc. I'm going," he said, his tone deadly quiet. He stared at her, his eyes narrowed.

She never backed down one inch, her gaze as unwavering as his. She grabbed his wrist and wrestled with him.

Tank closed his eyes, a knot of raw emotion climbing up his throat. He waited for the aching contraction to ease, then growled, "He saved us. If it wasn't for him, I wouldn't be here. None of us would. We were ambushed!" His voice broke and he swallowed.

She went stock-still against him, then looked at him, her eyes wide, her expression transfixed by a host of emotions. Her expression was strained as he held her gaze.

"I have to see him. I'm fine. You can't stop me. I have ninja moves you won't see coming."

Alyssa stared at him for an instant; then her eyes filled with tears and she hugged him like there was no tomorrow. His throat closed up completely, and he shut his eyes and turned his face against hers, hugging her back.

Trying his damnedest to get rid of the big lump in his throat, he ran his hand up her spine.

She leaned back, tight compression lines around her mouth. She released a long breath and tightened her hand on his wrist. "I didn't say you couldn't go. Just...for the love of God. Listen to me for once in your stubborn life."

He froze and locked on to those hot, tough, intense green eyes. "Talk fast, woman."

"Let me get the nurse and have her remove the IV, get you your clothes, and get you discharged. I don't need MPs chasing us down the hall and all the way to the airport.

Besides, you'll want to get dressed so that gorgeous backside isn't flapping in the breeze for everyone to see."

His mouth twitched with a flicker of humor. It wasn't lost on him that she thought his butt was gorgeous, but his need to get to San Antonio and Echo superseded everything, even this inconvenient attraction to Alyssa St. James. "You can bounce a quarter off my ass, lady. It won't be flapping anywhere."

A sparkle of amusement appeared in her eyes, and she tipped her head to one side. "I can't argue with that."

His mouth twitched; then he sobered. Tears appeared, and she looked at him, her heart in her eyes. "I'm not going to stand by when a hero is in jeopardy." With tears glistening in her long lashes, she caressed his face, infinite gentleness in her eyes, then leaned forward and whispered, "I promise that to you, Tank."

He closed his eyes and nodded.

She let go of him and backed away. "I'm the one who can help you now." She gazed at him, silently imploring him as she took the steps to the door. "Give me a few minutes.

Fuck. With those few words she turned his apple cart upside down. He'd only ever needed his brothers; his parents had let him down, but he had always been able to trust not only his biological brothers, but his brothers in arms. They had never let him down and would always have his back. But this beautiful, desirable woman was muscling her way in. He had to admit that he needed her. No one else had not only the guts but the connections to get him to see and save Echo.

He was expected to just simply give her his trust?

Women hadn't exactly been the most reliable parts of his life.

What made him think Alyssa would stick to her word?

All he wanted here was the status quo. He had to stick to the way it had always been, that was familiar, or he was going to have to deal with the consequences. It was much more than getting his ass in a sling with a violation of the UCMJ and the Navy.

He didn't have to wait long. Before he knew it, a nurse came into the room, followed closely by the attending physician.

"I understand you want to be discharged."

"Yes, sir," Tank said, his words coming out more belligerent than respectful. "I know you only have me here for observation. I need to be in San Antonio. My MWD—"

He held up his hand. "Your friend has already explained the situation to me, Petty Officer." He looked at Tank's chart. "My sympathies." Then he looked back up. "I'm willing to discharge you as long as I have your word you will rest."

"I'll make sure he does," Alyssa said, and her words should have made him want to chew glass, but her support only stabbed him right in the heart. Damn her.

"Make sure you watch him constantly." The doctor pursed his lips and was deep in thought. "I'm not crazy about you flying out of the state, but I understand the urgency. If you have any breathing issues or feel faint, I want to hear from you. Is that understood, sailor?" He pulled out a card and handed it to Alyssa as if she was his keeper. Tank bristled. No one kept him. He took care of himself and his brothers.

"Copy that, sir," he said, working at staying calm. Agitation wasn't going to get him to Echo, and that's all he cared about right now.

"The nurse will remove your IV and we'll get your discharge from the hospital started. Good luck with saving Echo."

He breathed a sigh of relief and allowed a begrudging gratitude toward Alyssa. "Thank you, sir."

He had to wait patiently for the nurse to remove his IV. When she was done with that, she got his clothes for him, then she and Alyssa left.

His chest still hurt from the blast. He suspected it was soft tissue damage from the impact. He was lucky he was wearing body armor and that shell had landed far enough away from them not to liquefy their organs.

He paused for a moment, remembering the way Echo had streaked across the compound, unearthed the man waiting for them, attacked, and valiantly risked his life for them. If that RPG had been fired straight at them. All of them would be dead.

Then there was Blue. The guilt ran through him again. He was supposed to have his back, and something had happened to him. He was sure Ruckus wouldn't rest until he was found and was even now making sure the search for him was thorough and a priority. The SEALs would pull out all the stops to bring him home. Tank felt as if he'd let Blue down.

Shaking himself out of his memories, he powered through getting his underwear on, then his jeans. Leaving them unzipped and unbuttoned, he shrugged into his shirt.

"They almost have your discharge papers ready. You just need to si—" Alyssa stopped and just stared.

"I'm moving a little slow."

She eyed him, then folded her arms over her chest. "Is that your roundabout way of asking me for help?"

"No, I don't need—"

She crossed the room and reached for his jeans, and that shut him up completely. He tried to ignore the heat settling in his groin while she zipped him up. A blush settled in her cheeks. This tough as nails woman blushed from a zipper and a bare chest? Maybe she wasn't as...sexually active as he'd been. That made him want to take her shoulders and turn her toward the bed and fall on her. The thought of getting her naked and pushing into her was not the most cooling thought right now, especially with her hands on him.

He knew how to make a woman scream, and getting down and dirty with a willing partner was as heady as combat. Until this moment, he'd considered it the best part about women. But Alyssa was the exception to the rule. She'd blown his rules to smithereens. As effective as lobbing a grenade at him and saying, *take that, sucker.*

She buttoned him up, then did up his belt, still focused on his chest, her hands brushing against the exposed skin of his waist. And it was a laser focus, as if she'd never seen a man's pectoral muscles before. Or was it that she had never seen him? He knew how he was built, and he was big everywhere. He understood his attraction to Becca. She was temporary and they both knew it. But his attraction to Alyssa was confusing. He'd always steered clear of the kind of woman that was looking for and demanded commitment. There was nothing that felt temporary about her. Not a damn thing. He'd known violence his whole life and she hadn't. Probably grew up in a nice neighborhood in with all that she needed.

He was wild, destructive, lethally dangerous when it came to his everyday life. It served him well as a SEAL, but as a potential significant other it felt negative when he thought about being with Alyssa. Would she think of his survival skills and his training negatives in a relationship? Why was he even thinking about this?

But the way she was looking at him said she wasn't *that*

innocent. He had to wonder about her inhibitions and what would happen if she let go of them. Their eyes clashed suddenly.

It was a wild woman looking at a wild man.

And he felt wild.

He wanted his mouth on her, everywhere on her, but especially where the heat of her would be the most scorching. He wanted to make her come, then take her and make her his.

He was damn near electrified with the closeness of her body, all those sensuous, silky curves pressed up against him, all that blushing innocence that he sensed in her flush against him with no daylight or breath between them.

He needed something—a freaking clue, her mouth on his, restraint, a drench of cold water to douse this heat, this need for this beautiful, sexy woman.

He was doomed.

"Alyssa," he spoke her name softly, like that could possibly save him from what he was feeling. His hand came up to cup her cheek. Yeah, he was on a freaking roll, and it was all rock bottom from there. "Pretty butterfly."

"Thorn," she said so softly, it was like butterfly wings against his skin. She'd crossed the line by calling him by his first name. An officer never used a rank and file's given name; it was considered familiar and could build the kind of bonds that would compromise her authority and show favorites. Not done in the military.

But she was so take-his-breath-away beautiful, looking up at him with that wild tumble of dark hair framing her face, her skin so soft, her gaze full of longing and locked onto his like she was drowning, he couldn't give a flying fuck.

"Thorn," she said again. "We need...we should—"

Yeah, he got it all right. They needed and should do anything they wanted, anything she wanted from him, give each other everything they had been missing. She was holding on to him like she was never going to let him go, had him up real close and personal. He could feel the rise and fall of her breasts on every breath, and so help him God, *hoo-yah*, it was fogging up his brain, giving him a bad case of tunnel vision, with her the only light at the end—those aching green eyes rimmed in thick dark lashes, so lush, her face devoid of any makeup. Stunning.

He was usually stronger.

But not today. Not when she'd vowed to save Echo and he was losing his cool and walking the knife's edge between this breath and the next.

It was the brotherhood he could trust, but Alyssa was making some pretty powerful inroads.

Once, he told himself, *kiss her once. Just one kiss to see him through.*

It was asking for trouble, more trouble than he could handle—and he knew it.

But that wasn't going to stop him.

Holding her gaze with his own, he lowered his mouth to hers and watched as her eyes drifted closed in readiness for his kiss. It was all so damn easy. He heard her hold her breath, felt the sensual heat of her draw him closer and closer—wild, dangerous butterfly.

He took his time, an eternity, barely touching his lips to hers, wanting to hold every breath of her inside himself, to savor every moment until he pulled away. In the past, he would have plundered and devoured, taken and demanded.

This was her fault. She was the one who was irresistible to him. It was all her, all the way, from the first crumbling of his outer wall of defense all the way through to his total surrender. He'd kissed more women than he could remember—so many lips, so many throwaway times.

But it wasn't any contest. She was the new yardstick.

Just the smell of her was enough to get him hard, and the taste of her...

He opened his mouth wider, took more of her, slid his arm around her waist and pulled her into him, and she was no damn help at all. She pressed herself against him, sliding her tongue along his and making a soft sound from deep in her throat that ran through him like fire, lighting him up from his brain to his balls.

The phone by the bedside rang and they broke apart as if they were both just waking from a dream. They blinked at each other and then Alyssa moved back. He reached for the phone. "We have your discharge papers ready for signature, Mr. Hunt."

"Thank you," he rasped.

He hung it up.

"We shouldn't have done that," she said. "I'll just pretend it didn't happen."

He let her think what she wanted, but he wasn't about to forget one moment of it. She was looking at his chest again. "The shirt's not going to button itself," he murmured, the smile on his face uncontrollable.

She raised her eyes to his and they were again a very snappy green. She reached out and he could feel her fingers shaking. Not as cool as she wanted him to think she was.

She focused on the buttons until she had them done up, each stroke of the back of her fingers a hot agony against his skin. Her blush was back.

He reached out and slipped his index finger under her chin. "How many men you been with, Alyssa?"

Startled, she blinked a couple of times, then her eyes narrowed. "What kind of question is that?"

"An honest one. I want to know."

She raised her chin, her eyes snapping. God, was it wrong that he loved that about her? "It's *none* of your *goddamned* business."

That struck a nerve. Her defenses were definitely up.

"I'm sure you'll need more than your fingers and toes to count your conquests."

"If you want to know, just ask me. I'll be honest."

"I'm sure you will." She reached for the sling, her movements jerky. Helping him get his arm settled inside it took only a few minutes, then she stepped back. "I'm going to forget all about all of this. You will, too."

Not damn likely, he thought to himself. He was going to be spending the next few days with her, and even with the knowledge that he was already way past crossing the line, he couldn't seem to pull himself together. She hadn't protested too loudly until he touched that very exposed nerve.

For the first time in his life, he was fascinated by a woman, snagged so thoroughly he couldn't seem to even preserve his own self. But she was worth the risk. All he had to do was minimize it. He'd like to tell himself it was all about getting her into bed. He wished it was about the physical. That would have been much easier to deal with.

BLUE WOKE UP, barely able to breathe around the pain in his head. He was under some heavy blankets on a flat, giving surface. He couldn't move, he was so exhausted. He opened his eyes to the rough beams above him. He reached for the memory of how he was injured but discovered...nothing. There was a blank space where his memories should be. It hurt his head to try harder, so he drifted back toward sleep. He woke up again, this time from the sound of someone close to him. With an excruciating effort, he turned his head and wasn't sure if he was seeing something real, or a gorgeous blonde angel minus the wings.

His beautiful savior had the kind of body with shapely curves that made him wonder and imagine what she'd look like naked, with nothing but his hands painting her supple, creamy looking skin with caresses. Then there was all that silky blonde hair the color of rich honey, those bright blue eyes that were full of life and light as if she glowed from within, and that sweet mouth of hers that looked like it would smile so guilelessly managed to fuel some fantasies of how soft and sensual her lips might feel sliding against his skin.

He pegged her at five foot five, a good eight inches shorter than himself, but the confident way she carried herself, combined with her angel beauty, made her seem larger than life.

She did look like an angel, but his thoughts were anything but saintly.

Her gaze locked on him and she smiled with a sweet, genuinely-happy-to-see-you grin curving her lips. "Hello," she said in English, but with a slight Slavic accent. "My name is Elena Sokolov. You're on my family's farm."

She had a bowl in her hand decorated with a navy-blue background, red fruit, and tan leaves. She knelt down with a smile. She had on a wool sweater that looked handmade, dark pants, decorative boots on her feet. Steam rose from the contents in the bowl. He groaned when he tried to focus, so he closed his eyes.

"What is your name?"

"I don't know," he said. "I can't remember." He realized that should upset him, but every time he tried to focus, his head would hurt even more, so he gave up.

She made a soft sound. "I'm so sorry. Hopefully, it will come back to you." He felt the spoon against his lips and he opened his mouth. Rich, savory broth filled his mouth, thick on his tongue as he swallowed.

"That's very good," he said, opening his eyes and once again getting caught up in the beautiful angel who said her name was Elena. "Thank you for helping me. What happened to me? Do you know?"

"You must have been in some kind of battle. You're obviously American and you're wearing a uniform. I found you in a field and brought you here."

Soldier? Battle? He reached for what he suspected he would have around his neck—his dog tags, but there was nothing there. "Did you take the small metal plates from around my neck?" he asked.

She shook her head. "No. I looked for identification, but there is nothing on your uniform. I suspect you are special forces. I removed it for safety. Your uniform and the one boot you were wearing are buried in the hay in the barn," she said. "What would you like me to call you?"

He didn't know why, but he said, "Blue. Call me Blue. Where exactly am I. What country?"

"Kirikhanistan. Boris and Natasha Golovkin run this area. If they find you here, I don't know what they'll do to you. Me, I will be executed for harboring the enemy."

He tried to rise, but she soothed him back down. "Don't worry. I am good at talking. They won't suspect you. We will get you to safety, but first you must be able to move and walk. Your injury was severe."

"All right. You saved my life and if I can't trust you, who can I trust?" he murmured, losing the thread of the conversation as he floated toward sleep.

He felt her gently touching his head, then the feel of something wet against the side of his head. As he drifted in and out of consciousness, he felt her wrap his head again. Then she pulled the blankets over him and tucked them around him.

"Rest now. You're safe here."

He fell back to sleep unable to hold onto anything concrete except for his beautiful and angelic rescuer.

6

Tank opened his eyes as the plane touched down in San Antonio. Home of the Alamo, the Spurs, and the famous Riverwalk. When they got to the hotel, it was also the host of Wurstfest, a ten-day salute to sausage.

"I'm sorry, ma'am. I just don't have any rooms left..." She looked down at her screen and back at him as if Alyssa didn't exist. It was amazing that the cute, perky blonde could do anything but stare at Tank. This had been the fourth hotel they'd been to, and it seemed the city was booked to the rafters. "I doubt you'll find anything available."

"Are you sure? He's a decorated Navy SEAL, just recently wounded. We'd prefer not to traipse around the city looking for accommodations," Alyssa said. Tank leaned on the counter, which flexed his biceps and shoulder. Oh, she went there and played the wounded warrior card.

The clerk's eyes went over his arm, then his chest, and she licked her lips, her eyes softening when she took in his sling. When they came back to his eyes, he winked, and she sighed. "I could put you in our Presidential Suite for the regular room rate plus a discount since you're one of our service members. We can make an exception for you. The only problem is there's only one king sized bed. The other rooms are being renovated soon and the beds and furnishings have been removed. Will that work for you?"

Alyssa hesitated in reaching for payment, but Tank beat her to it. He was sure she wasn't thrilled to be in a room with him. She did promise the doctor to keep an eye on him, though. He was also not exactly sure about this. He wanted her, and he wasn't used to denying himself what he wanted, especially women. Shockingly his last few times had been with Becca, but it had been sporadic and unsatisfying. The memory of sex with that sweet little cowgirl when he'd been helping out Wes "Cowboy" McGraw, his teammate in Cowboy's home town of Reddick had completely faded. He wasn't going to put any credence on the fact that he stopped enjoying recreational sex the moment he met Alyssa. Now he was again back in Texas. After all, they were here because of Echo. She was doing him a huge favor. The hotel clerk took his card and processed the payment. She then handed them two key cards. "It's on the top floor and has an amazing view of San Antonio."

"I've seen the view plenty of times," Alyssa mumbled under her breath, too low for the clerk to hear.

She smiled. "Please enjoy your stay, Mr. Hunt, and on behalf of all the hotel staff and management, thank you for your service."

They got into the elevator and Alyssa pushed the button. She was still standoffish with him, but he didn't miss the way her eyes flashed each time the pretty clerk sighed over him. "Why didn't you just whip off your shirt and let her see your impressive chest? I'm sure the tattoos and your heavy muscles would have gotten us an even better room."

"Impressive chest?" he asked. He shifted and leaned against the wall. He wouldn't admit it to her, but he was damn tired, the only thing keeping him going was the urgency to their being in San Antonio just over a day and a half after he'd been blown up in Kirikhanistan. He'd been flown to Germany, got stabilized there, his next stop, Coronado. It was to get to Echo, and if his sex appeal worked, he was going to use it. "Combine that with my gorgeous backside, I'd say you think I'm nicely put together."

"I'm not commenting on any part of your anatomy." She kept her eyes straight ahead, but there was that blush again. Damn if he didn't like that cute bodily response to his attraction more and more. She was so self-possessed, but when it came to men, attraction, and letting down her hair, she was so damn uptight. Fuck, he wanted to loosen her up.

"Hell, woman. I'd whip out my dick if it got me a room. I want to get to Echo."

Her lips compressed, and she gave him a scathing look. *Score*, that got her attention and at least a response that wasn't monosyllabic. "That would have gotten you a room all right, but I suspect there would have been bars on it and would subject you to being someone's bitch. The police frown on men whipping out their *dicks* in public."

He chuckled at her tone and the way she said *dicks*. She was full of surprises, least of all the way she didn't fawn all over him, get that dazed, I-want-to-fuck-you look he often got from his *conquests* as Alyssa described them. He was so primed for everything and anything she said because she gave him no quarter.

"I wouldn't be anyone's bitch, Alyssa. I'm an Alpha dog." He stated it without an ounce of ego. The elevator stopped, and the doors opened to a private corridor. Down the end of the hall, the double doors to the suite were large and impressive. They exited the elevator and she followed behind him, both of them rolling their bags. He was tired, but eager to get to Lackland.

"We'll drop off our stuff and head out immediately. Echo needs surgery and I don't want to wait one more minute to get to him."

He couldn't argue with that. Fifteen minutes later they were back in the rental car and on their way to the base. "We're heading directly to the Holland MWD Hospital. I've pulled strings with my commanding officer who has some chops in the service. It doesn't hurt that I'm up for the head of surgery for the facility."

"Doesn't that mean you'll have to be full-time Army?"

"I used to be active duty but transitioned to the reserves to have the time to open my clinic."

"Is that the real reason or did something else happen to sour you on active duty?"

"I got out after my separation from my ex-husband," she admitted. "I was tired and drained."

"You have to do what's best for you."

"Tell that to my dad," she said softly, then looked embarrassed at the outburst.

Not having anyone in his life who pushed him, the parental thing was alien to him. He spent a lot of his time alone or with his brothers, but all the drive to succeed came from inside him. He was surprised that Alyssa took direction from anyone, but it was true that people were influenced by their parents. He'd just wanted to get as far away from his own as he could.

"Your dad?"

"I'd rather not go into that."

"But you're from San Antonio?"

"Yes."

"And your dad still lives here?"

"Yes. Are you done, Oprah?"

He held up his hands. Getting to know her was going to be a work in progress. She glanced at him several times like she wanted to question him, too. But apparently, she was better at refraining even in the wake of her curiosity.

But then she smashed that barrier and said, "Tattoos are very personal, so you might not want to answer." He didn't say anything, and she continued. "I figured out the XXVI one is twenty-six and that's the atomic number of iron. What does the one on your shoulder stand for?"

"The ones on my impressive body?"

She snorted, giving him a half-amused, half-irritated look. "Yeah."

"The one on my shoulder was my sister's name, Jelsena. The roses are because she loved them."

"Was?"

"She died in a car accident when I was twelve. I was in the car and my dad ran a red light. He was drunk off his good-for-nothing ass."

"I'm so sorry. That must have been so hard on you and your brothers."

He nodded. "I don't talk much about the accident. Not even with my brothers." Jelsena had died in the back seat with him sitting right next to her. He'd watched the life drain out of her, and he'd never stopped blaming his father.

"Maybe you should. Maybe they need closure as much as you did before you got the tattoos."

It had never occurred to him that his brothers would hurt, not only at his silence about their sister's death, but being so young, didn't remember her life. Alyssa had a way of just cutting through the bullshit in his head. Maybe he should talk to his brothers about her.

They arrived at the hospital, and when they walked in, Tank stopped dead. In the lobby were all his teammates with the exception of Blue, an absence Tank felt down to his bones. "What are you guys doing here?"

"Alyssa called and said that you were coming here, and Echo is part of our team. We weren't going to let anyone make decisions about one of our team members without us having a say."

He took the time to look at each one of his teammates. Ruckus, Bowie Cooper, their leader, their LT who took the brunt of the failed mission. Who had lost a man in battle even though he'd argued vehemently against separating their unit. His decisions cost men's lives, but he bore that burden as he did everything else with a strong sense of duty and a healthy dose of conscience.

Kid Chaos, Ashe Wilder, might joke, but that clown went from a crazy, funny bastard to a dead-eyed killer in a heartbeat.

Cowboy, Wes McGraw, their Chief and touchstone. He was the rock that kept them moving, kept them honest and knit them together like a well-oiled machine.

Scarecrow, Arlo Porter, a charming bastard, but silent and the deadliest son-of-a-bitch with a knife Tank had ever seen, bar none.

Wicked, Orion Cross, calculating and strong both mentally and physically. He was a supernatural force to be reckoned with. He disappeared like a ghost and was as calculating as a serial killer.

Hollywood, Jude Lock, a smooth ladies man who turned into the enemy's worst nightmare, as deadly with any weapon as he was with his hands.

He took a small breath, and Blue, Ocean Beckett, a skilled medic, badass warrior and philosopher who could make you think hard with just a few words. The guilt of not being there for him, not knowing what had happened to him, hurt like a son-of-a-bitch. Had he neglected one teammate for the other? Was a human life more important than Echo's?

Echo, who was lying in this place somewhere, had not only saved these men, he'd saved countless lives.

Tank turned to look at Alyssa, and she smiled. There was no doubt in her mind that they would show up, which meant she understood the brotherhood—she got it that what they did was from their hearts, displayed in their actions, and was much stronger and louder than words.

He was floored, and it made him look at Alyssa in a different light. She was awesome in her own right, but this act of kindness, this understanding of how he was feeling, what he would need, did something to him that he'd never experienced before. She'd changed his perspective and burrowed her way a little deeper into not only his mind, but his heart as well. And he was so sure that he'd closed his heart a long time ago.

With that realization, fear surfaced. The kind of fear that he'd buried deeper than any fear that came after it. Fear of getting hurt, the fear of trusting and then being betrayed by the people who were sworn to love him. Of being alone.

He'd gone into the Navy SEALs because he thirsted for order. He hungered for cohesion and precision. He wanted to belong to something that meant something, something that was strong and filled an open hollowness in him. He'd found it in the SEALs.

Pushing himself to his limits, seeing how tough he was —not only his body, but more importantly, his mind. He'd navigated the mean streets of East LA by his wits and his brawn. He'd kept his brothers safe, protected them against gangs, drugs, and his sorry parents.

"Thank you for coming," he said.

Kid piped up. "Yeah, it's only part of it. When we heard there was a sausage festival in town, well, you couldn't keep me away."

"Yeah, now six guys are stuffed into two rooms," Wicked said.

"Then I guess you'd have to call that a sausage fest," Tank said.

Kid laughed along with the other guys, pointing his finger at Tank. "You stole my line, you bastard."

They all sobered when a man with a white coat and a stethoscope came through the door. Tank looked to Alyssa who had stilled near the front desk. "Lieutenant Colonel St. James," he said. "The dog is this way. Who is the handler?"

This was her ex-husband; this slender man Tank could break in two? Just the thought of him touching her, even in the past rankled.

"I am," he growled.

"Come with me," he said, as if this was a waste of his time. Tank wanted to haul off and deck the guy, but it wouldn't be worth losing his access to his brave buddy. He took them into a room and finally—Echo.

Tank relived the awful moment when everything had gone white. The feeling of helplessness churning through him when he spotted his fierce K9 warrior in agony. After waiting for so long, he had finally gotten to him.

As soon as Echo saw Tank, he barked, and Tank walked over to him. He braced his hand on the gurney and covered his eyes with his hand, finally giving in to the intolerable pressure in his chest. It was the panic that had unraveled him—and the awful tension that had dogged him every mile he'd been separated from his combat partner. And it was also the accumulated strain of hours of worry and moments of heart-stopping fear. For hours he had shoved the constant anxiety to the back of his mind, refusing to give in to it. His internal damn broke.

He bent his head down and buried his face into Echo's fur. His eyes filled, and Echo licked his face, his tail wagging a mile a minute. Something that had tightened the day he'd been separated from him loosened. Echo had always been there, doing his job, keeping people safe, working his ass off. He was the best K9 partner he'd ever had and the only thing in this world who had ever protected him. He wasn't going to stand by while someone told him his warrior dog wasn't fighting for his life.

ALYSSA MOTIONED for Stephen to exit the room. She closed the door softly, leaving Tank to spend some time with Echo. "Let me see his chart."

"He wasn't like that before. He was lethargic, and we didn't believe that he would survive the operation."

She'd never been a violent person, but she wanted to punch her ex-husband in the balls. How could she have married such a man? He was supposed to be a vet and an advocate for animals. She looked up at him. She grabbed the chart out of his hand. "What happened to you? When did you stop caring?"

"I do my job, Alyssa."

"Well, you go do that. I've got this." She stared at him stonily. But he didn't budge.

"That's the problem with you, Alyssa. You think you know everything there is to know. You always thought you were better than me. So this shouldn't come as any surprise to me that you're being such a bitch."

"Wow. You didn't even ask to speak freely." She lifted her chin. "I'm not responsible for how you feel, Stephen. You're responsible for that. What I do comes naturally to me. I don't think how my skills and expertise affect others. I don't answer to you anymore."

"No, as usual. You only answer to your father."

That hit like a nuke and exploded. Still not giving an inch even though he'd scored a direct hit, she stared him down. He shook his head. "If you need me, ma'am, just page me."

She looked down at the chart and the list of his injuries would heal, but the one to his shoulder had severed muscle, broken bone. She blinked rapidly, smarting from his jab. "I won't need you."

She looked up into his narrowed eyes. He stared at her for a moment then walked away. Alyssa took a deep breath. She didn't have time to think about what he'd said. She caught one of the lab techs walking by and said, "Prepare an operating room. I'm going to be doing surgery on this warrior."

"Yes, ma'am."

She took a breath and went back into the room. Tank was petting Echo and there was such a beautiful smile on his face that she had to catch her breath. This is what she was going to think about right now.

"Tank?"

He looked at her, the gratitude in his eyes profound. "Thank you for doing this, Alyssa. You'll never know how much this means to me."

"I think I do." She walked over and hugged him, his eyes red rimmed and swollen. He clasped her to him hard and held her for a few minutes, his hand cupping the back of her neck. "I'm going to need to examine him. Will you hold his head while I look at his wound?"

He let her go and stepped back, nodding. Fighting against the new wave of feelings jamming up in her chest, Alyssa looked away, her eyes prickling. The thump of Echo's tail almost made her laugh, but Tank caught her under the chin, forcing her face up. "I'll do anything to help Echo," he said, his tone firm. "He's ready to fight."

She unwrapped the bandages. This was a long and deep gash; the shrapnel had traveled from his ribs to the top of his neck. The largest muscle affected was his latissimus dorsi and she noted how deep the laceration went, but the good news was that he hadn't lost any muscle and the wound had been thoroughly cleaned. The guys over in Germany did an excellent job. She could fix this, but, she turned to Tank. "The good news is that this is operable, and I think I can give him a good range of motion, say eighty percent, maybe even ninety. But he won't be able to go back to active duty and he's probably going to have a limp. I'm sorry."

"Are you sure?" he asked, his voice breaking badly.

She nodded. "He's almost eight years old, Tank," she said gently. "He's done his duty. He needs to be retired."

He swallowed hard and she could tell he was having a hard time with this. "I don't want to let him go, but I understand."

When she turned around, six men stood at the window. With word from their commander, they all did a precision and hard salute. Tank leaned his head back against the wall and closed his eyes. She couldn't remember wanting to hold a man more.

"I'm going to get scrubbed up. You can stay with him until he's sedated."

He rubbed Echo's head and his tail went off again. "Good boy. You did an awesome job, buddy. You saved so many lives." His voice choked up, and she squeezed his arm, then slipped out the door. She faced the men in his unit.

"I'm glad you're all here. I'm going to operate on Echo, but I know that Tank would appreciate your support while he waits."

"Hoo-yah!" was the collective answer from them all. She smiled and went to the operating area, scrubbed in, and was gowned and masked. Soon Echo was wheeled in, the dog's breathing slow and steady. The anesthesiologist gave her the thumbs up. She sat near his head to monitor his vital signs.

Alyssa said, "Let's begin." She painstakingly sewed every severed muscle, nerve, and tendon back together with simple sutures that would dissolve as the muscles knitted. He wouldn't be one hundred percent, but she would give him as much mobility as her skill could give him. Eleven hours passed before she finished the job. She usually left closing to a resident, but she did this herself, taking that step for him, mending what America's enemies had sundered. She'd given him the vital chance he would need to heal and convalesce. She blinked back tears as she finished the last stitch. Silently she whispered to herself. *Thank you, Echo, for your service. Thank you for taking care of that big, beautiful lug out there waiting for you. Just thank you.*

She pulled off her gloves, leaned back to relieve the strain in her back, and turned to look back at the resting animal. The anesthesiologist came alongside her. She touched Alyssa's shoulder. "You are truly gifted."

That grabbed her heart and squeezed. She had worked hard to be what she thought Robbie would have been, what he would have done, the kind of dedication he would have given if he'd lived and become a vet. She smiled as the woman left the room. Something occurred to her. It hadn't been Robbie here saving Echo's life. It had been her—she had fought and bullied and called in every favor she was owed to get to do this operation on him. It had been all her. Immediately, she thought about her father and she had to wonder who he saw when he looked at her. Was it the past? Did he even think of her as an individual when he played the Robbie card her whole life as if his legacy would have overshadowed her if he had lived? It was a sobering and uncomfortable thought. How much did she really owe her deceased brother? Her emotionally crippled father?

She rubbed her neck after she took off her gown and disposed of it in the bin. Then she wearily walked down the hall to the waiting room. It was still filled with seven men, all of them sleeping, some in chairs, others propped against the wall. The duty receptionist smiled. "This is a lot of testosterone."

"Yes, ma'am. I tell you. It's been no hardship working tonight."

Alyssa smiled broadly and took in all that beautiful, sleeping muscle and handsome as sin faces. What a group of hotties.

But there was one face that was most dear to her, deny it as much as she might. Thorn Hunt was devastatingly gorgeous.

She walked over to him and sat down in the vacant chair. She touched his arm. He stirred, the soft noise of his wake-up sounds stimulating even after almost a dozen hours of bending over Echo. He opened those thickly lashed eyes and then, *boom*, he was awake. Combat awake as if he could turn it on and off. And maybe SEALs could.

"How is he?"

She wrapped her hand around his as he came upright. He looked so exhausted. "He's really good. Very good."

He let out his breath and closed his eyes. "Can I see him?"

"Yes."

They rose, and he grabbed her hand, walking down the hall together. Once they entered the recovery room, Tank stopped, then looked at her. Echo was on a pallet on the floor covered with a quilt that was made out of cute doggie material. He was hooked up to an IV and a monitor. But next to him was another pallet made up for Tank.

"Go on. Get some sleep. He'll rest better with you nearby. He knows your scent and he's probably going to be a little scared when he comes out of the anesthesia. Give him a lot of encouragement." She let go of his hand. "I'll check on him through the night. Rest."

She turned to go, but Tank's raspy command stopped her. "Wait."

She looked back at him and their eyes met. There was something new, something that looked as good on him as his tough look. A sweet sensation unfolded in her when she saw the way he was looking at her. It wasn't sexual. It was warmth she saw in his eyes—a warmth that was a mixture of gratitude and affection. That look created such a response in her that it was almost more than she could handle. And she wanted to touch him so badly that it was all she could do to keep her hands to herself.

A strand of hair came undone from her ruthless bun and slipped across her mouth, and Tank leaned over and lifted it away. Alyssa's breath caught on a wave of sensations, and she closed her eyes and grasped his wrist.

He rubbed his knuckle along her jaw, then reluctantly pulled free of her grasp and straightened. Alyssa rubbed her forehead; then drawing a shaky breath, she looked at him. "I wish," she said, trying to sound annoyed, "that you would quit doing that to me."

He gazed at her, that same mixture of warmth and gratitude and pure, unaltered sex appeal lighting his eyes. "You're even full of sass when you're dog-tired. Pun intended."

She groaned, then grinned at him. "You're a piece of work, mister."

He chuckled as he went to the pallet and lay down with his head next to Echo's.

She went to one of the empty offices and started to fill out the report, her eyes heavy and gritty. The words blurred, but she jerked awake. She looked at her watch and saw that she'd been asleep for about half an hour.

Time to check on her patient. She went back to the recovery room, and when she walked in, she had to take a deep breath. All of his teammates had migrated to this room. They surrounded Tank and Echo like a living, breathing shield. This was part of that brotherhood she understood. This was what these guys lived and breathed, covering each other's backs, being there when it mattered. Making sure all their buddies were accounted for. So it must have been doubly terrible to know that one of them was missing. Blue's bright blue eyes and strong, handsome face materialized in her mind. *God, please keep him safe until they can get to him.* She prayed silently, fiercely. *For their sakes and his. Give him the strength he needs to get through whatever it is he's going through.*

She maintained her cool as she checked Echo's vital signs. He was resting easy, and the color of his gums looked pink and healthy. He was doing phenomenally. What a fighter!

She kept it together until she got back to her office. She was a doctor and wasn't supposed to get emotionally involved with her patients, but Alyssa couldn't seem to separate herself from this one.

She fought against the thick feeling in her throat and chest. A small sob escaped, and she covered both her eyes with her cupped palms. It seemed like a long time before she had cried herself out, her harsh sobs dwindling to the occasional ragged one. Pressing the heels of her hands against her throbbing, swollen eyes, she forced herself to dredge up some control, then she reached for tissues, blew her nose, and closed her eyes and tipped her head back, waiting for her emotions to settle. God, she didn't know she could feel so involved, so exhausted, so emotionally twisted.

She folded down on the couch against the wall, her weary body shutting down, a terrible emptiness settling inside her. That feeling was compounded when she admitted to herself that she wanted to get so much closer to Tank. She tried to will away the ache that was pressing in on her heart. After seeing Stephen, she realized the contrast between the two men. Tank so larger than life, such a fierce and brave warrior, a gentle giant. In the beginning, she'd had hope with Stephen, but that had proved to be her undoing.

She sensed that Tank was alone, wary, and that created a serious fear in her that she could barely stand. Her imminent active duty change, the distance. It was as if history was repeating itself and she'd vowed, never again—never again would she be that vulnerable. He so desperately needed someone. Not to show him what love was—Echo had done that, those men in there had done that, and his brothers as well. What he needed was to offer that to a woman, something that wasn't all about getting his rocks off. Hit by a rush of emotion, Alyssa locked her jaw against the awful constriction in her throat. She had never realized until this instant that she wanted that woman to be her. She just wasn't sure if she had enough courage.

7

WHEN MORNING DAWNED, Alyssa woke up and then rushed to the recovery room. His teammates were already gone, and she was sorry she didn't get to say goodbye. Tank was sitting against the wall, and Echo's head was in his lap. Tank was petting his head, talking low and soft to him.

"Morning," she said, and Tank looked up. The pinched look around his eyes and mouth told her he was in pain. She might be a vet, but she was still a medical professional. He had been in an explosion less than thirty-six hours ago.

"It's time to go, Tank. You need to get some real rest. If your doctor finds out you've been sleeping on a pallet, he'll probably skin me alive."

"He took an oath. Cause no harm. Isn't that right?"

She chuckled. "Okay, so he might just blister my ears, then." She walked over and said, "How is our patient doing?"

"He's doing great."

"He just needed you here."

He nodded and gave her a full-blown smile and, yeah, okay, it was spectacular.

She walked over, checked Echo, then reached out her hand for him. He clasped it, and it was like moving a granite block with her pinky toe. It was a good thing the granite block was cooperating. Mr. My-way-or-the-highway, listening to her. That was also new.

Back at the hotel room, they took turns showering. Tank was already sitting on the edge of the bed when she came out of the bathroom.

"So, give me the lowdown on Echo. The whole story." He'd taken off the sling, and the medication had taken that pinched look away. He looked as relaxed as a man like Tank could get, the intensity still there, but banked.

She walked over to him and said, "He's in pretty good shape considering. There is good news. The supraspinatus and infraspinatus muscles, essential muscles which flex and extend the shoulder and prevent dislocation by stabilizing movement of the scapula relative to the ribs, vertebrae and forelimbs weren't severed. It's important to note because if these muscles atrophy or shrink, the spine can be affected, and the scapula loses its stability. Both muscles are rich in nerves and especially the suprascapular nerve. His tendons also were spared severe damage and should mend on their own. I can say with some confidence that Echo will be running after his beloved ball when he fully recovers."

For a minute Tank just stared at her. He blinked several times. Then he reached out and snagged her around the waist, pulling her across his lap. Her breath caught at the unexpected move. When she went to protest about hurting him, his mouth captured hers. She could feel the need in him, the aching, lonely need, and she put her heart and soul into the kiss, wordlessly telling him things she couldn't say aloud. A shudder coursed through him, and he drew a ragged breath, catching her by the back of the head, his jaw flexing beneath her hand as he responded. He moved his mouth slowly against hers, tasting her, savoring her, drawing her breath from her and leaving her weak.

It went on and on and on, until Alyssa felt as if she were suffocating from all the sensations pouring in on her, and she flattened her hand against his chest. Tank tensed and dragged his mouth away from hers. His heart was slamming, and his breathing was harsh and uneven, but he gathered her up in a cuddling embrace. Alyssa hung on to him, knowing that he needed her—needed her strength and comfort. Finally, she was able to get a breath past the frenzy in her chest, and Tank ran his hand up her back, pressing her to him. He turned his head, placing an unsteady kiss against the curve of her neck, then nestled her closer.

"Ah, Alyssa," he whispered unevenly. "I'm so tired and you feel so good."

She closed her eyes and hugged him hard, moved by his husky admission. Struggling against the feelings he'd created in her, she tightened her arms around him when she felt him move and settle against the mattress with her. She pulled the covers up.

"I just want to hold you. I know none of this is playing by the rules, but the rules can go fuck themselves right now."

"*Hoo-yah and hooah!*" she said.

She was rewarded with a husky chuckle and a hard hug. Unaccountably moved by the hug, even more moved by the protective way he tucked her head against his shoulder, she shut her eyes and struggled against the sudden threat of tears. There was an undercurrent of tension to his voice mixed in with the amusement. She'd felt it ever since she'd seen him this morning.

"What's wrong?" she asked. "Is it Blue?"

Resting his cheek against her hair, Tank continued to

rub her back, and Alyssa turned her face against his neck, saturating herself in his touch. How could anything this good be against the law? Finally, Tank released a long sigh, running his hand up the full length of her back. "LT got a call this morning. Three of the captured NATO members were killed and left out in the open," he said.

Alyssa opened her eyes, considering his comment; then the sorrow of those deaths washed over her. It must be even worse for Tank, who had known them personally.

"Two SEALs are still missing...Speed from Team Bravo and Blue. The guys had to go. They're going to be intensifying their efforts to find Blue and the Kirikhan rebels' stronghold."

"You're upset you can't be part of it."

Tank raised his head and looked at her, his gaze solemn. "Damn right. I should be with them." He shifted his gaze as he smoothed his thumb along her cheekbone, then looked at her, his eyes dark and worried. "I don't like feeling helpless. It pisses me off."

It had cost him a lot to make such an open admission. Alyssa could see it in his eyes, and it was all she could do to keep from letting her feelings get the upper hand. "What is it about Blue that you're not telling me?" she asked softly, holding his gaze. "What are you holding onto?"

He stared down at her. He lifted a wisp of hair off her face and carefully tucked it behind her ear; then he looked at her again. "I should have had his back, Alyssa. He's out there or he's captured and being tortured. I can't help blaming myself," he said huskily.

She smoothed her hand down his bare arm. "Weren't you blown back? Weren't you unconscious?" she whispered.

"Yes," he said, guilt shadowing the brown of his eyes.

"When I woke up, he was already gone. I was rushing to help Echo."

"You did what you could. You're not superhuman."

He nodded, and they were silent for a long while as he rubbed her arm, then something shifted, and it wasn't about comfort anymore.

"But you're the closest thing I've seen to it." She was actually surprised he'd corralled his raw hunger for as long as he had. She thought he wanted her and that made her feel both awe and shock. She wanted to touch all the hard places that were so forbidden and sexy. She wished he would kiss her again. Wait... Why did she have to wait for that? She was as caught up in what was happening between them as she thought he was. But when she shifted to move more into him, she saw that he was asleep. Feeling let down, she shouldn't be disappointed. He'd kissed her so passionately, tempered with his gratitude.

He made her want to embrace everything that made her feminine.

His warmth lulled her closer and closer into sleep. How many lines would she be willing to cross with this man? How many would he?

THEY WERE THERE for three days, visiting Echo every day—and he improved every day. He would stay at Lackland until he was fully recovered, receive his physical therapy there as well. After he was fully healed, he would go up for adoption. That's the part that hurt like a bitch.

They slept in the big bed, but Tank didn't touch her at all. She was beginning to think that his interest in her must have waned or it had never been that hot to begin with.

Ninety-nine percent of her was so god-awful disappointed, and that mutinous one percent bitch slapped her and told her to get a grip. *You aren't going to pursue shit because you don't have the guts. You wouldn't even know the first thing about seducing a man like that. He's so out of your league.*

The truth hurt. While people in high school and college were hooking up and getting to know the opposite sex, Alyssa had been studying and working her damnedest to become a vet. Every waking moment was about getting to her goal. But when she'd gotten there, it had been hollow. It had been someone else's dream. Maybe she had been wishy-washy about the job offer because she was now completely confused. Had this been something she'd wanted for herself? She couldn't say.

Had she settled with Stephen because it was easier to stay in her protected sexual shell even as she yearned to release that part of her and see where she would go?

Meeting Tank had kick-started her. Being near him had been stimulating because he was always so contrary. She'd have to be completely blind not to want him. But something special was happening between them these last few days. Friendship. Not something she'd expected from a man who had sexual encounters instead of relationships.

Jordan had warned her that his brother wasn't boyfriend or husband material. He didn't want to see her get her heart broken, but he'd smiled and said he wasn't worried. She was too smart to go down that road.

She looked at herself in the bathroom mirror as she packed up her toiletries. "Yeah, I have a Ph.D. in How to make Myself Miserable. The dissertation was a complete downer."

When she came out of the bathroom, he was sitting on the bed looking out the window. His suitcase was packed and ready to go. His gorgeous profile made her heart beat faster.

At the sound of the door, he turned to look at her. "I guess you'll have to get yourself a new mascot, Doc."

He was back to calling her that as if he was working at distance. That clinched it. He was looking for a way to get out of seeing her. She should have known she couldn't tempt a man like that. She was such a ninny.

"You don't want to do it anymore?"

He gave her a disapproving smile. "I don't currently have a dog."

"How about we worry about this once you've gotten better and are reassigned a dog."

He looked down, then away. "What if I don't want another dog?"

She came over to the bed. There was a rebellious slash to his mouth and a hard look in his eyes. "You don't mean that. I know you believe in the MWD program. You've been helping me for a while." Was this Tank closing down, pulling in because of what happened to Echo? It had been easy to see that his wounding had torn Tank apart. She was sure he wasn't used to being this vulnerable. Maybe he recognized that. "Tell me what's really going on."

"Nothing. I just don't want another dog." He rose and grabbed his suitcase. "It's the end of this particular discussion."

The my-way-or-the-highway Tank was back, only this was worse than before. He seemed locked up.

She rolled her suitcase to the door. "Tank...I just want to help."

Her world tilted when he was there filling her vision, backing her against the wall. She looked at him, the tension humming in every muscle and nerve.

"Well, you're not helping right now, especially when I can't keep my mind on anything other than you."

His intense eyes caressed her face in a coarse and unsettling way—a rousing good way. She was so inexperienced when it came to connecting with her sexual side. She lived so much in her head. Her intellect was her armor, but with Tank, being smart didn't seem to be working. She had slept in the same bed with him. That wasn't exactly a genius move. Even knowing they were probably already violating the UCMJ, she couldn't seem to think, once again, that it was wrong.

"I'm having the same problem," she murmured.

He brushed his knuckles over her cheekbone, then his hand traveled down her neck to encircle her throat.

"I'm not going to give in to my need to fuck you so hard you'll forget about any man you had before me. Make no mistake, Alyssa, I want you. I usually take what I want if the woman is willing, and even with our constraints, I already know you are. I don't have to touch you to know your core is aching and you're wet and hot for me." The slight, sinful smile that curved his mouth told her that he knew how hot and restless he was making her. "I'd have you begging for me, and that's when I'd go down on you and use my tongue to make you come and come and come."

She made a soft gasp at the rough way he was talking to her. His eyes flashed as if her helpless sound of wanting pleased him. "Your unimaginative ex-husband had no idea what to do with you. I can taste the innocence in you, and I'm not a missionary kind of guy. I'd take you in every possible way a man can fuck a woman."

She was melting, her sex tingling where she wanted his fingers against her swollen flesh, and even though Stephen had fumbled around down there, she knew Tank would be masterful.

"You'll want to fuck me with your mouth, suck my dick so hard it'll drive me crazy, knock me to my knees, turn me upside down and inside out. I know you have that kind of power."

It was all she could do to keep herself from straddling his waist and locking her legs around him for direct contact.

His breathing was ragged, and his hand tightened on her throat as he tipped her head back. "You want to know why I'm restraining myself? Why I don't just do it?" His mouth hovered over her lips, his hot breath making her mouth ache for the pressure of his. His tongue slipped out and ran over her mouth, lust simmering in his eyes when she sucked on him. His lips grazed along her jaw, all the way to her ear. He pressed his cheek against her, the electric scrape of his stubble on her soft skin an erotic sensation that heightened the sexual tension rising between them. She closed her eyes, leaned more fully into his hard, lean body.

"Why?" she whispered.

"Because, I don't want this...our relationship...to be about sex. And sweetheart, that's the most dangerous thing about you."

He opened the door and slipped out as if he could ninja his way out of any more conversation. She closed her eyes to rein in her temper. After all they shared, this is what he was going to do? Shut her out? Like hell.

She marched out the door and he was already at the elevator. She stalked down the hall and faced him, her body still tingling, reacting to every hot and heavy word he'd said. God, she closed her eyes for a moment thinking how she wanted to be fucked by him, have that hot, wet mouth every-where. "This is a dangerous path we're on. We need to cool it before we both end up regretting it. We have already crossed so many lines."

"Agreed," he said.

She ran her hand over her hair to smooth it down. She nodded. "Good. That's settled. But not the dog handling." She had to get away from the relationship talk and back onto even ground if that was at all possible. "It would be wrong for a man like you, with your training and your way with dogs, to get out of the program. What else is going on?"

"Newsflash, Doc. You're not my keeper, my LT, or my therapist. So back the hell off. Touchy-feely time is over."

"In other words, you don't want to face that kind of situation again."

He sighed and stared at her stonily. The elevator doors opened, and he stepped inside. "You coming? I can't drive with my shoulder like this."

She gritted her teeth and ducked inside before the doors closed. He was right. Touchy-feely time was over.

He was silent and stoic the whole way back to San Diego, and he didn't say anything until she pulled up to his house. He sat there, lines of strain etched deep beside his dark eyes that combined with the shadow of his beard to make him look tough and dangerous.

He turned to her. "Thank you for what you did with Echo. I meant it. I'll never forget it, Doc."

Was this goodbye? She turned to him not sure where they really stood. There didn't seem to be any way to move forward, and God help her, there was no way to go back.

Her jaw locked against the sudden ache in her throat, she tried to will away the awful fullness burning in her eyes. They had shared so much in the last few days, and she had to ease in a deep, hard breath. She was strong enough for this. She knew that from experience. She didn't want to let him go.

His gaze stormy and intimate, he stared at her, his eyes alive with longing. Something flickered in his eyes, his expression hardening. "Take care of yourself," he said, his voice husky.

Left with nothing but this achy, hot feeling that filled her with dissatisfaction, she nodded, turning away, her throat tight. *Just let me get through this without coming apart in front of him.* Then she remembered. There was still a tie between them. Jordan worked for her, and it made her feel marginally better for some stupid reason. Regret filled her for his health scare. Tank was already overloaded with the loss of Echo and Blue missing. Hearing about Jordan must have been another terrible blow. Anything she could do to lessen his worry was worth mentioning. "You, too. If you ever need help with Jordan, let me know."

He paused half his body already out of the vehicle. He settled back in the seat and frowned, black hair tumbling across his forehead. "Why would I need help with Jordan?" he said, his voice little more than rough smoke.

"Doctor's appointments, treatments."

His face blanched and she realized in the split second before he said, "What treatments?" that she had just placed her foot in her mouth.

Tank's eyes narrowed a fraction, and he stared at her. Leaning in closer, his gaze suddenly dark and serious. When she just stared at him, a feeling of apprehension unfolding in her belly, he caught her chin. He didn't say anything, but she could feel the tension in him, and her apprehension turned to dread. "What treatments, Alyssa?"

"You should talk to Jordan, Tank."

"I'm talking to you and I want to know what's going on with my baby brother," he growled.

"I really think—"

"Tell me."

Feeling shaky inside, she had to resign herself to the fact that he wouldn't relent until she told him. He had a right to know, but it should have been Jordan who had told him. This was such a damned awful way for him to find out. She needed to give Jordan a piece of her mind. "He had a blood test that indicated he might have cancer."

He closed his eyes and swore viciously. "What the hell are you talking about?"

"I thought he would have told you about it. I'm sorry."

His voice gruff with hurt undertones, Tank said, "Fuck. I've got to go."

"Tank, I'm really sorry."

His face etched with anger, he slammed the door and walked across the lawn, slamming the front door so hard she heard it even at the curb.

For a moment, she didn't want to leave. But he had made it quite clear that he didn't want her help, not emotionally, not with Jordan. Not with anything.

She hunched her shoulders, filled with pain and remorse, but there was no outlet for it. She put the car in gear and headed home.

Her breath caught on a little sob, but she kept driving. There was nothing to do but move forward. She'd done that enough in her life.

Her moral conduct was safe, her career was safe, and her heart was safe.

Somehow that didn't cheer her up at all.

BLUE WOKE UP, the smell of wood burning and the heat of a fire warm against his face. He was in the same small room, the rough-hewn rafters above his head. The smell of something rich and delicious was in the air. He stirred and had no idea how long it had been since he'd been hurt. His sense of time was completely out of sync.

The door opened and closed. Then footsteps. Elena was above him. "*Yaxshi*."

That was *good* in her language. He knew Russian and he knew this dialect, more Uzbek than Russian. It made sense because the countries had once been one before Kirikhanistan had split. So he was fluent in languages, because after thinking about it, he knew French, Italian, and Spanish as well as several Middle Eastern ones to boot.

"What time is it?"

"It's after ten. You've been in and out for days. I was worried. For safety reasons, I don't even trust our local doctor. I couldn't risk you. There's no guarantee even he wouldn't turn us in, and believe me, you'd rather be dead if the Golovkins get a hold of you. Natasha is a sadist and her husband likes to watch. They are animals and they terrify me." Her voice was solemn with undercurrents of fear. "People disappear and never return."

"I understand. I'm feeling better, more alert."

"Things coming back to you?"

"Not yet. Still fuzzy."

She smiled, and God, but she was beautiful when she did that. He wasn't about to fall for some sweet angel who had saved his life. He was just feeling the effects of gratitude. That was all. "By helping me, you've put yourself in danger."

"*Da*, I have, but I don't leave wounded men lying around to die. You were very far away from any help. I'm not sure how you walked that far with your injury. I guess you're very fit. There were rebels everywhere. Not safe for either of us."

"How did you get me here?"

"I got you up and got you into my horse drawn cart that I use to drive my wares into town. My car was stolen, and I don't have any other mode of transportation. I drove you here. It was a job to get you into the house, but we managed." She smiled at him again and he wasn't sure if it was the concussion that made him go into idiot mode. "I think I'm more American than Kirikhan."

"Why is that?"

She rose and shrugged. "I worked as a translator at the UN in New York City. I loved it there, but when my parents were murdered by the state for suspected treason, I came back for the funeral and to sell off the land that was left after the state took the best part for themselves. Really, the land grab has been initially why the Golovkins came to power. It was a small rebel force of disenfranchised landowners. I like that in America once you buy property and pay your bills, no one can take it away from you by force or corruption."

He pushed himself to a sitting position, bracing his back against the wall. She helped him, then rearranged the covers over him. He expected her to smell like animals and hay, but instead she smelled clean and flowery. He breathed deep of her scent as she backed away. "Why do you stay here?"

She walked to the stove and with a potholder took the lid off a pan. Immediately steam rose and Blue's mouth watered at the delicious aroma, at the delicious view of Elena. She was both beautiful and intelligent. She spoke English fluently with just a slight accent. Possessing both brains and a body that was soft, lush, and womanly made him lose his train of thought. Apparently, he had shit for brains.

He was a big guy, all over—from his wide shoulders, to his large hands and long fingers, to his taller than average frame. And because of his size, he liked women amply proportioned to handle and complement a man of his size. She would be a perfect fit for him, in every way. Everything in him dictated that he should keep this platonic. Keep himself from getting involved.

She wore a white peasant shirt with a deep V that showed a helluva lot of cleavage. Her faded jeans sat low on her curvaceous hips and hugged the rest of her shapely figure, and her smooth, rounded ass was a fine example of how that particular part of a woman's anatomy should look.

She captivated him with the graceful sway of her hips. Fascinated him as she swung her long, blonde hair over her shoulders. The strands looked silky and shiny beneath the overhead lights, and the golden color accentuated her beautiful, and striking, blue cornflower eyes. A slight smile curved her lips as she glanced his way, and there was something in her eyes that made his heart pound.

He couldn't want this woman. Acting on his desires wasn't an option. He had obviously been here on a mission for a branch of the service. He was on foreign soil, behind enemy lines. Those were reasons enough to be smart.

She picked up an orange bowl and dished up the contents of the pot while she answered his question. "I've been denied travel because of my parents' questionable ethics. But, now that the rebels control a lot of this area, I fear I will never get out." She walked back to him and set the bowl in his hands. Their hands accidently touched, and she handed him a spoon. He could have sworn he heard her suck in a quick, startled breath at his unintentional caress.

"Go ahead and eat. Don't wait for me."

"It smells delicious."

"It's solyanka soup made with ham, cucumber pickles, tomatoes, onions, olives, capers, and spices. It's sweet and sour." She handed him a plate with thick bread on it, then poured him some hot tea from a pot that was sitting on the small table that was obviously used for meals. She set the tea on the windowsill. "I hope you like it."

"Why can't you leave the country?"

She prepared her own bowl, and regardless of her urging him to do so, he couldn't start without her. She smiled at his manners and sat down in a chair near the bed. "The government likes me to be aware of what's going on and report back. If they find out, the rebels will kill me. But it's been the carrot they have held over me. I have no choice but to comply until they grant me the permission to travel."

After she took her first bite, then chastised him for not eating, he took a mouthful and savored the sweet tangy goodness exploding on his tongue. The ham was tender and melted in his mouth. He swallowed and said, "I'm sorry."

She shook her head. "Thank you. You are a kind man and I will do everything in my power to get you out of here as soon as you are well. I have a contact in the government. I don't want to risk your exposure to any leaks. I simply can't trust anyone. Not until you are well and, if need be, can fend for yourself."

He took a bite of the delicious bread and washed it down with the hot tea warming his insides. He didn't know where it came from, but he wasn't going to leave her here. There was something ingrained in him, a sense of right and wrong that he couldn't overlook. It had to make up his character. He liked that about himself. "Elena, I promise I will help you escape as well. I won't leave you here if you wish to defect."

"Would you? That is unexpected. I don't know how

much longer they're going to leave me and this small farm alone. It's not safe here. But I don't need to defect. I am already an American citizen."

"I'll return the favor. I promise."

"Did you like the solyanka?"

"Very much." She served him blini after that, a savory crepe-like pancake topped with strawberry preserves that she had canned herself. He watched her lick a dollop of whipped cream off her upper lip and felt his entire body tighten with the urge to taste her. Clearing his throat, he shifted on the bed and focused on the dessert. "You're a good cook," he said, his voice husky. "Thank you for sharing your home and food with me."

Pleasure filled her eyes and she smiled. For a moment he couldn't seem to pull his gaze away. It was Elena who turned away, a blush staining her cheeks. He was captivated. He was feeling tired after that, so he laid back down.

He had to keep his wits about him.

This wasn't a tryst for God's sake.

This was life and death.

Yet he couldn't seem to get her beautiful blue eyes out of his mind as he fell back to sleep.

8

TANK RIPPED OFF THE SLING, then cursed as his shoulder wound protested. He threw it and his bag across the room. The suitcase hit his coffee table and it overturned, sending a glass bowl hurtling across the room to smash against the wall. Multi-colored glass tinkled and chimed as the demolished pieces of the bowl spread across the carpet.

He grabbed his cell phone and pressed Dan's contact. The call connected, and Dan said, "Hey bro. Did everything work out with Echo?"

"Yeah, he's good. Really good."

"What's wrong? You have your teeth clenched and your ass-kicking voice going."

"I need you to pick up Jordan and come over right now."

"What's wrong?"

"I'll tell you when you get here. I can't drive right now. I need you to do this, Dan."

"All right. I'll get him—and we'll be there in a few. Chill, man."

Chill? Dan had no idea his world was going to be

altered. Jordan hadn't told either one of them. He knew Dan wouldn't have kept this from him.

He paced and finally gave in and got some of the pain medication from his bag, took the tablets, and sat down on the couch, cradling his head in his hands. He'd been afraid to take it after that first night with Alyssa. God, he'd wanted her. It was still an ache from his balls to the tip of his dick. Kissing her had been a big mistake. Now he knew what it was like to have that mouth, all soft and moist. She kissed like an angel.

He'd been uncharacteristically chatty that night as well. He blamed the damn drugs. He wouldn't have ever talked that much. He didn't do the bonding thing with women, and crying wasn't his thing. He'd never expected that beauty to blindside him. The tenderness he felt for her lay like a constant ache on his heart.

He knew his limitations. They were intense.

Dealing with the loss of Echo as a partner was mild compared to losing him to some unfeeling asshole who was too fucking lazy and incompetent to understand that Echo had just been through a traumatic situation. He'd been separated from his handler, and it had been as hard on the Malinois as it had been on Tank. If he hadn't been medicated, his Navy career might just be over. He would have beat that jerk to a bloody pulp. He clenched his fists. The sexual frustration mixed with the devastating news that Jordan may be sick ratcheted up the tension in him to unbelievable levels.

He had to see the damn shrink tomorrow, and he wanted to go like he wanted a root canal or bamboo under his fingernails. Making the decision to bail on the MWD program was his own business. Alyssa had been completely right. There had been underlying reasons, but not hidden ones. First, he couldn't even fathom another dog matching Echo's skills, smarts, speed, and intuition. Secondly, the pain of almost losing him was something he hadn't expected. He knew they were part of the military, not pets. But trying to stay detached from an animal who needed affection and attention was impossible.

Now Echo was out of the picture and he had no idea how he was going to handle that. Right now, he was just hanging on, trying to accept that things were changing in his life. Jordan was sick. Echo was recovering, and Blue was still missing.

He'd thought once he'd put East LA in his rearview, he'd get a handle on what he was feeling. But it wasn't going to work that way. He couldn't outrun all the things that were chasing him. And he sure as hell couldn't outrun himself— or images of her.

Every time he closed his eyes, he saw Alyssa as she'd been the night she'd saved Echo: a tough, fierce protector of his buddy. He'd watched her tell off her ex-husband through the glass. Every nuance of her face, her disgust and anger so evident in her lush mouth and expression.

Her ex-husband hadn't deserved her, but Tank wasn't sure he deserved her either.

He remembered that awful stricken look in her eyes when he'd left her after she'd spilled the beans about Jordan.

He made a soft sound in his throat, the changes in his life challenging him. He had strived so hard for the status quo, to keep everything balanced, and now that was shot to hell and it was a brave new world.

And he didn't like it one damn bit.

He had learned a long time ago how to erect barriers; especially as a kid, he'd perfected the fine art of putting on armor to protect himself and his brothers. He'd relied on that when he'd had to shut Alyssa out or drag her down on top of him and do her like he wanted to. Now everything was shifting around like loose baggage, and it scared the hell out of him. He knew deep down in his gut there was no future for them. There was too much crap in the way. He relied on the brotherhood. That's what he did.

But damn, no brother ever smelled like her, no brother could soothe him, no brother could be what she was to him. Hell, friendship with a woman, one with respect and a deep abiding gratitude—he'd never seen that coming.

The fact that he wanted to sleep with her over and over again only made him feel even more out of control in situations that were taxing his ability to cope.

When he heard the car pull up outside, he went to the door and threw it open. They were coming across the lawn, and Dan was laughing at something Jordan said. The accident came back to him like it was yesterday. The crash of metal, the car rolling, windows smashing, and his little sister's cries cut off abruptly.

He closed his eyes and waited. "Hey," Dan said as he passed Tank. "You look like hell. You should get some rest."

Jordan came right behind him, and Tank slammed the door, grabbed his little brother by the shirt collar and growled. "Why the fuck do I have to hear that you have cancer from Alyssa?"

You could hear a pin drop in the instant that it registered on Dan's face. Along with Jordan's realization that he was going to have to do some fast-talking because Tank was in his roll-over-anything rage.

"Calm down," Jordan said. "I know I should have."

"You're telling me to calm down when my little brother is sick! This isn't a broken bone, Jordan!"

"I know."

"You know."

Jordan struggled out of Tank's grasp and walked into the living room. Dan was evidently speechless because he just sat down on one of Tank's big leather chairs and stared at Jordan. Jordan righted the coffee table and sat down on the sofa.

Tank couldn't sit down.

"I've spent my life protecting you, Jordan. I've been there for you."

Jordan's mouth compressed and his dark brown eyes flashed. "No you haven't, Thorn. You've been playing war games."

Jordan had been too young to remember Jelsena. He'd spent a lot of his younger years trying to get their old man's approval. Tank had tried to fill his father's shoes.

"You told me what to do, and sure you protected me, but I never felt your support. You were always deployed. I think you love that dog more than me."

Tank stared at him, his face rigid, then swung his gaze to Dan. "You feel the same way?"

"Jordan, Jesus, really man. If it wasn't for Thorn, both of us would have been dead by now, just another statistic He was there for us."

He turned his attention back to Jordan, a look of pain on his face. "No, Dan, he was separate from us, not accessible. I feel sometimes I don't even know you."

Tank stared at him, the muscles in his face taut. Jordan's words were like physical blows, and Tank folded down into the other leather chair. He closed his eyes. What was happening here? They were splintering, and his family was falling apart. Or—a twist of pain wrenched his gut—had he ever had a family at all?

A look of anger and frustration on his face, Jordan shook his head and stared off into space. Finally, he looked at Tank, the defiance replaced by fear. "I didn't tell you about the cancer because I didn't know how. I didn't want to do it while you were training. You seemed so far away most of the time, like you're fighting a war in your head. I get it. The SEALs are tough, and you belong to Uncle Sam. But you belong to us, too, Thorn. You belonged to us long before the SEALs. I need more than your protection. I need your support. And after you came back, after Echo was wounded, I thought I should just wait. It's not like the cancer is going away."

"You know something, Jordan? I don't give a damn what your reasons are. We can deal with those later. I'm your brother and I do care about you. Christ...it's killing me to know you could have cancer."

"Try having it," Jordan muttered.

"He's right. You should have told us. Regardless of all the shit it seems we need to work out, we are a family. We have stuck together through some pretty terrible, harrowing stuff. We made it out of a shithole," Dan said.

"Look, I'm sorry. That's how I feel."

"You have a right to your feelings, but you should have brought these up to me a long time ago. How can I address something I don't know about?"

Jordan grudgingly looked at him. "You have a point."

"I don't like that you think I'm not supportive or accessible. I'd do anything for you, little brother, or Dan. Anything."

Jordan leaned back, his face contorting. "I know." Tank rose and walked over to the couch. He grabbed Jordan by the back of the neck.

"I'm so scared," he whispered. "So scared."

Dan rose and grabbed Jordan's shoulder in silent support. Tank did his best to be the support Jordan said he needed as they talked about the next steps, like finding the best damn doctor they could. Sometimes the strong exterior slipped—for all three of them—but Tank refused to let himself completely break down when his little brother needed him most.

Hours later he was lying on his bed, and he tried like hell not to miss her warm heat, her presence. But it wasn't working. It hadn't been the fraternization that had held him in check...it had been his deep-seated fear. Fear of showing any affection for anyone, fear of laying open his heart and having it stomped on.

It was different with the brotherhood. That was men bonding over war, over life and death decisions. There was an expected and silent code that they would have each other's backs. But they were men, and a relationship with a woman was infinitely different. He loved and trusted each of his teammates. But he had to wonder how they were all feeling now.

His armor was so damn thick. Had been until Alyssa had showed him what real support was, what real and true friendship was, what tenderness and care looked like. He got a glimpse of what he could have with her—not every woman was like his mother. Then, Jordan had pierced what was left of his armor with his words like blades, cutting him up. But even then, Jordan was his brother; they would work this out. Now that his eyes had been opened, he saw clearly for the first time in his life, and if he didn't try to be a better man because of it, he would die inside.

Just maybe he needed more than the brotherhood.

Because of Alyssa, he couldn't seem to get his detachment back. Who was he kidding? He'd never had it with her.

The way he'd left her haunted him and would haunt him for a long time. He didn't know if it was guilt or regret, but his throat closed up every time that image took shape in his mind, and the hollow feeling in his chest spread a little more. It had, without question, been one terrible way of saying goodbye.

He had never, ever thought of himself as a quitter. If he had, he would have rung that damn bell and washed out of BUD/S. But right this moment, that's what he was. He'd go into a million battles without fear, but the tenderness and care of one woman sent him into a tailspin. He had been a temporary lover. That's how he defined himself. A good fuck with nothing to give. Sex. Hot and dirty.

But now he wanted to be something more. If he didn't overcome this fear, what would that make him now that he'd acknowledged it?

A coward.

Plain and simple.

Navy SEALs weren't cowards.

Plain and simple.

AFTER HIS LEAVE WAS UP, he went back to active duty. He made sure he said all the things the therapist wanted to hear. He was still working out shit himself. Jordan had an appointment with another oncologist. He hadn't been happy with anyone so far. Tank was still struggling with the fact that Jordan hadn't told him something so important, but he was willing to fight alongside him against this disease.

His own grief, he buried. He had to have his mind in the game or he was going to end up dead. He arrived at the hospital, and when he rounded a corner, he ran right into a candy striper. He grabbed her arms and steadied her, ready for an apology.

"Becca?" His jaw dropped open and he gaped.

"Thorn. Hi."

"You work here?"

"I volunteer. What are you doing here?"

He was still trying to get his head around the pretty pink princess working at the hospital, emptying bedpans and playing fetch. "My brother's sick."

"Dan or Jordan?"

Again, Tank was floored. He had no idea Becca even remembered their names. Something else that he had overlooked.

"Jordan."

"Oh, God, I'm so sorry. What does he have?"

"Maybe cancer. They're still doing a lot of tests."

Her face twisted into a horrified grimace. She was sure going to have to work on her bedside manner.

"Look, my daddy's a patron of this hospital. I know the best oncologist. You should get an appointment with her. I can pull strings. She's had a fabulous success rate. Let me get you her information. Where are you going? I can bring it by."

He told her where they would be. "What has gotten into you?"

"You mean me volunteering?"

He nodded.

"It's your fault."

"How is it my fault?"

"I saw the work you were doing for the MWD charity and I read up on SEALs. I was so impressed by everything you had accomplished. I looked at my life. All I cared about were cars, partying and shopping. I could do so much more.

I was a spoiled brat, but now I'm taking an interest in my daddy's company. I think I almost gave him a heart attack. Philanthropy, I think, will suit me. But before my daddy starts letting me fundraise, he wants to make sure this isn't a whim. So, I'm proving it." She grinned. "At least the uniform is pink."

He chuckled.

She reached out and ran her hand down his arm. "I know it's over between us. But we're just friends with benefits anyway. And, to be honest, I want someone long-term and committed."

Did this little bit of a thing just blindside him? He was starting to think the same thing, but with the obstacles in their way, he wasn't sure how it would resolve with Alyssa.

She patted his cheek. "I've got to run, but I'll see you in about twenty minutes."

True to her word, Becca showed up with a card and information. She flushed when she met Dan and there was a decidedly just as interested look in his eyes. But then it was gone, and he thought maybe he was seeing things.

WHEN HE WALKED into the ready room after getting a summons from Ruckus, he found it empty. His LT sat at the head of the table on his laptop. "Hey, boss? Any word on Blue?"

"No, not yet. Intel in that area has been difficult at best, but the brass isn't giving up. As soon as we have a location, we're going in to get him out."

"Copy that. Where's everyone else?"

"They're not coming. This is between you and me."

"Oh. Okay. What's up?"

"You've gotten orders to report to the kennel to start training with your new dog. Are you ready for that?"

"I got cleared, LT."

"Is that what I asked you, Tank?"

"No, sir."

"Are you ready?"

"I'm not sure."

"Why?"

"Echo tore me up. I know I'm not supposed to treat him like a pet—" He looked away, his voice thick. He blinked rapidly and knew the man he'd been before he'd met Alyssa would have been embarrassed as hell showing this type of emotion, but fuck it. He loved that damn dog.

"Fuck that shit." Ruckus was just as moved. "He was part of our team, an integral part. If he hadn't taken that insurgent down, we wouldn't be here right now. The EOD guys found a long line of explosives buried in the ground. It would have taken most of us out if he'd detonated those explosives. It would have been a massacre. They were waiting for us."

"An ambush. That's exactly what it felt like."

"We have reason to believe that there's a leak. The Kirikhan government is as corrupt as I've ever seen, but they've been straight shooters with us. They were the ones who suggested it was on their end. So, any plans we have won't be going through them. We have free rein to work this as we see fit. After all, it's to their benefit if we take out the Golovkins."

"Fuckers."

"Yeah, but that's what we have to work with. So, getting back to what we were talking about—"

"Am I ready?"

"Before you answer, let me say that we value having a dog handler on this team. It might bump you out if you decide not to take on that duty again. But, more importantly, you excel at that job better than anyone I've ever seen. You and Echo worked in tandem. He and you are both being decorated for saving us. I got the word you're receiving the Navy Cross and Echo the K9 Medal of Courage. Congratulations, Tank."

"Thank you, sir, but Echo is the real hero here. His instincts were on point."

"Have you thought about adopting him?"

"Hell, yeah, but with my deployments, it wouldn't be fair to him." It hurt like hell, but Tank had to let Echo go to a good home where he would get the love and attention he deserved.

Ruckus handed him the orders and Tank rose. "One more thing. I'm not blind. Is there something I should know about Dr. Alyssa St. James?"

"Not yet, but if there is, I'll let you know."

"Tank."

He looked at Ruckus and finally gave in. "It's like a Dana thing," he said and Ruckus's expression smoothed out. His boss had fallen head over heels for a tough, spunky reporter during a harrowing jungle adventure who didn't take any crap from his intimidating LT. Tank was in the exact same boat.

"I can look into it for you."

Tank nodded and left the room.

He immediately headed over to the kennel, deciding that getting back in the saddle again was what he had to do. He was just gun-shy because it had hurt so much to lose Echo. It would be difficult to forget the years they'd been together and the work they had done to save lives. Tank also didn't want to go to another squad. He didn't think he would fare well with a different leader.

He reported to the kennel master who took his orders and told him what kennel the dog was in. He said, "Her name is Bronte. She's a three-year-old and well-tested. You've been especially selected for her, Petty Officer. She's an exemplary animal, agile, fast, strong, and hard-hitting. Alpha all the way, just like you. But where she excels is her detection capabilities."

"Thank you, Master Sergeant."

Tank headed to the kennel, and once inside, he moved down the row of metal pens. A dog started barking the moment he entered, and he followed the sound right to Bronte. She was a rich mahogany with black-tipped hairs and a black mask and ears. She regarded him with curious but guarded brown almond-shaped eyes. He could tell she was intelligent.

He squatted down and she kept her ground, but he was prepared for her to be a bit aggressive. "Easy, girl," he said. She didn't know him yet. "Bronte, sit." She ignored him at first, but then he said it in a firmer voice, but kept his words modulated.

She sat down. He opened the door, watching her intently, but she sat calmly. He gave her a moment to get used to him, then bent down to snap on her leash. He felt as if he was betraying Echo's trust but had to school himself to remember that Echo was retired. He and Bronte would have to become pals, find their footing.

A female dog, he thought. The universe was laughing at him.

He took her out to the training field and started putting her through her paces, but she balked and acted confused at his commands. The same thing happened day after day.

Maybe she wasn't the right match for him. Finally, he got frustrated, and without warning, she lunged at him and grazed the back of his hand. It hurt like a son of a bitch, but he'd been fast enough to avoid too much damage. A Malinois could break bones if she really latched on.

He put her down to the ground and immediately to her back. He said nothing, letting her understand that he was the boss. She struggled at first, and he wrestled with her until she was still. As soon as she accepted his authority, he let her up. He took her back to the kennel and decided to hit the vet clinic. They could take care of his hand.

He walked inside, and a woman was standing with her back to him. "Excuse me," he started. She stiffened and turned around. It had been weeks since he'd last seen her, but the impact of her beauty hit him between the eyes. Every damn time.

"Tank?" she asked, then she saw his bleeding hand.

"I got bit."

"Come on back. I can handle that for you."

He followed her through the clinic into a treatment room with a table, cabinets, and several chairs.

"Let me see it," she demanded, gripping his wrist and dragging him to the sink. Pushing his other hand out of the way, she lifted the paper towel. There was a nasty gash across the back of his hand where Bronte's teeth had scored him. She carefully turned his hand over and saw another gash.

He was studying her face, her touch electric, but she was all business—or so she seemed.

"This must hurt," she murmured, turning his hand back over.

He held her gaze for a moment, then smiled. "Like a bitch."

"You decided to take on another dog?"

"We're getting acquainted." His focus this moment wasn't on Bronte. His eyes went over Alyssa in a slow slide.

"The gash is deep, but luckily, you don't need stitches." She let go of his hand and opened a cabinet. "I want to clean this with some antiseptic first," she said, digging through the well-stocked cabinet. She thoroughly irrigated the wound, the water in the sink turning red.

"That should do it," she said, setting the bottle down. Her shoulder brushing against his arm, she tore open a sterile pack and blotted the wounds, then pressed fresh dry pads against them to staunch the renewed bleeding. He was keenly aware of how close she was, of the warmth of her arm against his, and he closed his eyes, the heat from her body igniting his blood.

She glanced at him, giving him an encouraging look, but there was sizzle in her eyes. Her touch was robbing him of common sense. Her closeness overwhelmed his senses, and she swallowed hard, obviously struggling against her attraction to him.

His hand jerked when she touched his palm, and as she wrapped his hand with gauze, he said, "I've missed you."

She stilled and turned toward him, searching his eyes. "I missed you, too."

Before he could even think what to say next, she grabbed his face and her mouth was hot and urgent against his. The bolt of pure, raw sensation knocked the wind right out of him. Tank shuddered, and he widened his mouth against hers, feeding on the desperation that poured back and forth between them. She made another wild sound and clutched at him, the movement welding their bodies together like two halves of a whole, and he nearly lost it right then, only remembering that they were in a public place, tucked away, but still not exactly the best timing.

He broke the kiss, trying to regain some control. He tucked her head against his neck, holding her with every ounce of strength he had, fighting for every breath. She clutched him tighter as if she was trying to climb right inside him, and any connection he had with reason shattered into a thousand pieces.

The feel of her heat against him was too much, and he clenched his jaw, turning his head against hers. His face contorting from the surge of desire, he caught her around the hips, welding her roughly against him. God, he needed this—the heat of her, the weight of her. He needed her.

9

For what seemed like an eternity, they stood together, holding each other. Finally, Alyssa moved and closed the treatment room door. She leaned back against it, her face thoughtful. "We have to talk about this...this thing between us."

"Attraction, Alyssa." She blushed, and he wanted to take her home, strip her down and see if that blush suffused her whole body. "This isn't exactly the best situation here," he said.

"No," she made a soft, half-amused, half-exasperated sound. "What do you want to do about it? I intend to talk to my commanding officer today about our options."

"It's a good thing we're in a public place or I'd show you exactly what I want to do about it." He sighed. "I've already mentioned it to my LT. He's looking into it."

She nodded looking pleased. "I'm not naïve. I'm aware of what kind of man you are."

"What kind is that?"

"Temporary," she said and looked away. "This is pretty complicated, Tank."

"Maybe I want to find out where this goes, and temporary isn't factoring into this *thing* we have." He crossed the room and cupped her face, his thumbs caressing her cheekbones. "I can't get you off my mind. I've tried. I told myself this was too crazy, too difficult. Doesn't do any good. I want you...for more." He leaned his forehead against hers. Exhaling heavily, Tank drew her fully against him, resting his jaw against her head as he began slowly running his hand up and down her spine. Alyssa tightened her arms around him, and he could detect a light quivering in her as though she had the same feelings. He wanted to get her take on it. It floored him that he even cared what her opinion was. He usually dictated his terms in a no-nonsense way. The fact that he'd held off getting her into bed said volumes to him. He didn't want to mess this up with sex, but he also knew he wanted more than friendship from her. "Maybe you should tell me your concerns."

Shifting his hold, he cradled her head firmly against him and brushed a gentling kiss against her temple. He didn't know what in the hell was going to happen. And if he'd realized anything when it came to Alyssa, it was that he couldn't let it go and he wasn't sure how to move forward or even if they could legally do so.

A snatch of conversation sounded out in the hall and Alyssa drew him away from the door. "To say that you've caught me off-guard is an understatement. But this is probably not the best place for a private conversation. Can we meet somewhere later?" When he opened his mouth, she said hurriedly, "Preferably in a public place."

"You don't trust me?"

She looked at him for only a split second, then she covered his mouth in a kiss that was raw and honest. Tank went still. Then with a soft exhalation, he yielded, opening his mouth over hers as she clutched at him. He slid his hand along her jaw, a fever of emotion sluicing through him.

Dragging her mouth away, she trailed a string of kisses down his neck, then caught his head again and gave him another hot, wet kiss. His breathing ragged, he tightened his arms around her. She drew back and said solemnly, "No, I don't trust myself."

He smiled. "You're killing me, babe."

"Yeah, well, the feeling is mutual. Now get out of here before we get into any more trouble. I have a feeling that's your middle name."

"Just as soon as you tell me where you want to meet?"

"How about the coffee shop across from my practice?"

"Roger that. Time?"

"Eighteen hundred hours?"

He nodded. "I'll see you then."

He left the clinic, his thoughts and body in turmoil. He glanced to the practice field, toward the kennel, and his chest felt hollow. He still couldn't shake the sense of betrayal he'd experienced while working Bronte. She was the most difficult dog he'd ever met in the program. When he'd trained Echo, they had been like one, handler and dog, moving in tandem. He trusted the master sergeant. The kennel master knew what he was doing, and Tank respected him. But maybe he'd been wrong assigning Bronte to him. A hard, hollow ball of longing lodged in his chest, taking up valuable air space, and he scowled and did his best to smash it with a mental mallet. He and Echo were no longer a team. His buddy was fighting his way back from a debilitating wound. He'd have to rehabilitate, heal, learn to walk again. He would go up for adoption. That was the reality Tank had to accept.

Then there was Blue. He was never far from his thoughts

as well. He still couldn't seem to let go of the guilt that dogged him. Still not sure what decision he could have made after the RPG blast. The satisfaction of foiling a devastating plot that would have left most of the combined NATO, Green Berets and SEAL teams dead part of the victory, but losing Blue had been the price. The needs of the many outweighing the needs of the few. He loved Blue like a brother, and if he'd been harmed or killed in action, those rebels would get no mercy from SEAL Team Alpha.

Pushing the dark thoughts from his mind, he turned his attention on Alyssa and all the little puzzle pieces he had yet to find to complete his picture of her. She had the tenacity of a pit bull and the grace of a gazelle. She wore baggy, neutral clothes, her hair always ruthlessly contained, but even with the way she downplayed her beauty, she looked so feminine and graceful. He shook his head, a wry smile tugging at one corner of his mouth. He wanted to let down all that hair, see it soft around her face like at the ball, those forbidden days in that hotel room in San Antonio.

She so wasn't his type. Not at all. He went for the bad girls, curvy women with big breasts and uncomplicated dispositions, women who wanted nothing more from him than a good tussle between the sheets. He didn't know what Alyssa St. James would cost him. She drew on him like a magnet. Instinct told him his curiosity would be dangerous, but the warning wasn't strong enough to overpower the attraction. Besides, he told himself smugly, he couldn't get in any deeper than he wanted to.

He went back to his locker, the cut on his hand throbbing. The rest of his body throbbing, his dick hard. In the past he wouldn't have waited. To hell with that shit. He would have found a way to get what he wanted if the woman was willing. But that was before he met Alyssa, before he found that his way or the highway was not any way at all to act.

He respected her and her position.

And she made him rethink everything he'd ever known about risk, about duty, and about the fairer sex.

He'd get some shooting in or maybe PT. Physical exercise sounded like a good idea to him. Maybe he could find some of the guys at the gym. He changed into his workout clothes, not sure he was focused enough for the range today.

As Tank exited the lockers, LT called out, "Tank. Wait up."

Tank paused and let him catch up. "What's up?"

"I checked in with the powers that be about your fraternization situation. They told me that there was no violation because she's a reservist and a different branch of the service."

Tank took in the information. "I can see her?"

"Yes."

"I can see her."

Ruckus laughed softly. "Sure sounds like a Dana situation."

ALYSSA'S HANDS were still shaking, her body in an uproar that she'd let him go when she wanted nothing more than to take him home and find out what she'd been missing with Stephen. Deciding that it was too important to wait around for information, Alyssa called her commanding officer's assistant and got an appointment.

Soon she was standing in front of Colonel Johnson's desk. "At ease and have a seat." She set her hat on the corner of his desk and sat down. "What did you need to see me about?"

"It's personal and professional."

His head came up at the sound of her voice. "Don't tell me you're not going to take the job in San Antonio. I'm not going to accept it."

She smiled and shook her head. "No, it's not about the job. I still need more time."

"Elaborate then."

"Remember the request I mentioned regarding the Navy SEAL who asked for my assistance with one of the working dogs, Echo?"

He nodded. "Yes, he was severely wounded recently, and it doesn't look good for him returning to service."

"I've deemed him disabled. The muscle in his shoulder was too damaged to fully repair. He's going to limp for the rest of his life."

"I'm sorry to hear that. This Navy SEAL..."

"Chief Petty Officer Thorn Hunt."

"Hunt must be having a tough go."

"He is, but that isn't what I wanted to talk about." She shifted and looked away her stomach tied up in knots. "He and I are...attracted to each other and wish to pursue a romantic relationship."

He steepled his fingers, frowning. "I see. Well, the policy is pretty clear for the Army, but there are still loopholes even thing. But for the reserves I can't really dictate to you how you spend your free time when you're not on duty. But I do have to ask you these questions because it's important for the smooth running of the command and my duty to ensure that it continues to run smoothly."

"All right."

"Article 134 states in general it might not be an offense.

The surrounding circumstances dictate here. He's in the Navy and you're in the Army. So your relationship doesn't compromise the integrity of supervisory authority or chain of command."

"No, sir."

"Would you say that there is no actual or perceived partiality of unfairness, improper use of rank for personal gain, exploitative or coercive activity, adverse impact on discipline, authority, morale, or the ability of command to accomplish the mission?"

"No, sir. None of those conditions apply in this circumstance."

"Then you're free to engage in a personal relationship with Petty Officer Hunt. But, if you decide to go active duty, that might change. We could definitely talk about it more, but have you thought about that?"

"Yes, I have."

"This is an amazing opportunity. Think about it carefully and what it would mean to your relationship if you decide to take the position at Lackland."

"I understand, and I haven't totally ruled out Lackland... it's just that I like him very much."

He nodded. "You have to do what is best for you, Alyssa, but your country does need you in this position, our K9 warriors need you."

She gave him a look, knowing that he was campaigning for her to accept. "That was a nice touch. I promise I'll consider everything."

He nodded, his expression hopeful. "I'm sure you will. I appreciate you bringing this to me to make sure there is no impropriety, but that doesn't surprise me in your case, Lieutenant Colonel. Your exemplary record reflects your dedication to duty."

She blew out a breath. "Thank you, sir."

"You were saved by Article 134, but that in no way diminishes your service, Dr. St. James, nor gives you the latitude to act inappropriately in public while in uniform."

"Yes, sir. Thank you."

"I'll make a note of my approval in your record and wish you good luck in your budding relationship. If there's nothing else…"

"No, sir. We're done." She rose and picked up her hat and exited his office. She had to stop and lean against her car in the parking lot. She felt a rush of adrenaline and a giddiness she hadn't felt for a long time. Maybe she hadn't been too open to Stephen's needs, maybe she hadn't comprised enough. This situation with Tank opened her eyes, made her look at herself in a different light. She had to take this chance with him or she feared she might die inside.

Closing her eyes against the longing to take this thing with Tank into the deep end of the pool contrasted sharply with her experience with her ex-husband. She took a breath. That was between them. Here, now, this was between her and Tank. She looked at her watch and noted her meeting with Tank was coming up fast. She couldn't let her baggage interfere with the potential for something amazing, solid and passionate. There was no doubt in her mind that's what this would be.

But she was still scared to death.

WHEN HE ENTERED THE GYM, Hollywood, Scarecrow and Wicked were working the weights. When the team's safety and security depended on how fast they could move with all the gear they might need to do a job better than anybody else in the world, the words "being in shape" took on a whole new meaning.

"Hey, slacker," Hollywood said as he came over to them.

Tank gave him a narrow-eyed look. "If anyone's slacking, man, it'd be you." He watched as Hollywood's head turned when he heard the sound of female voices as a group of beautiful women entered the gym. Part of the CIA contingent on base.

Scarecrow smiled. "He's like a homing beacon."

Tank laughed, but when he looked at Wicked, he was watching the group with a taut, predatory stare. Wicked didn't talk much. He was more the strong, silent type. But his body language was giving off a very intense vibe. He'd seen badass dangerous men give Wicked a wide berth.

There were four women: two blondes, a brunette, and a drop-dead gorgeous fiery redhead. Wicked was staring at her. Tank got that—she was lean and sleek, clear she was an operator, had the kind of moves that served the shadowy players who populated the spy world. He'd never seen her before on base. But she was making Wicked twitchy. She was tall and looked badass, but what she had was power. It pulsed through her in a steady, unending beat.

It was there in every line of her beautiful body...survival —they'd all been trained for it, trained to do whatever it took to survive. But this beauty took it up a notch.

She was so sleek in her clinging workout clothes, all black like a ninja siren, her body sculpted by lengths of hard muscle with a strength of heart that shone out of a pair of whiskey amber eyes.

He glanced at Wicked again and his mouth hardened. She never even glanced his way, but Tank was sure she was also very aware of him. There was history there for sure.

"He sure has the radar for beautiful women," Scarecrow continued, breaking into both Tank's and Wicked's regard of the redhead.

Wicked turned back to the bar and picked up a couple more plates and slammed them home. Hollywood turned and said, "Jesus, Wicked, you must think I am the man of steel."

"You need to take that testosterone and put it to good use. Nothing can come of approaching any one of those women. You'd be much better off steering clear of anything to do with the spooks."

It was the most words Wicked had strung together ever. The guys gave each other looks and Hollywood grinned. "I can handle spies, Wicked. I can handle any damn woman."

"Sure you can," Scarecrow said, "until one of them blindsides you."

"Not going to happen."

"Right, ask Ruckus how well that went for him." Hollywood lay down on the bench after giving Scarecrow a sour look. "Kid maybe?" Hollywood grabbed the bar and Wicked helped him steady it before he started to do his reps. Scarecrow crouched down. "Cowboy?"

With a giant heave, Hollywood's muscles bulging, he replaced the bar. Sitting up, he gave Scarecrow another scowl. "It won't be me. Ever." Then he grinned that cocky grin. "I conquer. I don't get conquered."

Wicked looked back at the redhead and said under his breath, "Don't say never; those words will get force-fed back to you and you could choke on them."

Scarecrow glanced at Tank and sighed. "Even Tank is succumbing, and I don't think he's happy about it."

"Leave me out of this," he growled, taking his turn with the bar. His realization about Alyssa was a little too new, too raw right now to have it bantered about within his team's gritty and raucous minds. It wasn't that he was averse to commitment. He'd committed plenty. It was that Alyssa was a future he didn't know was there and one that he hadn't realized until now he wanted.

"Well, it's Tank's business," Hollywood said. "But putting your career on the line for a piece of ass is reckless."

Before Tank could even realize what he was doing, he got into Hollywood's face. "Shut the fuck up about the Doc. She's not a piece of ass."

Hollywood's eyes narrowed, and he pushed back. "She's a fine piece of ass, but you're out of your mind if you mess with an officer."

"You don't know what you're talking about," Tank said deep and low.

"No, I don't get it."

"I like her, Hollywood. I know that's not something you're interested in, but sometimes things change."

"So, maybe you should put a sock in it," Scarecrow drawled.

"Look, man, I'm sorry. I can be such an asshole, but I got your back."

The tension defusing, Tank backed up off his teammate. He was sure there would never be a time where he was willing to go to war with one of the brotherhood over a woman, but Wicked had been right. Never was a word that had to be eaten, and damn if it didn't stick in the craw.

He walked out with Wicked and indicated the sultry redhead with his chin. "What's up with the her?"

Wicked grunted. "Officer Kat Harrington. I knew her a lifetime ago before I was on this team."

He hadn't really expected a response. When Wicked didn't want to talk, he didn't answer and that was that.

"What the hell did you do before you came to us?"

He looked at Tank, then looked away. "It's not common knowledge, but I was with Team Six."

Team Six was the common name for the United States Naval Special Warfare Development Group commonly known as DEVGRU. "You pulling my boot?" Usually one of its elite operators went out two ways after snagging one of the coveted spots on that team—retirement or a body bag.

They entered the locker area. "No, I was with DEVGRU. We deployed with Delta. Let's just say Kat and I have bad blood between us."

"Mission gone wrong?"

"Something like that. She hates my guts." Wicked changed and slung a bag over his shoulder. "A little advice. If you find yourself a woman you can love who wants to support you, give you a couple of kids, you should grab that with both hands, man. It's the golden ring."

Wicked clapped him on the shoulder then headed for the exit. Tank watched him go. Who would have thought it? Wicked had layers and he wanted a family. What the hell? Still waters did run deep, and he'd learned more about the guy in this short exchange than he'd learned from him the whole time he'd been on their team. He wondered what kind of beef Kat Harrington had with the deadly gunslinger. Looked like she could hold her own with him. Maybe one day she would have to.

At the agreed upon time, Tank entered the coffee shop and looked around, but Alyssa wasn't there. He waited for fifteen minutes, then walked up to the counter. "Has Dr. St. James been here?"

The clerk smiled at him. "She was about thirty minutes ago, then she must have left."

"Thanks," Tank said, wondering if Alyssa was okay. Maybe she'd gotten cold feet.

He walked across the street and went inside the clinic, but she wasn't there either.

Now he was beginning to worry.

He went to her place because she wasn't answering her cell phone and he was really starting to stress over her whereabouts.

He knocked on her door, resisting the urge to kick it in, and to his utter relief, she answered it.

"What the hell, Alyssa? You gave me a heart attack. Why weren't you at the coffee shop like we agreed? Have you changed your damn mind?"

She backed up as he advanced, slamming the door behind him. His worry made him cranky, and he realized right here, right now that he was actually in much too deep, that if LT had told him he couldn't have her, he would have broken the damn law, risked his career, risked anything to have her. This beautiful, skilled, caring woman that took his thoughts and rules and turned them on their head. He hadn't understood what support really was until she had been there for him during his worry over Echo. He regretted that he hadn't realized that his protective need to shelter his brothers had led him to distancing himself from the people he loved. In his desperation to keep from losing them, he had lost what it was to really be a family and lean on them for support; giving that support was all there really was.

"No," she whispered. He noticed that she had on a silky robe and was barefoot. His heart started to pound harder. "I have two reasons I wasn't there."

He set his hands on his hips, trying not to jump to conclusions or jump her for that matter.

"They are?" he prompted when she didn't continue, just stared at him as if she hadn't seen him in a year.

"The first one is because I wanted to see if you'd come after me. To see if you really wanted it as much as I thought you did."

"I'd follow you to the ends of the fucking earth," he rasped. He stepped closer. "And the other reason?"

"I don't want to waste another minute talking about this. My commander gave us the green light. God, help me, I don't care if you haven't heard yet."

Before he could respond, she pressed him back against the wall with a hot, open-mouthed kiss that knocked the wind right out of him. All he could do was groan, caught up in the sweetest, sexiest moment of his life.

10

Alyssa was sick of playing it safe. Sick of acting like she didn't have needs and desires. Sick of making believe that she couldn't experience something wholly wonderful with Tank. The soft growl he made deep in his chest gave her great satisfaction and he flipped her around, so their positions were reversed. Stephen hadn't responded to her like this, and it was like she was a virgin all over again. He buried his fingers in her hair and pressed her up against the wall with his hard, undeniably aroused body. With a low growl, broadcasting both his frustration and urgent need, he slanted his mouth across hers and sank his tongue deep, kissing her just as recklessly as she had kissed him only moments before. She loved his big body, the rough way he looked. His mouth promised sin and unrestrained sensual pleasure, and she matched him stroke for stroke, chasing his tongue with her own, letting him know that she was with him all the way.

She was touched by the way he'd been stressed out when he couldn't find her. It was a dick move on her part, but she wanted to know that she wasn't just convenient, just a conquest. She wanted to know that he wanted to be with her, not just a warm body.

The feverish intensity between them was sizzling hot, the strength and immediacy of her arousal making her knees weak. She slid her arms around his waist and skimmed her hands down to cup his buttocks through soft, worn denim. The muscles tightened under her palms, and the long, hard length of him pushed insistently against the apex of her thighs. She felt the bite of his belt buckle against her hip, but she was too swamped with desire and need spiraling tighter and tighter within her to care about the minor discomfort.

With his lips still devouring her mouth with aggressive, utterly devastating kisses, he shoved open the robe. Then he stilled and looked down.

"Jesus," he whispered as he took in her naked body, the robe slipping off and pooling on the floor. She shivered and moaned as his big, warm hands closed over her breasts, rubbing and massaging the mounds of flesh, then rolled her hard, aching nipples between his fingers.

He lowered his head and closed his mouth over her taut, throbbing nipple. He laved it with his tongue before nipping it with his teeth, then sucked her strong and deep, until she felt that same seductive, pulling sensation in the pit of her belly. An electric jolt zapped through her, exploding in heated ripples that thrummed across her nerve endings.

Her skin tingled everywhere, hot and alive with sensation. She twined her fingers in his soft, thick hair, feeling breathless and dizzy and unable to do anything but hold on, let him have his way with her body, and give into too many months of wild, pent-up passion between them.

He wedged his foot between hers, widening her stance. One hand left her breast and slid down her ribs to her belly.

She sucked in a quick, tormented breath, and her heart raced in anticipation as his hand slid between her thighs and his mouth returned to hers, hot and hungry and demanding, allowing her no escape. His fingers skimmed along her skin and delved through her damp curls, gliding into her soft, swollen sex.

A blunt finger slipped easily into her, followed by a second that seemed too much to take all at once. She gasped into his mouth at the exquisite pleasure, but then his thumb pressed against her core, right where she'd wanted him for so long, both soothing and arousing her at the same time. This man of violence, this warrior, so gentle with her.

As soon as she relaxed, he pushed deeper, filling her, and her inner muscles contracted tightly around his fingers in an involuntary surge of sensation. She could barely catch her breath. Her head rolled back against the wall, and she panted for air, wondering how his hardness would fill her up even more.

His big body shuddered, and he buried his face against her neck, his ragged breath hot and damp against her skin. "You are so fucking tight, so hot and wet," he rasped in her ear. "I want inside you."

Wanting that just as much, she pleaded, his magic fingers bringing her closer and closer to release. "Please, Thorn. God, please."

"Say my name again," he rasped.

"*Thorn*," she said in a strangled voice as her hips jerked hard with a tingling throb and she came in a blinding, intoxicating explosion.

When she opened her eyes, he was staring at her, enraptured, his face drawn, his eyes intense, warm with desire. He fisted his hand into her hair, twisting her head back, covering her mouth with a kiss that was meant to incite, to ignite, to devastate, and Alyssa made a low sound. Adjusting the fit of his mouth against hers, he absorbed the sound, running his hands up her rib cage, rolling her hardened nipples with his thumbs.

She'd wanted to touch him for so long, and with the edge off, but building again, she slipped her hands under his T-shirt and shoved it up. Velvet skin over hard, thick muscles. They were everywhere, his abdomen, the heavy pectorals of his chest, the thick column of his throat. He raised his arms and then grabbed the cotton and pulled it off.

He was so heartbreakingly beautiful. There was no other way to describe him. He was all rugged angles and tattoos. He had the street in him. He was hot-blooded yet always in control with a raw presence, all of it sculpted into layers of muscle and sinew—the power of long legs, thick, bulging biceps, broad shoulders, and six-pack abs with that patch of hair that trailed down and disappeared beneath his waistband.

He was strong, always getting stronger—tough, then even tougher. It's what they all did. It's how he was trained, how they stayed alive in the places they went, in doing the jobs they were tasked with. And all Tank's strength and power were finally in her arms, surrounding her, warming her skin on the outside and causing a meltdown inside.

She wanted to see all of him. Finally, all of him. Have all of him.

Tank's hands went to her hips, holding her immobile. His face dropped and buried in the tumble of her hair, then finally he took an unsteady breath and raised his head, brushing his mouth against hers with agonizing slowness. Alyssa tried to move against him, to bring his head down to increase the pressure of his mouth, but he resisted. His mouth barely touching hers, he ran his tongue along her bottom lip. "God, you taste so damn sweet."

Fighting for every breath against the frenzy inside her, she drank him in, drawing his tongue deep, then deeper still. Gasping against his mouth, she fumbled to release the heavy buckle on his belt, then ran her fingertips up the thick, hard ridge under his zipper and molded her hand against it. Tank made a hoarse sound deep in his throat, thrusting hard into her hand. She undid the front of his jeans as his hips moved again, his breathing harsh and labored. He rested his forehead against her as she pushed his jeans and underwear off.

His full, thick erection jutted from his body, a ring pierced through the base of the head and through the tip fascinated her. Shivering with anticipation, she reached down to touch him, and when her fingers fluttered over the broad, velvet head of his shaft, gently depressing the ring, he sucked in a hissing breath. Grasping both of her wrists, he pulled her arms up and pinned them above her head, giving him complete control of the situation.

Drawing air through clenched teeth, he pressed his body against hers. "It's called a Prince Albert. Does it bother you?"

"No. You're so beautiful, so sexy. It turns me on."

He covered her mouth with a blistering kiss, his heart hammering against hers. She needed more, so much more from him, and he held onto her wrists as he deepened the kiss, then slowly, so slowly, flexed his hips against hers, aligning the thick, hard ridge of his arousal against her pelvis. She sobbed against his mouth, thrusting her hips up to increase the pressure.

At her muffled cry, he let go of her and cupped her butt,

making another foray into her mouth, his touch wet and tormenting.

Feeling as if she was drowning in the thick, pulsating sensations, Alyssa shuddered and turned her face against him as he worked his way down her neck, his touch turning her boneless. Sinking into sensation, sinking into unbelievable pleasure.

He lifted her, using his big body and the wall as leverage, the slide of his muscled body against hers making her pulse leap higher and faster. Her arms went around his neck, her legs around his waist, locking her ankles together. He covered himself with a condom, fitting himself to her, pressing his erection intimately against her, nudging his way in, stretching her with an exquisite pressure that was making her lose her mind, the metal at the head noticeable, adding to the pleasure of his sliding into her. She stared into his heavy-lidded eyes. With a dark, fierce expression, he crushed his mouth to hers and kissed her passionately as he buried his shaft to the hilt in her slick heat, possessing her completely.

He held her as if she weighed nothing, his huge biceps bulging, as she ran her hands over the thickened muscles. She couldn't feel the ring, nothing but the delicious friction of his hard heat inside her, intensifying her sensual tension even higher.

"Good?" he whispered.

"Yes," she managed, then groaned when he pressed in again. The way he communicated with her about her pleasure turned her on even more. She felt more pressure, the glorious sensation twisting her into a mind-bending orgasm. She cried out, her body arching hard against his.

"Fuck me. That was beautiful..." He bit her jaw, rubbing his stubble against her skin, then returned to her mouth, kissing her with a thoroughness that went on and on. Dragging his mouth away, he shuddered and turned his head against hers, the muscles in his back bunching as he flexed his powerful hips against her one more time.

It was so much and not enough as Alyssa cried out his name and arched against him, her body tightening, tightening as she clutched at his back and lifted her hips. Tank thrust his arm behind her hips and shifted; then with an agonized groan, he thrust into her, burying himself in her swollen, wet heat. His whole body went rigid, and he roughly adjusted his hold; then gathering his strength, he thrust into her again and again. Alyssa came apart in his arms, the tightness coalescing into one throbbing center, and on one deep, urgent thrust, that center exploded, and convulsions ripped through her, making her arch and cry out. Tank locked his arm around her hips, thrusting again and again; then he made a ragged sound and shuddered violently in her arms, his release as catastrophic as hers.

Alyssa hung on to him and turned her face against his neck, the emotional aftermath as wrenching as the release —she felt raw and was in a million pieces. Tank was so damn strong. He never let her slip or lost any of his power as he adjusted his hold, his hand splayed wide at the back of her head, holding her with such absolute tenderness that it made her throat close up. He could turn her inside out, and God, she cared so much for him.

He held her for a long time, until his breathing leveled out and she stopped shaking, until the aftermath softened into something less intense.

"Bed," he muttered.

"Second door on the left down the hall," she whispered, kissing the side of his face, his jaw, behind his ear. He tasted salty against her tongue. He pushed away from the wall and carried her to her bed. Once inside, he pulled the comforter and sheet down and settled them onto the mattress all without her having to let go of him, the light in his eyes possessive and bright with banked desire. That was good, because she didn't want to let go.

Bracing his weight on his forearms, he cupped her face, his thumbs caressing her cheeks, still intimately joined with her. Then he lowered his head and gave her the sweetest, softest kiss. Releasing another sigh, he lifted his head and gazed down at her, a glint of amusement lightening his eyes. "Is that what you had in mind, babe?"

She smiled up at him, swallowing the clog of emotion. She smoothed her hand up his long, muscled back. "It's as if you read my mind."

He smiled. "Read your body, every curve and inch of it. Jesus, Alyssa, you take my breath away with your beauty."

Alyssa closed her eyes and held on to him, unable to stop the tears from leaking out and slipping down her temples into her hair. He made her feel so feminine with his huge body and the easy way he manhandled her. His raw masculinity turned her on in so many ways. He made her feel like a woman, desired and attractive. He'd made love to her like he'd seen her, knew her, wanted her with a desire that had never shown so hotly in Stephen's eyes. For so many years, she repressed so much of herself. How could she give herself fully to any man until she embraced her femininity, until she opened up and let everything out?

"Hey," he said gently. "What's going on there?"

She opened her eyes, blinking at the blurry image of his handsome face, the intensity of his brown eyes, now the softest she'd ever seen them.

"It's embarrassing," she murmured.

"You can tell me anything, Alyssa."

"I used to say being a girl never got me anywhere."

"Yeah, why is that?"

"When I was five, my brother died. He had a heart attack at fifteen. It was a genetic defect that wasn't detected. My parents were devastated. My father changed so much my mom couldn't deal with it and she left. She lives in Arizona with my stepdad, but I don't get a chance to see her much. She left me with my dad because he needed me more. I think he wanted to mold me into being what he'd hoped my brother would've become. Whenever I would cry, he would say that I needed to be a big girl, keep emotion hidden. He enrolled me in sports, and as a result of his disapproval of makeup and dolls, he didn't allow me to have them. He pushed me to excel, which isn't a bad thing. I had a lot of drive. He never came out and said it, but he wanted me to downplay my femininity. I didn't realize until now that I was being brainwashed into his way of thinking. But now I wonder if I'm living someone else's life instead of my own."

"Now that you're aware, there's nothing stopping you from figuring it out, deciding what you really want. We're just getting to really know each other, but I'm re-evaluating some stuff, too, that's been dogging me for all of my life. Getting involved with you is a big change for me. Protectiveness is my knee-jerk reaction, but I'm getting the idea that there's more to family than being protective. We just need to be honest with each other and ourselves."

She nodded. "I'm starving. How about we order something to eat?"

"I'm not quite done here," he said as she felt him hardening inside her. "The piercing is okay. It's not hurting you?"

"If hurting me felt this damn good, I'd become a masochist."

He chuckled.

She cupped his silky jaw. "You recover fast, sailor."

"SEALs always have to be on point and ready for action," he said, and she laughed softly as his mouth covered hers.

Later, after they ordered a pizza and made love again, they showered together. He got out first, leaving her to finish washing her hair. It took her the usual time to comb out the tangles. When she came out of the bathroom, he'd already dozed off. She wanted to curl against him while he slept, but she couldn't seem to relax, so she stood there, trying to work through her discomfort. The floodgates had been opened and part of her was angry, the other part feeling a bit lost. She had a lot to think about and Tank was a colossal part of it. She'd need to work through her repressed feelings. There was still the fact that she had this job change hanging out there, that active duty may change her dynamic with him. She knew her skill was special, and the military service needed her at Lackland, but the thought of going back to San Antonio, being close to her dad caused her turmoil. Her father would tell her to put her emotions aside and use her head, but that just didn't work for her anymore. Her heart was engaged. She was allowed her emotions and feelings. She was allowed to be confused and unsure.

At this moment, she was glad she cancelled her plans to go home for Thanksgiving.

In sleep he still looked fierce and ready for action. If he had the slightest inkling that something was wrong, he'd be wide-awake and ready for action. She walked to the bed, her skin still damp, her hair a wet rope down her back. She settled on the bed. He'd fallen asleep upright with his back against the headboard, his hard body bare to her eyes. She reached out and brushed her fingers over his sensual mouth, traced the line of his very nice nose to the place between his forehead that tended to wrinkle when he was deep in thought. His long lashes fluttered, and he opened his eyes.

They stared at each other in the semi-darkness, saying nothing, but communicating so much. Their first night together and she wanted to be bold and strong. Now that he'd released her from her neutral chains, she was free to explore that side of herself. Tank had given her so much more than he realized.

"You are such a beautiful, sexy man," she whispered.

"Show me," he said, his eyes daring her to be the woman she had set free.

She lifted her chin and he smiled like he knew she was going to accept his challenge.

Settling between his legs, she leaned forward and captured one of his rigid nipples between her lips. She laved the erect nub with her tongue and grazed the tip with the edge of her teeth. A groan rumbled up from his chest as she traversed her way lower, spreading hot kisses on his taut, flat belly, her tongue licking over the hard ridges. She encountered a few scars along the way, some round bullet holes, others long and slim. She caressed each badge of his service, of his courage, with her tongue and heard him suck in a surprised breath in response to her tender touch. Finally, she came to his thick, straining erection, and even that part of him was as gorgeous and magnificent as the man himself.

She wrapped her fingers around his hard length and felt him pulse in her tight grip. A drop of moisture appeared, and she spread the silky drop over the head of his cock.

She wanted to give him such pleasure.

She took him into her mouth, his skin hot and salty against the stroke of her tongue. He shuddered and tangled his hands in her damp hair, and she sucked him, taking him deep, the metal ring just as warm as his skin. It felt different, arousing and dangerous. She played with it, loving his reaction as he jerked against her mouth. She pleasured him some more, teased him with her tongue until his breathing was ragged, his whole body shaking with his restraint and against the need to let go.

"Christ, woman," he breathed and frantically tried to tug her back up. "If you don't stop now, I'm gonna come."

She had more things she wanted to do to him, so she complied. With one last irresistible lick and a flick of her tongue against the metal ring, she kissed her way back up his body and crawled onto his lap, covering his hard sex with latex. She straddled his hips and directed his shaft upward. She was so ready for him from the foreplay, and with deliberate slowness, she sank inch by inch on top of him, until he filled her completely and her sex stretched tight around his width.

His nostrils flared, and stark desire heated his eyes. He clutched her waist with his hands and rocked her tighter against his straining body, setting a rhythm she knew would take him to orgasm. She reveled in the feminine power that she had over him.

"Touch yourself," he said. "Come for me."

When her fingers slipped down her stomach and between her splayed thighs, she gasped at the fullness of her core and the pleasure that streaked through her. His chest rose and fell heavily, his expression fierce and hungry as he watched her caress herself for his eyes only.

She felt the hot, spiraling sensation, and she rocked into Tank, increasing the pleasure and the friction. She pressed down on his erection hard and deep, and came on a soft, shivery moan before collapsing against his chest.

"So fucking beautiful," he said raggedly.

She locked her arms around his neck, locked their

bodies from chest to thighs. She could barely breathe as she pressed her mouth to his, kissing him with each roll and glide of her hips against his.

He gripped her hips, but his big, warm hands let her set the pace. Shameless felt damn good. His thighs tensed beneath hers, his stomach muscles rippled. His groans and deep moans increased with her tempo. Grabbing his thick hair in her fists, she pulled his head back and raked her teeth along his throat. Then she sucked and bit him. He bucked upward one last time, hard and strong, and his groan of surrender in her ear was the sexiest, most empowering sound she'd ever heard.

Once his tremors subsided, he tipped her back against the mattress and stared down at her with a serious, fierce look on his face. "I'd say you are pretty aware of your own power, babe."

"Thank you for that," she whispered, working at ignoring the glimmer of adoration in his eyes along with the emotional tug on her heart that warned her she was falling for Thorn "Tank" Hunt.

She had a measuring stick for this feeling, and compared to the lukewarm feeling she'd had thought she'd felt for her ex-husband, this was off the charts.

That might be the most empowering feeling of all.

THE NIGHT WAS pitch black as Ruckus and his team approached the area where the bodies had been reported. He lifted his arm and clenched his fist for his teammates to come to a halt. He didn't like this feeling of being two men down, and for the time being, he'd have to endure another

SEAL dog handler until Tank was back with his new K9 warrior.

The dog handler sent Rex out, and they followed him. Showing no signs anyone was lying in wait, they approached the clear outlines of several bodies on the ground.

"Base, this is Alpha One," he rasped into his mic.

"Go, Alpha One, over."

"We're approaching the kill zone. He looked at Wicked and he held up three fingers.

"We have three bodies, over. We're checking them out."

As Kid crouched down in sniper mode and the other's fanned out, Ruckus, low to the ground closed the distance between him and the motionless heap. When he got there, he turned over the first man and his mouth tightened. His face had been so badly beaten, he couldn't make out who it was. The same went for the other two dead men.

"No ID, base, over," he said into the mic through clenched teeth.

"Chopper incoming," Base responded.

As they waited, there wasn't one man on his team who wasn't wondering: Was one of these men Blue?

11

DURING THE DAY, Tank worked with Bronte, and he spent his nights with Alyssa, his thoughts not far from Blue, especially now that those bodies had been found and identified. All SEAL Team Charlie members had been executed. It was just a matter of time before he and his team would be back over there, and when they found the people responsible for the deaths, there would be justice. Blue was still MIA. His absence was always felt, like reverse space, his calm presence missed at every training session, pressing against Tank's conscience. To date, there had been no trace of him except his dog tags had been found near where he had been standing. The blast had destroyed the laces of his boot, and the dog tags nestled inside where special ops placed them during covert missions had been left behind. His whereabouts were still a mystery.

Tank was working on not letting his frustration and impatience get the better of him. For him, the status quo had been blown to smithereens both in his private and professional life. The events had both stimulated him and challenged him. Maybe he'd grown too complacent and what he really needed was a challenge. Working with Bronte hadn't gotten any better. In fact, she seemed to be even more contrary and had snapped at him a couple times. He kept remembering his ease with Echo, how well they had been together. The more he felt like he was failing with Bronte, the more he thought about Echo. He called Lackland several times to find out about his health. Once he was told Echo was out of the woods, Tank stopped calling. He had to do this cold turkey.

But Echo was his way of getting through those sessions, and the more that Bronte fought him, the worse it got.

He was at his locker, getting changed so he could get home, shower and change to go with Jordan to meet his new doctor. After many tests and still no definitive answers, it was frustrating as hell. Just as he closed and locked the gate, Ruckus walked in. "Hey, we're pulling out at in an hour. Got a lead on Blue."

Tank swore softly under his breath. "LT, I need to talk to you. It's about Jordan."

"What's up with him?"

"He's sick. They don't know what's going on yet, but he's meeting with his new doctor today. I want to go after Blue. It's killing me to ask this, but I need to be there from my brother."

Ruckus shifted and went thoughtful, his understanding tempered by his orders. Wheels up was wheels up. "I can delay for about half an hour, but your ass needs to be on that tarmac by then."

"That's enough time. Thank you!"

"Thank you? What happened to my Tank...you going soft?" Ruckus smiled.

Tank shook his head as Ruckus left.

He raced to the hospital. Jordan looked up when he

walked in, his face showing his surprise. "I didn't know you were coming," he said. Then they both turned at the sound of Dan's voice.

"We wouldn't miss being here for our broski."

Jordan took a breath and looked away. "Thank you for coming...I'm pretty scared," he admitted. "So many tests and no answers. It's getting old."

"Yeah, we're right there with you," Tank said. "We've always been. I might not have shown it, Jordan, but I do support you. I was just trying to keep everything together. Our parents were no help at all, they lived the gang lifestyle, high most of the time. When Dad caused Jelsena's death, I thought it was up to me to keep us all safe. That's all I could focus on."

"You don't talk about her at all," Jordan said. "I've always wanted to know more. I was pretty young when she died."

"Me, too," Dan said. "I do remember she loved to sing and she had the best smile."

Tank smiled, remembering his sister not as a tragedy, but as she once was. "She was sweet, funny, and loved roses. She'd shove her nose into one any chance she got. She was pretty awesome." As he talked the pain of her death eased more and more. Sharing her with his brothers was what he had needed. He just hadn't been aware until now.

Two weeks after he'd slept with Alyssa, he decided to go back to the basics. He projected calm, kept his cool, and they practiced, practiced, and practiced some more. He worked her hard for an hour, but by the end of it, he was beginning to think she was not the dog for him. "Good girl," he said, trying to project a positive mindset. The navy-blue tug that he'd used after almost all of his sessions with Echo as a special treat was in his back pocket. He went to reach for it, but then stopped. Rewarding her for her behavior today wasn't procedure. The tug stayed where it was. After he kenneled her, he saw Alyssa at the gate.

She handed him a bottle of water. "Hey, you looked like you were struggling out there."

The last two weeks with her had been eye-opening. Damn, but she was intelligent and funny. There were times when he couldn't wait to get to her, to touch her, hold her and make love to her. Yet, right now there was a strained silence between them. He really needed to be alone to think this out. The Navy wasn't normally accommodating when it came to dog handlers. They expected him to handle the situation and train the dog. This whole situation with Bronte had yanked him up short, and with Blue, Jordan, and Alyssa heavy on his mind, he needed time to assimilate it all. "I don't think she's the right dog for me." He looked off into the distance, opened the bottle, and took a long pull.

She shaded her eyes and looked up at him. She leaned back against his truck and folded her arms. After a moment, she said, "I think you're selling yourself short."

He rolled his shoulders. He was done for the day, a heavy training session with his teammates, range time, and hitting the gym all taking its toll. He needed a shower and something to eat. "I don't want to talk about this right now."

Alyssa gave him a level gaze. "Tank, you quit on her before you even started working with her."

He stared at her, then looked away and exhaled heavily. He looked back at the kennels, the dusky quiet perforated by the sound of chickadees. He considered Alyssa's comment, then let go another exasperated sigh. "That's not true. I've been here every day since she was assigned to me. I'm making a rational decision. Not every dog works with every handler." He unlocked his truck door and decided that he would withdraw from this discussion before he let the irritation building inside him bubble up. He needed to decompress. "I'm going home to shower and change. I'll see you later."

He got in his vehicle and resisted looking in the rearview mirror. Her assessment stung, just as Jordan's words had stung when he'd been confronted about being sick. It drove it home to him that he had made mistakes with his brothers. Working hard to keep them safe was rooted in his unresolved feelings regarding his little sister's death. There was a reason he'd tattooed her name on his arm. He never wanted to forget that she had died because of neglect and recklessness. Once again, he realized that he hadn't exactly been supportive toward them. When he pulled in his driveway, he closed his eyes and leaned his head back against the headrest. Bronte was an exemplary dog. Why was he having such a hard time with her? He was a seasoned handler. It should have been an easy transition. But nothing was easy with the loss of Echo. He felt his partner's absence as keenly as he felt Blue's. He was relieved that Echo was recovering, but there was this ache he couldn't seem to make go away.

He swallowed against the tightness in his throat. He had to stop thinking about Echo. He was no longer able to serve, and he was retired now. Someone would adopt him, and he'd live his life out with someone who loved him. He deserved that.

He clenched his jaw and tightened his hands on the wheel. He wanted to be the one to adopt Echo. *You can't. He needs someone there for him twenty-four/seven and your schedule is too unpredictable.*

Out of nowhere his throat closed up with a painful cramp and his vision blurred. He was trying to be rational, but he hated the truth when it came to Echo. He had to consider the needs of his furry friend and not be selfish about it. Yet he couldn't shake the sense of being incomplete.

Suddenly, the scene played out once again: Echo discovering the insurgent, his shouting, Echo streaking across the compound, then the explosion, blacking out and coming to with Echo's high-pitched cries filling his ears. Pressing the heels of his hands against his eyes, waiting for the memory to settle, the fear and helplessness surging back, he attempted to reel in his emotions. Could he have done anything differently? He reached down and released his seat belt as he heard a car come to a stop behind him.

Alyssa wasn't about to let him get away with this. She got out of her car and slammed the door. He was halfway up his walk, his strides clipped. Damn him and his obstinance. "Tank!" she said. "Don't you dare walk away from me."

"Give it a rest, Doc. I'm done for today."

"No you're not," she said. When she reached him, she grabbed his arm and spun him around. "This is what it's going to take to get back into shape. You've got to work with Bronte! She's ready. You're the one holding her back."

"No, dammit. We don't mesh and I'm not in the mood to discuss this anymore."

"Thorny?"

Tank stiffened and turned around.

"Becca?"

Alyssa took in the small, beautiful younger woman dressed to the nines in designer clothes.

"I haven't heard from you in a while. I was worried. I wanted to talk to you about Jordan."

"I'm fine. Jordan is doing all right, everything considered…" He trailed off.

"How is Echo?"

"He's recovering."

Her eyes welled and the surprise on his face said it all. She clutched his forearm, giving Alyssa an anxious look. "Now isn't a good time, Tinkerbell."

Tinkerbell?

He had a relationship with this woman, and everything in her tightened, a bad case of the green-eyed monster stabbing at her.

She gave Alyssa another anxious look and nodded. "Would you call me?"

He nodded. "Yeah, I'll talk to you later."

He opened his front door and went inside. Before he could shut it in her face, she inserted her boot. He let out a breath and let go of the door. She came into the foyer and shut it behind her. No reason to give his neighbors a show.

"Who was that?"

He didn't say anything, just gave her that flat, annoying Tank look.

"Are you seeing her, too?" She couldn't keep the distress out of her voice. Here she was putting her heart on the line by getting involved with him and he was already involved. When he set his hands on his hips and looked as stubborn as all get out, she realized that she wasn't quite strong enough to deal with a man who slept around. It was true that he hadn't made any promises to her. She should have gotten it straight. "You're right. I should go," she murmured.

She turned, and he grabbed her arm and spun her. "It's not like that. She's not my girlfriend. We just hang out in between deployments. She's a rich little daddy's girl who used to get me off."

She huffed out a breath.

"It's mutual. It's all about me being a SEAL. She's a strap hanger, a groupie, Alyssa."

"I see. You don't like change and she does it your way."

He dragged her against him. "You challenge me." He hit the back of his head against the wall. "Every day, all the time like a freaking drill instructor."

"Oh, how flattering."

"It's not her I think about. It's not her I want," he ground out. He closed his eyes. "I wouldn't hurt you like that."

Her heart melted at his passionate tone. God, she was showing how insecure she was when she knew Tank wouldn't do that to her. "You wouldn't. I'm feeling a little stupid right now. So, I'm sorry I accused you of that."

"It's all right. This whole thing is making us both crazy. I'm just not sure about Bronte, Alyssa. It doesn't feel right. We don't mesh."

"That's not true. She's trying and you're not. She's never going to be Echo, Tank."

His voice got thick and his eyes went moist and she felt like a hard-assed bitch. Damn, maybe she was being too hard on him.

"You don't understand. I love Echo, he's part of my family! I don't know how to do this again," he shouted.

She instinctively wrapped her arms around his neck. "I'm sorry. That was so insensitive. Please forgive me. I'm just trying to get you to see that you have to find a way to get past this, for yourself and for your team."

"I've been with Echo for ten years, ever since I came into the program." He swallowed. Before her eyes, this big man disintegrated. "He saved us; he gave up everything, almost lost his life."

He buried his face in her neck, his skin damp against her

throat, his mouth pressed just under her chin, his hair a silky slide against her jaw. Her resolve broke. The hard part of her that refused to give in, gave in, caved, crashed, tumbled. Serving together had broken her marriage, and she'd been gun-shy for so long. Getting involved with a SEAL, one who wasn't even in the army where they could at least try to get postings together, it seemed so impossible, but none of that meant anything. The feel of him beneath her hands felt so damn good. Before she knew it, he spun her, his mouth hot against hers, backing her up against the wall, devouring her lips as if he was going to eat her alive.

His mouth even after two weeks was so familiar, the way he kissed her driving home that he was telling the truth. Tank was an honorable man. And he lived his life by that creed. She had always been aware of it, but she had never really thought about it. Now that she had, she realized it was one of the traits in him that she respected most. And she recognized that he measured everything by that.

Feeling as if she had just stumbled onto something very significant, Alyssa wondered how his sense of honor had affected them. As long as she had known him, he had been upright and honest in his dealings with everyone. She doubted if he had ever betrayed anyone—certainly not his brothers. Never his fellow SEALs and certainly not her—

But the choice he thought he'd made on the battlefield dogged him. He'd gone to Echo as he'd been trained to do. Dog and handler were a unit. Even though he was part of a bigger team, Echo was his responsibility, and he had followed through.

But his teammate, Blue, had been lost. All these things must be pressing against him each day. Getting back to working an unfamiliar dog wasn't like picking up a new gun. Whether Lackland or Tank's command thought he should just soldier on and exchange one K9 warrior for another, it wasn't Tank's perspective. Tank loved Echo more than he could ever love any piece of his gear. Echo was a living, breathing member of their team. He'd saved so many lives that day, including Tank's.

A funny feeling unfolded in her belly, and Alyssa straightened, the sensation buzzing through her. But what if he felt that he was betraying Echo, who she was now convinced he considered as much a part of his family and an integral part of his team? She was suddenly so aware, she felt as if she had received a deep insight into a complicated man. What if he did feel that, and what if that was why he was struggling with Bronte?

She pushed against his chest, even as he deepened the kiss, but the moment he felt the pressure, he released her. "Making love to me isn't going to make all this go away," she said gently.

He stared down into her eyes and something shifted there in those deep brown, so intense depths. Where in the past he would withdraw and gloss over anything to do with what he was feeling. He backed away from her and slipped his hand into his back pocket, one of his fists clenched, and he huffed out an unsteady, heavy breath.

"You are tenacious, and believe it or not, you don't know everything."

"Maybe I don't. Maybe I use that to keep people at a distance so that they don't really see me for who I am. But this isn't about me. This is about you, Echo, and Petty Officer Beckett—Blue."

"Ocean," Tank said, his voice strangled. He blinked rapidly. "He's a surfer, you know. Knows how to become one with the ocean. He said his parents, hippie surfer people, named him after their favorite part of Mother Nature. They thought it would make him a strong man when he grew up."

"There's still no word about him?"

He walked to the front window and leaned against the casement, passing his hand over his eyes, then rubbing at his rough jaw. "No. Not a thing. It's like he disappeared off the face of the earth."

She came up behind him and wrapped her arms around him, setting her face against his heavily muscled back. "That was a very tough op for you, especially because of Echo."

"It's war, Alyssa."

She squeezed him. "I know that. Combat is organized chaos. Your instincts, all your senses and your training had you focus on Echo. He was your responsibility. I'm sure that talking about your feelings wouldn't be your first choice, but Tank, deciding to help your K9 partner isn't in any way the wrong choice."

"I didn't really make a choice, Alyssa." He took a ragged breath, his voice clogged with emotion now. "I reacted to Echo in distress, a threat still not neutralized."

"Agreed. If you hadn't, all of you would have most likely died if that rebel had set off the detonator in his hand.

He nodded. "Still doesn't make it any easier for me to deal with Blue missing. My responsibility was to him, too."

"I understand. Losing him doesn't make it any easier. Then your loss of Echo...we're not talking about equipment here or weapons. Those are inanimate objects. Echo is as loyal and fierce a warrior as you are. You've been with him for so long, and the bond with a dog goes so deep, I don't think we really realize how deep. Your whole routine, everything you did on a daily basis involved him. There is no status quo here anymore, and everything has changed both within your team and within your established unit. It's more than losing a partner, he's family. Now you have to deal not only with loss in your everyday working life, but you have to deal with the personal and very real emotion that goes with it. You have to deal with those dog prints on your heart."

"Yeah," he whispered.

She experienced such a rush of feeling for him, for Echo, and for Bronte who, from what Alyssa could see, wanted to please him. But that resistance in Tank was confusing her when he needed to bond with her. He was still raw from Echo, from dealing with his feelings at both Blue and Echo's absences, and Alyssa understood the kind of grit and determination it took to set that aside and do his job.

"Everything you're feeling is going down that leash to Bronte. She's sensitive like all dogs. You might not be conscious of it, but your resistance is very clear to her, and that causes a disconnect. She doesn't trust you because you're not trusting her."

"You're right. I'm struggling with this. Echo was my shield. I protected everyone in my life, but he protected me. We relied on each other. Nothing feels right without him."

"Oh, Thorn, I'm so very sorry." She couldn't say anything more as she circled him and put her arms around him. Pulling his head against her shoulder, she eased in a careful, constricted breath, her tears, like his releasing the pressure in her chest.

For an instant he simply stood there in her arms. Then he let his breath go and put his arms around her. Alyssa closed her eyes and cradled his head against her, tears slipping relentlessly down her face.

Sensing how raw and stripped he felt—knowing without a doubt that it wasn't in his nature to lean, that he had been the rock, the foundation in every life he'd touch—

she hung onto him, finally, finally understanding the source of his reserve, his wariness. She wanted to be within that select circle of people he depended on, that he cherished, that he trusted.

Dashing away her tears, Alyssa swallowed hard, struggling to achieve a degree of self-control, an outward calm. It wasn't finished. Somehow, she had to find the key to unlock the rest.

Stroking over his thick hair, she closed her eyes and forced herself to get the words out. "Tell me how you're feeling," she whispered, her voice breaking. "I want your trust, Tank."

His chest expanded, then he tried to pull away, but she simply tightened her arms around him, determined not to let him go. Waiting for another contraction in her throat to ease, she cupped the back of his head, pressing her face against his. "Tell me," she whispered. "You're safe with me."

He remained rigid and silent in her arms, then he took a deep jagged breath and started talking. She wanted to absorb everything he said.

"I'm afraid for Blue. If he'd been killed in action, it wouldn't be so torturous. We would all know. We talk around his absence. We declare that we're never going to leave him behind. We make sure that we maintain that warrior status quo. Talking about our fears isn't easy for us. It's something we bury to keep going. I don't have to outline the horrors of being captured by someone as ruthless and depraved as the Golovkins. They have members of Team Seven, and we're already planning to go after them as soon as we discover where they're being held. But Blue is our medic, and like Echo, there's a strong bond, and even though that guy can take of himself, we're protective of him.

He's a badass warrior, but he's so much more and I love him like a brother, like I love them all."

Meeting her gaze, he toyed with her hair, straightening a tendril that had escaped her tight ponytail, his expression drawn. The effect of telling her had taken a toll. And his eyes—oh, God, his eyes. Refusing to give in to the feelings churning inside her, she freed her arms, then took his face between her hands, wanting him to understand. "I'm here for you—twenty-four/seven. Don't ever feel that you can't come to me whenever you need to. I will never judge you. Like Echo, you have my unconditional attention."

"That's significant, Alyssa. I would never dismiss that offer." Shifting his gaze, he caught one of her hands, then carefully laced his fingers through hers. His voice was husky and a little unsteady when he went on. "We have every intention of getting all those team members back." His voice wavered, and he stopped and rubbed his eyes; Alyssa felt him try to swallow. It took a while before he could continue. "I swear that, but we'll pull out all the stops to find Blue and the rest of them and bring everyone home."

Alyssa had been fighting the good fight; she'd thought she had everything under control, but that roughly spoken admission, that statement of commitment, completely did her in. Unable to see, unable to speak, she clenched her arms around his shoulders, and Tank held her hard, his face turned against her neck.

It was a long time before Alyssa could ease her hold. She felt as if she'd been wrung out to dry.

"I have no doubt you will do everything humanly possible to bring those men home alive," she whispered unevenly. "But don't forget that you need self-care and to think about moving on from Echo to Bronte. I know that you love what you do. I see it in your eyes. Training with her will save lives, and your team needs you and her to work together for them."

His chest expanded sharply; then he hugged her so hard that she couldn't breathe, and she hugged him back, knowing that if Thorn "Tank" Hunt had ever needed to hear that, it was now. She held him until she felt the awful tension ease and then shifted her head, smoothing her hand up his neck. He needed her. He needed sweetness and solace. And soft, soft loving. "Let's go upstairs," she whispered. He went still; then he inhaled sharply and gathered her up in a hard, enveloping embrace.

Later that night, Alyssa lay in bed in Tank's arms, listening to his rhythmic breathing. His bedroom was masculine and rugged, the big bed warm and comfortable. She absently fondled his hair, thinking it would have been a perfect night for a walk on the beach. But they had made long, leisurely love instead and then had watched the stars in the black night sky before he'd fallen asleep. She smiled. At least she assumed he was asleep. He'd been boneless and quiet for the last thirty minutes.

Shifting her head, she gazed at him, liking the feeling of his big body next to hers, the possessive way he held her with his arm tucked around her waist. Her face was turned toward his, and she smoothed her thumb along his temple, through his glossy beard, then tucked her chin and brushed a kiss against his sexy mouth, smiling when he made a soft humming sound.

He made her feel so damn beautiful with the way he touched her, the way he looked at her. Owning herself, that was something she had always done intellectually. Her mind had been her vehicle. But she'd only discovered the physical was just as potent, something she'd downplayed for so damn long. Her father's disapproval made her squirm inside with a restless need for freedom from this need to not disappoint him. Like Tank had said, it was better to do that than disappoint herself. Her father wanted her to make it in a man's world on his terms.

Now, after experiencing Tank who made her think, she wanted to experience the world on her own terms. She'd just have to figure out for herself what that meant.

12

BLUE SPREAD around the chicken feed like Elena had taught him. The hungry hens made clucking sounds as they gobbled up the yellow mixture. She was gathering the eggs of the recently abandoned roosts, placing them in a basket she'd made herself. He marveled how resourceful and accomplished she was.

The sun was just breaking fully over the tree line in the far distance, at the back of the lower fields, making him shade his eyes

He couldn't seem to stop looking at her. She was so beautiful that she took his breath away. She moved with a deliberate grace, no waste of energy. His breath fogged the air as he dragged his eyes from her.

He grabbed up the cart with the feed and drove it over the rutted path back to the main barn. A heavy mist hung in the air, chilling his skin. He understood why he was having these feelings. It was clear from the way he'd assessed the injury to his head that he was a medic in one of the branches of the military. At least he could only guess, since he had no recollection of who he was or what happened to put him here. He could have stolen the uniform Elena had carefully hidden.

He was making use of her father's clothes that were just a tad too short and a bit baggy. He looked out at the unfamiliar landscape, feeling suddenly a bit shaky and unsettled. This wasn't his country. Her farm was nestled in a fertile valley she'd named Vskhozhiy. Huddling in her father's coat, he stared out across the panorama, the jagged gray mountains covered with snow, and he shivered. He realized even if he was home in the US, he would still be looking at unfamiliar sights.

She'd told him that mass cotton cultivating farms, introduced by the Soviets, dotted the valley, but after her parents were murdered and their land taken, she didn't have enough real estate to grow cotton, so she'd focused on grains, fruits and vegetables.

He could attest to her ability with all three. The fresh dishes she made were not only filling, but so tasty.

While he went to the barn to milk the cow, she headed to the house to take care of the eggs. She'd also taught him to do this. He was sure he'd never done it in his past. It seemed that technical things like his ability to pull medical data from his brain would make the information on how to milk a cow second nature. He was no farm boy.

She came into the barn. "I will throw down the hay," she said.

"Want me to do that? Those bales are heavy."

She smiled at him and nudged him with her hip, sending heat traveling to all parts of his body. "How did I ever manage without you?" she asked wryly, then laughed and climbed up into the loft. She was right. She'd been working this place since she was a little girl and had taken over after her parents' deaths.

A couple of bales hit the barn floor just as he finished the task. He rose and went to them, but looked to see her climbing back down the wobbly ladder. He went to her and steadied it, but she lost her footing on the last rung. An instant later, his hands were around her slender waist, steadying her as both feet reached the ground. Putting his hands on her might steady her, but it was doing crazy things to him. He tried to keep his thoughts neutral, but they had a mind of their own as he thought about putting his hands on her while they were both naked amongst tousled sheets.

Then he was turning her around, and she was so close, her blue eyes level with his. The temperature seemed to rise several degrees.

Even in her farm clothes, the woman looked like she'd just stepped off the pages of the latest Ralph Lauren ad. She made farm worker look so damn sexy as he worked to fight off the waves of desire she inspired just by breathing.

"Looks like you needed my help after all."

Her hands clenched on his shoulders as if she was having a difficult time forming words.

A smile played around her lips. "Looks like I did. Thank you."

He should have removed his hands; their situation was complicated enough as it was, and he was susceptible to her beauty and the way she had nursed him to health with her care and attention. Hell, he had no idea if he was married or had a girlfriend. His ring-less left hand made him think that he wasn't involved with anyone.

He released her, and they walked to the bales of hay and started pulling them apart to feed the cow, pig, goats and horses—a ravenous lot.

He could feel her behind him, his awareness of her ass finely tuned as his senses were to his surroundings. Except with her, there was all that sexual energy jacking things up. He cleared his throat and steeled himself. The light was bright behind her, caught her golden hair and set it aglow, setting her face in shadow, enhancing how impossibly thick her eyelashes were.

He tried to stop looking at her mouth. But the sensuous line of her lips kept drawing his eyes. He was sure if he could remember, he bet his knees had never been this weak. The morning air might have cleared his head, but his body hadn't gotten the message at all.

Walking to a small room, they both reached for the buckets to fill with grain. "Oh, sorry," he said as their hands collided.

"My fault," she said in a flustered way that just wasn't like Elena. She waited a heartbeat too long for him to move first. He couldn't seem to get the command to register in his brain.

They stared at each other; the silence in the enclosed barn crackled with energy, singeing the air between them. The space seemed to shrink down to the two of them from one heartbeat to the next. The sun hadn't risen enough to slice through the panels of the roof, leaving them deep in shadows, with thin beams of gray dawn providing the only light. There was a light bulb overhead, but the switch was behind her and he didn't dare get any closer.

She stepped forward. "Blue—"

"Elena—"

They spoke at the same time, then both broke off.

She said, "Let me go first. I think you feel that same way I do, but at the risk of making a fool out of myself, I think we should be cautious. There are so many unknowns and you don't even have your memory or are fully well."

"None of that seems to matter. And if you're a fool, so am I."

He might not have his memory, but he didn't need it to know that the way she was looking at him wasn't about making sure he was healed. There was nothing that innocent in the visceral way he felt when he looked at her.

She took another step closer, and his breath suddenly felt trapped inside his chest.

"We don't know what tomorrow will bring," she whispered. "We could be running on borrowed time." She stepped closer, still invading his personal space. Again.

"I know. We might not get out of the country alive."

"I can't go with you, Blue. They won't let me," she said with sorrow, tipping her chin up slightly as she shifted closer. He felt the solid wall at his back.

"I'm not leaving here without you," he said, his voice flat and firm.

She closed her eyes, desperation on her face. "Don't say that. You must go. You would never be safe here."

Her eyes were so dark, so deep, he was drowning in them. And her sad expression made his heart clench.

She lifted her hand, barely brushing against the length of his jaw, before trailing her thumb over his mouth. "You are the most beautiful man I think I've seen," she whispered. "I think about you when I shouldn't. I shouldn't take advantage of your situation, your vulnerability. It's not fair to you."

His skin tingled as if the words themselves had brushed against him.

"You saved my life, but how I feel about you is clear. My mind isn't clouded about that," he said fiercely as his mouth lowered to hers. His lips brushed across hers, and she gasped softly when he slid his fingers along the back of her neck, beneath the heavy fall of silky hair. He coaxed her to kiss him back, but she backed up, tears welling in her eyes and slipping down her cheeks.

"I can't. It's too difficult," she said, then grabbed the buckets and filled them with grain. After a moment, he helped her, his heart heavy. He'd been serious when he'd told her his mind was clear. He was falling for his rescuer, and there was nothing he could do about it.

After the chores were done, she cooked breakfast, cleaned up the house, and did some wash.

He grabbed his coat and left the cabin. The ground was hard, the new snow creaking beneath his borrowed boots as he aimlessly walked through the fields. The branches of the trees glistened with white as he made his way down the trail through the trees along the brow of the hill. He inhaled deeply, the sharp, cold air scoring his lungs. But it was good to move. The physical activity good for his muscles. He'd been serious when he'd told her he wasn't leaving without her. If the rebels got even a whiff of a clue that she'd been hiding him right under their noses, they wouldn't hesitate to make an example out of her. He couldn't risk that, and he couldn't, in good conscience, go home and figure out his life while she was here in constant danger.

He ducked his head to avoid a low hanging branch, shivering when cold snow hit the back of his neck.

Elena was just coming out of the house when he rounded the barn. It was clear she was looking for him.

Tucking a stray curl back into the loose knot of her hair, she wiped at her cheeks, then broke into a run. She threw herself against him, and he stood there absorbing the feel of her.

He slung his arm around her shoulder, pulling her close. Once inside, they sat down to eat, and she taught him how to play Durak, a Soviet card game.

Finally, as it got late, she got up and stoked the fire. Looking over at him, she whispered, "I'm sorry about refusing to go, but you have to understand. This is going to be so risky as it is. I have to get you safe. I couldn't bear it if something happened to you."

He let her believe that he was okay with it for now, but there was no goddamned way he was leaving here without her. He was prepared to throw her over his shoulder and take her with him with or without her consent.

TANK STOOD at the entrance to the kennel. He'd done some heavy thinking after his talk with Alyssa last night. In the past, he'd gone his own way. He always had to be in charge because his life had been so out of control with the constant moving, the unpredictability of his mom, the disappearance of his dad, the loss of his sister and his fierce need to protect his brothers. One feeling was prevalent in all those situations: his feeling of powerlessness. It caused him to rebel not only in his manner of appearance or in his music, but sent him into a spiral in the opposite direction. In an effort to take control of his life, he'd lost the definition of what it meant to be supportive.

He'd assumed the protector role as second nature, and joining the SEALs only extended that need to be the shield where anyone or anything met its match. He'd dismiss the term hero because he was part of a team that embodied all that he held dear.

He should have known that she would understand, and he experienced a huge amount of relief that she'd forced the issue with Bronte. He should have known it wasn't the dog's fault. He was the one confusing the hell out of her.

He was broken up about Echo and he'd needed the time to come to acceptance that his stalwart companion was no longer a part of his life. He had to wonder if he'd feel that emptiness forever.

She understood so much about him, and her acceptance mattered more than he'd realized.

He'd had no idea what it could mean to be part of a relationship, something real and intimate between a man and a woman. He'd thought he'd only needed close male relationships in his life, that women were nothing more than a way to fulfill his physical needs. But it wasn't females in particular, it was exposing his vulnerability. It was easy as a man to keep his personal thoughts and his heart guarded when he'd only allowed himself close male friendships and his brothers were just like his SEAL buddies. Emotion was masked or glossed over with humor. But a woman didn't accept that kind of crap. Alyssa was an exception, and it was a huge, shocking revelation to realize that her opinion mattered the most. With sudden clarity, he knew that was part of the reason he'd avoided her for two months, because his subconscious had obviously known what his emotions hadn't been ready to face or accept—that this woman who challenged him at every turn, who was there when he needed her, and who gave of herself so openly and generously when they made love, could very well be the one for him.

And more than losing Echo, more than handling combat stress, more than anything in his life, he feared getting deeper with Alyssa. With her life in flux, her opportunities that could take her away from San Diego. But it might be too late. She had herself wrapped around his heart.

It had been a gradual thing until now. Now it was a complete forest of tangled vines.

He hated that he was afraid and vulnerable. It brought back that feeling of being out of control and helpless.

He took a deep breath and released the latch, stepping inside. There was something exciting about being in a place where canine warriors lived and thrived. If there was one defining trait, one successful characteristic of all Navy SEALs, it was that they couldn't stand losing—and they refused to quit. Ever.

He'd had a low point with Echo. He still missed him like hell, and he'd been unfairly comparing Bronte to Echo. She wasn't Echo, and his baggage regarding his first K9 companion had to be jettisoned. He could say that she did have the needed trait that reflected every Navy SEAL in the Teams. She just wouldn't quit.

He stopped in front of her kennel and she immediately focused on him. Her attention was razor sharp. She was telling him that she was ready to work even if he was being an obtuse asshole. That was good, because he was ready to really commit and put Bronte through her paces.

He put her on the leash and they exited the kennel. He'd asked the kennel master to set up the most difficult course of explosive detection he'd ever dreamed up. But before they got to that, he sent her through agility.

Before they had been caught in an unforgiving triangle with Echo at one of the apexes.

As painful as it was, he took Echo out of the equation. This wasn't a threesome with Echo's influence affecting the way he perceived Bronte. This was what he had and wanted to build: a partnership between him and her.

That was all it was, except in this equation, one plus one didn't equal two. They equaled one strong meshing of man and dog into a single, unstoppable fighting entity.

He worked her for twenty minutes to tire her and then really give her a chance to show him what she was made of.

He took her through the kennel master's course and she found every single explosive.

Back at the field, he pulled a ball out of his pocket. To her credit, she didn't move, but her whole body shivered with anticipation and pent-up desire for the object he was holding. She was beautiful as she sat there, her dark muzzle cocked, her whiskey dark eyes riveted on him.

Her prey instinct was off the charts. He resisted comparing her to Echo. He was out of the equation, and Tank wasn't using his memory and emotions regarding his beloved partner to score Bronte.

He threw the ball, and before he'd even released the object, she was racing after it in a show of blazing speed. For the first time since Echo had been wounded, Tank smiled as he watched Bronte, taking sheer pleasure in the caliber of dog the Navy had entrusted to his care.

She was bold, powerful, stubborn, and dominant. But what made his heart sing was that she was absolutely crazy about getting that ball.

He approached her as she chewed on the object. Reaching down, he said, "Release." She immediately complied. She gazed up at him, once again focused like a laser on him. He crouched down and grasped her head, "Good girl. We're going to work together, you and I. We're going to do what's necessary to complete every mission we're given. You up for that?"

She barked, and Tank laughed softly, the part of him that had unconsciously walled himself off from Bronte embracing what he had here. The females were filling up his life, and if he couldn't have Echo by his side, then Bronte was an exemplary new warrior to fight with him on the battlefield. She wouldn't hesitate at all. She would use that nearly out-of-control pursuit in the field and charge into unknown environments without fear.

"You're pretty focused, Bronte," he murmured. Her unflappable disposition was golden. "That's good because we're needed. We save lives and you're going to love my team and they're going to love you."

With a hitch in his chest, he reached back and pulled out Echo's favorite toy. The navy blue tug. "Come get it," he said releasing her from her charged immobility. She lunged at the square piece of sturdy stuffed cloth and clamped down. As he wrestled with her, his trust in her grew when she twisted her body and took him down to the ground. Then she gave him slobbery kisses as if to say, *no hard feelings, but I'm going to bring it every time.*

He wouldn't want it any other way.

After showering, his cell rang and he saw it was Alyssa. "Hey, babe."

"Meet me at Juniper and Ivy in fifteen minutes. It's on the outskirts of Little Italy. I'm taking you out to dinner."

He smiled. "I'd rather have you here in some interesting position so that I can have my way with you."

"Afterwards," she teased before laughing softly and disconnecting the call.

He dressed in what made him comfortable: khaki pants a cross between joggers and cargo pants, tight to his hips with slim legs, pockets, and a drawstring closure; a black sweater beneath a quilted jacket with a hood and ribbed cuffs. On his feet, black laced-up combat boots.

He drove downtown and entered the three-story, open-beamed warehouse-sized restaurant. It was full, but he saw Alyssa was already there in the back. When she rose, he had to take a moment to admire her. This wasn't the same woman he'd dumped coffee on the first time they'd met, all buttoned down and neutral. No, this Alyssa was vibrant with color, her hair in soft waves down her back, her face subtly made up, even lipstick on her gorgeous mouth. He thought the caterpillar had absolutely turned into a butterfly with that rich coral and the uneven skirt of her dress adding the perfect ethereal touch to an already striking woman.

They embraced and the scent of her went deep inside him. "You look stunning," he whispered.

"You look good enough to eat," she whispered back. He was loving the way she was embracing her flirty side.

They settled into seats and a waiter poured some wine into their glasses. "I took the liberty of ordering," she said.

He took a sip and let the flavors of blackberry, raspberry and sunshine in the Cabernet she'd chosen roll around on his tongue. Nodding to the waiter, he picked up his menu as she picked up hers. "I saw you briefly on the training grounds. You and Bronte looked awesome."

He smiled, feeling lighter and freer than he had in years, and Alyssa was the reason. He stared at her, met her green gaze and wanted to tell her everything he'd just discovered about himself and how much he wanted her to be a part of his life, but he was fairly certain she wasn't ready to hear something so life-changing, even worrying a bit that she wouldn't find him a suitable, permanent choice. They both had work to do. If he'd learned anything about Alyssa, she was just coming into her own, dealing with her own personal issues with some work still ahead of her. She was a kick-ass woman, but stuff from her own past needed to be addressed. Anyone dealing with that kind of emotional baggage was vulnerable. From his own revelations, she'd taught him to treat those emotions with care.

"Mostly because of you. You taught me that being

protective wasn't enough, offering support and putting myself out there even though it was uncomfortable would break me wide open. You were right." He was wide open, and it was scary in a good way. "I had a good session with her once I stopped using Echo as a shield against bonding with another dog."

She leaned forward and placed her hand over his. "What you do isn't easy. The training, the dedication and the effort. But nothing prepares you for bonding with an animal. It's uncontrollable and such a necessary part of a partnership. You can't skimp on it one bit or you run the risk of real danger. No dog will ever be able to hold back on unconditional love. They're just not wired that way. It takes a very strong person to do the job you do, not just as a SEAL, but as a military working dog handler. I admire you so very much for pushing past your loss of Echo and moving on with Bronte."

He turned his hand and laced his fingers with hers. "It's been hard, but the only easy day was yesterday," he said, repeating one of the SEALs favorite mottos. Those words were truer now that he'd been through the transition from one dog to another. But he had a feeling that his relationship with Alyssa was going to be the one that ultimately could make or break him.

Their meal was delicious, and he followed her back to her apartment, anticipating loving her until they fell exhausted into each other's arms. They were almost past the point of no return when someone knocked on her door. To their surprise, the lock twisted, and Tank barely got his pants up over his thick erection before grabbing and covering Alyssa with the throw on the couch before the door opened.

A tall, older man came in, wheeling a suitcase, but

stopped dead, his expression changing from one of anticipation to shocked surprise, then a disapproving frown as his eyes went over him.

Alyssa jumped up from the couch and said, "Daddy!" They all just stared at each other until Alyssa said. "Wait here." She hurriedly grabbed up their clothes in a bundle, and with as much dignity as she could muster, she pulled him into the bedroom.

"What is he doing here?" Tank growled.

"I cancelled my Thanksgiving plans with him because... well, I just didn't feel up to going. I have too much on my mind to deal with my dad's...advice."

"I'm just glad he wasn't carrying a shotgun...if he had come in five minutes later, he might have gone looking for one," Tank said, his eyes dancing.

She giggled, then wrapped her arms around him. "Believe me. Back home, former Colonel in the Army, Kyle St. James has one in his truck. I don't think he toted it from Texas."

"That's something." He laughed softly, then groaned softly when she pressed up against him. His dick was so hard and aching, any pressure against it sent him into pleasure overload.

"Oh, dammit."

"I'm so sorry," she whispered, kissing his mouth, her cheeks still flushed from his arousal of her and her embarrassment at having her father walk in on them. "You'd better go."

"I'd rather come," he said, and she giggled again.

"He'll know what we're doing up here."

"Yeah, right. Finding a half-naked guy in his daughter's apartment probably tipped him off that you're having sex. I don't give a crap what he thinks. You, on the other hand, I care very much about."

"You are so bad, but I am a grown woman. Leaving you like this is just a plain waste of a mind-bending, body-rending fuck." Then she looked up at him, a hot, mischievous twinkle in her eyes. "Screw it. He can wait." She reached for his pants and pushed them down and off him.

13

HIS ERECTION CAME free and she wanted to go down on him, but there wasn't enough time. God, what had happened to that repressed woman she had been? Tank had helped her find her inner bad girl, and she couldn't get enough of her brave new inner world.

He kissed her, the throw dropping from around her body, and he crowded her to the bed. "I'm so hard for you, babe," he whispered hoarsely.

She couldn't even answer him, couldn't even tell him how desperately she wanted him. All she could do was hang on to him, trying to surface above the heavy throbbing that threatened to swamp her. She wanted him now, needed him now. One hand clamped around the back of her neck, he slid his hand over her butt and drew her hard against his pelvis, his hold viselike, the feel of him wrenching a broken sob from her. A shudder coursed through him as he lifted her up and carried her to the bed.

He dropped them down onto the mattress, bracing their fall with one hand, Tank's deep moan vibrating from his wide chest. She buried her face in his neck, her breath coming in shredded sounds as she arched against him. She was so primed for him, so desperate, that the instant she felt the weight of his arousal against her core, she locked her legs around him. He fitted himself to her and she emitted a low, tormented cry as he entered her. He withdrew and thrust back in to the hilt, finally filling her the way she longed to be filled—beyond what she believed was possible for her to take. And he didn't stop there. He increased the tempo of his strokes, each one a little faster, harder, deeper than the one before.

"Fuck, Alyssa."

She closed her eyes and shuddered. His words were just as urgent as the unbearable pressure building between her legs and setting her aflame once again, as reckless as the demanding, aggressive way he plunged into her again and again and again. Two more thrusts—two long, controlled thrusts were all it took—and the pressure splintered, her whole body convulsing around his, her clenching release detonating his. He hung on to her as tremor after tremor coursed through him, but in spite of her frantic urgency, he didn't let his own need take control.

Alyssa was trembling so badly that she had no coordination left. Tank enfolded her more securely against him, and even though she was nearly incoherent, she felt this man all the way to her heart.

A heart that was falling in love with Thorn "Tank" Hunt.

It took her a long time to surface from the blinding release. But the thought of her dad waiting for her just outside the door sent adrenaline rushing through her system. She felt that she'd been burned so hotly in Tank's fire, she was now tempered steel. It was time to face the music.

Once they had recovered, Tank dressed; the sound of his

cell phone going off on the end table near the couch sounded ominous behind the closed door. It's ring sent him out of the bedroom sooner than her. She heard him answer as she did a quick wash, pulled her hair back and threw on a pair of sweatpants and a green T-shirt with ARMY across the front in white.

Tank was near the front door, his jacket in his hands. Her father had brewed a pot of coffee; she could smell the aroma. She glanced at her dad, who was sitting at her dining table reading on his laptop while sipping from one of her mugs.

She went to Tank. "What is it?"

"I've got to go." He cupped her face in his big hands. "I'm pissed that I have to go right now when I wanted to curl up with you and just hold you."

She kissed him deeply, hungrily, desperately, striving for mindless pleasure to chase away her doubts and uncertainties. With her dad showing up, she could no longer ignore what was right in front of her. Her future with Tank or active duty. *Duty.* That word made her want to swear like a sailor. Duty was hanging over her now, and in the past, she'd chosen it over her marriage. Just as Stephen had done the same. Physical intimacy with Tank wasn't just mindless sex. There was a hard, strong connection she couldn't deny. But it was all the other emotional chaos swirling within her that made her feel as though her carefully guarded life was spinning out of control.

Being a girl had never gotten her anywhere. That phrase haunted her. She nearly broke down right there, but after years of being strong and holding herself together, she was conditioned to keeping her emotions locked away tightly.

"When I get back, we need to talk about where we go

from here." He kissed her again, a slow, lingering kiss. "I'll call you when I get back."

"Stay safe," she whispered.

When the door closed after him, she realized that he was going to be in harm's way. It drove home to her what it meant to be in love with a military man and the hollow feeling every time they were apart. It brought up the memories of living apart from Stephen on all those deployments, the lonely days and the even lonelier nights. But Tank didn't fully belong to her. He belonged to the SEALs, to the US government they both served.

Her father closed his laptop and rose. He went to the kitchen and poured her a cup of coffee. Coming back to the table, he set it down. "I'm sorry I barged in here, Alyssa...I had no idea you were..."

"You could have waited until I said something. Geez, Dad, that was embarrassing."

"I get it. I had no idea you were seeing anyone...who is he?"

She sat down next to him and picked up the cup, taking a sip. It was rich and delicious. Her dad did know how to brew a cup of coffee. "Thorn Hunt."

"That Navy SEAL you have as the spokesperson for your charity?"

"Yes."

"Doesn't that cause complications? He's enlisted."

"Apparently according to Article 134, no."

"Will that change once you go active duty?"

Her mouth dropped open. "How did you know about that?"

He chuckled and crossed his ankle over his knee. He was still a fit man, no extra belly hanging over his belt, always neat and groomed. She felt like a wreck next to him, still tingling from Tank's lovemaking. "I still have friends in the Vet Service, honey. Just because I'm retired doesn't mean I don't hear things."

"I haven't decided if I'm going to make the transition yet. I have my practice and the charity. I don't know."

Her dad's eyes narrowed. "And your tattooed hunk."

Why did he have to mention Tank and her mind wandered to the image of Tank with just those pants on, that dark stubble shadowing his jaw. He'd been ready for an army to come through that door, and she had no doubt he would have been able to handle one. Instead, it was worse.

"I started seeing him a few weeks ago."

"Exactly. He shouldn't factor into your decision. Don't let soft emotions derail you again."

She stiffened. "Stephen didn't derail me."

"Yes, he did. You transferred to the reserves after your divorce. You let him affect you, and you've lost time in your career, Alyssa. You're being offered exactly the position you wanted. You can go far from there. Don't let a barely-there relationship lead you to a bad decision."

She drained her mug. "It's not a barely-there relationship, Dad. I'm still thinking about what I'm going to do."

He rose and grabbed her mug and took them to the sink. "Don't wait too long or this opportunity will be gone, and you'll regret it."

She thought about Tank on his way to someplace dangerous. His service to their country was steadfast, unwavering, and he would never shirk that. Could she do any less? The command needed her to step up. Did she have to give up the man she wanted for a job that she'd been working towards? Had her life taken a different path? Should she go back?

"What brings you to San Diego?" she asked, knowing

full well that he had been expecting her for Thanksgiving next week in San Antonio, but cancelling her plans probably ruined his tactic of getting her home and exerting his opinion, except it was never an opinion when it came to her dad. "Did you just come here to lecture me?"

He came back into the room and folded his arms, leaning his hip against her counter. "I figured it would be easier for me to be here for the holiday than have you come back to San Antonio. I should have offered instead of demanding you come home. You know, you could have called me and let me know you were there."

"It was a business-related trip and I had someone with me who needed me."

"Hunt?"

"Yes. His dog Echo was wounded in battle and I went there to make sure he wasn't euthanized."

"I thought they didn't do that anymore. Have things changed?"

"No, they haven't changed. I had to argue with the attending vet."

"You saved the dog?" He watched her face. "But something tells me it was more than that. Who was the attending vet?"

"Stephen."

"Ah, I would have paid good money to see you take over a case from him."

"He wasn't happy, and he was sullen and uncooperative as he could be without being overtly rude."

"You always threatened him, Alyssa."

"What? No."

"Yes. He was jealous of you and your skill, the way you surpassed him. Why do you think he took that assignment at Fort Benning?"

He had said that it would help with his advancement, but Alyssa couldn't understand why he was willing to go so far away from her when the Army would work with them as a married couple. It wasn't guaranteed, but he didn't even try to change it. It wasn't possible that Stephen had been intimidated by her. They had a great marriage.

The pain and hurt from her failed marriage had faded, but this revelation that Stephen had resented her couldn't be true. He'd loved her. He'd promised he had by taking vows. How had things gone so wrong? She immediately thought of Tank. If she stayed here and gave up this opportunity, would she resent him? Would it undermine any relationship they had?

Tank was career SEAL. She was well aware of that without even asking him. Was she going to have to choose again between love and career? Could she give up the budding, endless possibilities with Tank to advance in her career, to fulfill her goal and make her dad proud? There were no answers.

She looked at her watch. "It's getting late and I should turn in. The guest room is ready for you and there are towels in the bathroom."

"Thanks, honey, and good night."

WATER IS ALWAYS IN FLUX. *When you move with it, you understand its currents and flow.* The man standing next to him as he watched the water ebb and crash against the shore smiled, and Blue really liked his smile, his face, the way his eyes crinkled at the corners. Deep down he knew this man was important to him, but his name, his context escaped

him. He had a surfboard tucked under his arm, and Blue
found that he, too, was carrying one.

He urged Blue into the water. When they were out quite
a ways, Blue bobbing on his own board, the man
disappeared.

The sea enclosed him all around. But just as he was
starting to feel as if he too were liquid, the sleek gray head of
a dolphin broke the surface. The animal watched him, and
Blue connected to the one dark eye on the side of his head,
intelligence shone as sure as the silvery sheen of the moon
on the water.

You've been away from yourself too long, he whispered.

Do you know who I am, Blue asked.

You have your own proof. Discover truth.

Blue woke up with a shiver to the heady smell of
jasmine, the sound of snow hitting the small house like the
scratching of rats in the walls. The dream was still vivid in
his mind, the warmth of the water, the hot breeze that blew
across his skin. The wisdom of the dolphin's words. He had
to wonder if Zen had been a part of his life. But when he
reached for the memory of that man on the beach, there
was only a dark, blank wall. Frustration took hold and he sat
up. Pushing the curtain aside, the landscape was frozen and
uninviting. One of the logs in the fireplace snapped and
popped, and he looked toward the glow. His breath backed
up in his throat.

She was standing in the fire's glow completely naked.
She ran a soapy cloth over her neck, down over the indenta-
tion of her collarbone, down over the tight peaks of her
nipples and breasts, the water dribbling down over a flat
stomach to the shadowy cleft between her slender thighs.
Her body was toned from the manual labor of running the

farm, from the walking and trekking over the hard ground. From hours of hard labor.

Her honey hair flowed down her back, unbound, ribbons of silk that shone in the glow of the fire. He got hard, his dick reacting to the sight of a naked woman. A completely normal male reaction. But his heart, it tripped and stumbled, marveling at this woman who was brave enough to stand up not only to a corrupt government, but a slew of goddamned cutthroat rebels. She knew more than one language, a testament to her intelligence.

He was half in love with her.

His rational mind wanted him to think it was irrational as he barely knew her—he barely knew himself. That his emotions were tied up in her rescuing him from certain death from either exposure to the elements or the end of a rebel's rifle.

His head had stopped aching and was finally, for the first time since he'd woken to this rough-beamed cabin, clear. He watched the water trickle down her body and wanted to trace each glistening path with his tongue.

Elena turned her head and their eyes met in the semi-darkness.

Her presence offered a strange mix of contradictions. Verbal silence, but silent communication. Distance, but a strange kind of closeness. And Blue drew on her silent strength, repeatedly trying to get his mind to let go of his secrets. They were, after all, his.

He got out of bed and walked toward her, her eyes beckoning him as if she'd uttered the words, "Come to me."

Without modesty, without shame, she never attempted to cover any part of her. As if he had the right to gaze on her stripped naked. When he stopped in front of her, she reached for his shirt and unbuttoned it, pushing it off his shoulders. Then she reached for the drawstring pants and one pull loosened them so they pillowed around his feet.

He reached out and drew her against him, her fire-warmed, damp body making his body come alive.

"You're wet," he whispered, his touch caressing as he smoothed his hand up her back. Elena moved deeper into his embrace. Relief that she was safe and the unexpected feeling of love mixing into a fierce surge of emotion caught him off-guard. Did he really love her? Or was he reacting to her care of him? Her hand splayed across the taut muscles of his back, and she pressed her face against his neck, holding him with every ounce of strength she had.

"You are so beautiful," she murmured. "I have thought about this often, so often," she said with a sob caught in her voice.

Catching her by the back of the head, he kissed the curve of her neck. "Shh, babe. I know. I know," he murmured huskily. "It's been tough for both of us." Pulling her up against him, he nibbled a trail along her skin, tasting the dampness of her shoulder, the scent of her as intoxicating as the sight of her had been. "Jasmine."

She closed her eyes, and he sank into the sensations she set off in him. Smoothing her hand up his rib cage, she arched her head back, giving him access to the side of her neck, the soft brush of her mouth sending a shiver of fire and ice along his nerve endings. He stroked her back, loosening every connection in his body when she trailed her fingers over his chest and raked her nails across his abdomen.

She arched and moved against him, the rhythmic, kneading pressure setting off pinpoints of sensation that saturated him with an ache deep in his gut, rippling along his erection, settling in his heart.

His fingers tangling in her hair, Blue turned her head, leaving a line of kisses up her neck, pulling him deeper into a swirl of sensation. Then down to each hard peak, lingering, laving her with his tongue and sucking her into his mouth, tasting her arousal, her gasp a sensual goad.

She wrapped her hands around his shaft, the up and down motion making him groan with the intense pleasure of her soft palms.

He bent down and picked her up, moved toward the bed, and settled her against the mattress, catching her hips and moving her beneath him, molding their bodies together as he eased into the cradle of her thighs.

Her breath catching, she cupped his buttocks in both of her hands, urging him, and he responded by settling himself deeper between her legs. Bracing his weight on his arms, he bracketed her face with his hands, then slowly, so slowly, brushed his mouth against hers. Elena lifted her hips, opening herself to him, and with deliberate care he slowly, slowly eased into her. "You feel so good, babe." He tightened his hold on her face and brushed his mouth against hers again. "So damned good."

She flexed her knees, urging him up as she smoothed her hand across the bunched muscles in his shoulders. "Move higher," she whispered brokenly. "I want —ah, Blue—"

Tasting her mouth with tormenting lightness, he rocked his hips, impaling her with his thick, hard heat, and she tilted her hips, taking him inside her. Blue drew a deep, unsteady breath, his whole body tensing; the feel of her was so exquisitely erotic. He thrust, then bent his head and took her mouth in a deep, slow kiss that turned her breathing ragged and made her moan long, low, and beautifully feminine.

With an uneven sigh, he lifted his head, caressing her temple with his thumb. Laying a trail of soft kisses along her jaw, he moved again, a single rolling thrust that made his breath catch, his dick going even harder inside her.

In a soft stream of Russian, she whispered, "More, Blue, please. Take me more."

Slipping his arm under her hips, he pulled her up against him, his voice rough and low as he murmured huskily, "All of me for you." He withdrew, then thrust deep inside her again.

She met his thrusts, arching her head back, the tension in her telling him she was so close. He increased his tempo, reached between their bodies, and stimulated her. He locked her hips against his. His breathing ragged, he covered her mouth with a kiss that comforted, that promised, that incited. With infinite care and controlled deliberation, he made sure she experienced it all, and when her shimmering climax came, his soon followed as he gasped and emptied himself deep inside her.

For a long time they held each other, the sound of snow now soft with a brushing, soothing rhythm. They were warm and sweaty from their exertions. He slid to the side, bringing her with him.

She broke the silence. "I cherish you and I barely know you. But I'm determined to see you safe."

She rubbed her hand over his chest, her touch warm and soothing. But at her words, his heart tightened.

"I'm not leaving without you."

She breathed a sigh and said, "I want to go with you if you can manage it. I have missed the US. I want to go back where people are civilized and not horrifying monsters." She pushed up to her elbow and kissed his mouth. "I will go to town tomorrow and talk to my contact. I don't trust using my cell if I could even get a signal. Once I have his coopera-tion, I will come back, and we'll prepare to make the journey back home."

The thought of getting back where he belonged filled him with hope and light, and in that instant, he knew who that man had been on the beach. It was a boyhood memory, and the man was his father. He smiled at the memory of his dad. With that came the faces and names of his sisters, Bay, Raina, and Fen, and his beautiful mother. Other boyhood memories flowed along with an idyllic family life, but his own name eluded him still.

He'd discovered truth, hope following on its heels that all his memories would return.

14

By the time Alyssa was in bed and already had been asleep for two hours, Tank was in a C-130 heading back to Kirikhanistan. This would be his first mission with Bronte. She was on the seat next to him, prone, her head on her paws as if this was second nature to her. Nothing seemed to faze her, and damn if that didn't remind him of Echo.

When he'd arrived at the ready room, Ruckus had explained they were tasked with going back in and clearing the rest of the minefield. They had strong intel that the rebels were holding the captured SEALs in the heart of the city. There were pockets of rebels giving the NATO forces and the Green Berets a hard time.

When they landed, they loaded up in Humvees and drove through the eerily quiet town that had already been secured. When they passed the place where Blue had disappeared, and Echo had been injured, Tank clenched his jaw against the rush of anger and remembered fear. He buried his fingers into Bronte's fur. He was already in love with this K9, too, and they had jobs to do. He wouldn't dwell on what could happen to her. They were SEALs and would do what needed to be done.

Even with her calm presence, he missed Echo like hell, and it escalated his worry over Blue. He'd been missing now for almost six weeks.

When they got to the camp, there wasn't much there, no real security perimeter. They spent nights sleeping under Humvees and patrolling. An hour of sleep here and a twenty-minute power nap there was about all the shut-eye anyone got. Nearly every moment was punctuated by gunfire, shouts, or some other disruption. By the third day, sleep deprivation was taking its toll.

The clearing operation they were doing to neutralize mines and remove other obstacles was particularly difficult. This time, Ruckus got his way and they moved together as a team. Ryuu "Dragon" Shannon—the sniper who had done that pilot extraction in North Korea with them while Kid had been vacationing in Bolivia and who had lost Justin "Speed" Myerson from his team—was assigned to them to fill in for Kid who was on sniper duty in a different sector. They also had the Bravo Team medic, Robin "Hood" Ballentine, whose brother had been captured by the rebels. It must have been difficult without their tough LT, Ford "Fast Lane" Nixon. So far, other than Charlie team members, none of the Bravo SEALs had been found or bodies discovered. The rebels were being tight-lipped about their prisoners.

Tank could imagine that Hood was as worried about his teammates as Tank was about theirs. They pressed forward with determination, hoping for any clue as to their whereabouts.

They were taking a break so Tank could water and rest Bronte. "How you holding up?" he asked Hood as they rested their backs against one of the walls of a half-erect house.

"Staying positive that we'll find out where Pitbull and the others are and go get them. My brother Pirate and I knew what we were getting into. So did Pitbull."

"Doesn't make it any easier to have team members missing, especially with one of them being your brother. I have two and I would be out of my mind."

"No, it doesn't. I'm trying to stay positive."

Bronte rose, her attention fixed on a house that was across the street from them. Her intent focus had Tank and the rest of the team rising. "LT, she's onto something."

Tank approached the doorway. Immediately, Bronte's ears pricked forward, then went back and she sat down.

Ruckus motioned for Hollywood and Scarecrow to head around back.

"LT, caution, there's ten rebels inside," Hollywood said. "They're heavily armed. Doesn't seem like they know we're here."

"Copy that," Ruckus said. "Do you have a clear shot, Dragon?"

"Affirmative. Clear shot."

"Take down as many as you can. Hollywood and Scarecrow be ready to catch any of them fleeing from the back."

"Copy," Hollywood said. "LT, hold! Friendlies inside. I repeat, friendlies inside."

"How many?"

"Two, no three. Maybe more. I can't fully see into the next room."

"Our guys?"

"I can't tell. It's too dark in there, but it definitely looks like prisoners."

Tank wasn't going to get his hopes up. They had missing

Army and NATO soldiers as well. The intel on their guys was, according to LT, solid.

"I can send in Bronte," Tank said. "She can distract them while we breach."

Ruckus stood there for a few minutes, then nodded. "That's a good idea. Send her in. Dragon, take out tangos at will. If our guys are in there, they'll know to keep their heads down."

Tank knelt down and unclipped the leash, his hand in her soft fur. In that split second, he closed his hand over her ruff. He'd always put his trust in Echo. It was unwavering, and his love for his injured partner would never die. There was no more holding back, no sense of betrayal as his will solidified. He took a breath and let it out—success depended on his bond with this dog. When he finished releasing his breath, he had no doubt that she could do the job.

"Tank, send her in."

"Bronte, seek," he said, and she shot through the door. Immediately after her entrance, they heard shouts and Bronte growling. Then shots as Dragon started to pick them off.

"Breaching," Hollywood said as he and Scarecrow went in the back. The rest of them went in through the front.

It was over in ten minutes. Rebels down. Tank followed Ruckus inside at the all clear. Bronte came over to him, and he went to one knee to check her over. She had blood on her muzzle but otherwise was unharmed. "Good girl," he said, rubbing her head.

"Blue?" Tank asked, looking up as Ruckus came into the main room. He shook his head.

"He's not here. As far as we know, there's a second group

of prisoners at the outskirts of town. We're headed there now."

Tank tried to swallow his disappointment. Every single one of them worked at keeping it contained. He wasn't going to give up hope. Not for a minute.

Their team pushed ahead, moving toward their Humvees. Once inside, they convoyed their way out of the city. When the lead vehicle stopped, Tank exited with Bronte. He saw a structure some distance away. He walked along the rutted road to where Ruckus was looking through a pair of binoculars. "We're going to wait until nightfall, then we're going in. Get some sleep," Ruckus said.

Tank took the time to remove Bronte's harness, give her a quick brush, feed her, and play tug with her for a bit. Then he leaned against his pack and closed his eyes.

He missed Alyssa with a deep ache. Bronte made a soft sound and settled her head in his lap. He immediately rubbed her head. She was feeling his longing, and her comforting eased his ache for Alyssa, if only slightly. It drove home to him that he could get past Echo's wounding, work with another dog, and move on with his professional life.

He had Alyssa to thank for opening his eyes, not only to the possibilities of working with a new partner, but his own blindness to opening his heart to the kind of love he thought was too risky to grab for.

He couldn't shake the feeling that her dad hadn't shown up just for Thanksgiving. His gut told him Kyle St. James had a hidden agenda.

He'd never thought he'd be here. In the same boat with Ruckus, Kid, and Cowboy. But watching Cowboy fall in love with the lovely Kia Silverbrook had affected Tank. Deep down, he had wanted what Cowboy had found with her.

It was as simple as that, and he wasn't going to fight something that felt so amazingly right to his heart and emotions. He'd denied himself long enough, and he admitted it was a huge, life-altering revelation, both scary and exhilarating, but he was a SEAL, and they didn't back down from anything. The status quo could go to hell. He wanted to complicate the hell out of his life.

But Alyssa had her own demons and her own personal achievements to fulfill. He wouldn't dismiss that at all. She was a dedicated and phenomenal veterinarian. She'd saved Echo's life, hadn't hesitated a moment to go all the way to Texas.

She was all woman, tough and beautiful, but she ached for the love and approval of her dad, searching for a way to make her duty to her country, to her profession, and to herself count. She wanted a life that was stable and safe and filled with unconditional acceptance.

He wanted to commit to her, throw away the empty sex and the life he'd been living like he could control a damn thing, least of all how he felt.

He shook his head at how ironic it was that he was the one who now wanted that white picket fence and everything that came with it.

He finally understood what his teammates had found with the amazing women who were now in their lives, two of them married, one of them engaged. Tank had been afraid of opening his heart, and he'd masked it with a gigantic lie—the only family he needed was his brothers and the brotherhood. He knew what he'd been missing by giving in to the control he thought he needed, the resistance to change he thought he could avoid, and the emotions he'd buried to stave off the fear of intimacy. But what he hadn't realized was how easy it would be with the right woman.

He had fallen hard and fast for her. Whatever decision she made, he would support her because he could do no less. But he also wasn't going to just let her go without a fight. It wasn't in his nature.

He just hoped he hadn't run out of time.

BLUE PACED, the hair on the back of his neck in a permanent state of prickling. Elena was due back an hour ago. It had grown dark, and he had a nagging feeling that he was being watched. He should have insisted he go with her, but she'd been adamant that she would be more invisible alone. He hated that her cell phone, and her landline were probably not safe. She had to go into the capital to speak directly to her government contact.

He couldn't wait around anymore. He realized that he was a man of action, that he had always been, the kind of man that did what needed to be done. Memories assaulted him, the soft sand beneath his feet, the ache in his body from sleep deprivation, trial and test, one after the other. BUD/S. The acronym came to him in a flash—Basic Underwater Demolition/SEAL. He was a Navy SEAL.

He walked to the door and grabbed his coat. He wasn't going to leave her out there by herself for one more minute. Just as he reached for the handle, the door swung open.

"Blue," she rasped, breathing hard. "You must go. Now."

He clasped her upper arms. "What is it?"

"I was delayed in coming back because they are coming for you. I don't know how they found out, but they were on the outskirts of the property. I'll cover for you, but you can waste no time. She pressed a card into his hand. "This is my contact. Go to him. He will help you."

"I'm not fucking leaving here without you. I'm certainly not going to leave you defenseless against those bastards."

The sound of vehicles coming up the driveway had him looking out the front door. Men with automatic weapons were jumping from the vehicles. He slammed the door. "Guns."

She ran to the corner of the room and pried up the floorboards. "I found this with you. There's not much ammunition." She pulled out a handgun and clips, slamming one into the magazine. "We'll do this together."

He grabbed her around the waist, his mouth captured hers. "Thank you for risking your life for me, Elena."

She cupped his face as a voice shouted from outside. "Make this easy on yourself and just come out with your hands up. We won't harm the woman."

Their eyes met. Everything flowed back to him. The fact he was a special operative, a Navy corpsman, and there was no way he was going down without a fight. Faces flashed through his mind. Men he'd served with, men he would lay down his life for—members of his team. He had pledged to serve, and he would do that now. He would do everything in his power to protect Elena.

Or die trying.

SOMEONE KICKED TANK'S BOOT. He woke with a start. There was frantic movement around him. "What's up?" he asked Hollywood.

"We just got word. Blue is just miles from here. We're going after him."

"What about the other hostages."

"Team Bravo is on the way. Let's move."

They ran to the Humvees and they pulled onto the main road.

Ruckus swore from the front seat.

"What?" Tank asked as their leader turned to look back at him. "They just got a satellite image. The house where Blue is...it's surrounded by rebel forces."

"Fuck!" Tank said.

"Move it," Ruckus said to Wicked, who was driving. He hit the gas and the armored vehicle sped up. This couldn't be happening. They couldn't be too late.

Blue was coming home with them...tonight.

ELENA WAS A CRACK SHOT, Blue thought as he popped his head up and discovered that the rebels weren't deterred.

"I'm almost out," she said. "Maybe we should take our chances and make a run for it. We could go through the barn. It leads to the fields beyond. It's our only hope."

Blue nodded. "I'll cover you while you make a run for it." His voice was solemn.

She grabbed the lapel of his coat. "You're not coming with me, are you?"

"It's me they're after."

She shook her head, her gaze terrified and frantic. "They'll use me against you. I can't have that. I won't be the person who makes you give up your secrets." Tears streamed down her face. "You have to go. We don't have any choice."

He pressed his mouth to hers, his heart aching. He'd just met her and now he was going to have to let her go to keep her safe. As they parted, Blue lifted his head, the faint smell of smoke drifting through the walls of the cabin. The bastards had set it on fire.

The whole side of the cabin near the bed ignited into a wall of flame. The wood crackled and charred, the flames hot against his exposed skin. They couldn't stay in here. He rose and grabbed her arm. Pulling open the front door he came out shooting, spraying the area in front of him. Several rebels went down, and he shoved Elena towards the barn. "Run and don't stop," he shouted.

She hesitated for only a moment as more rebels came running. "Elena, go!" She turned and started to run, but one of the rebels stepped out from the corner of the house and grabbed her around the waist. She fought and struggled. Blue started for her, but three rebels surrounded him. He dropped the empty weapon. They came for him as they dragged Elena toward one of the waiting vehicles. The house behind him was now a conflagration lighting up the night.

Fear for Elena gripped him, and without conscious thought, he started to move. The first man went down after a palm strike to the nose. Blue's training came back to him from one breath to the next. He whirled, keeping his enemy off balance, striking hard and moving away. A punch to the windpipe removed the second threat as the man choked, backed up, and fell to his back.

The third man threw a punch, but Blue blocked it and, quick as lightning, stepped behind him, grabbed his head, and with a quick jerk, broke his neck.

The man dropped at his feet, but three more rebels came at him. He lunged, going for another throat punch when a gun discharged. Blue looked toward the noise and saw the man who had fired off the shot point his gun and press it against Elena's temple. The rebel holding her smirked at him. The two rebels had her effectively captured.

He dropped his arms to his side. The look on her face

was heartbreaking, and as their eyes met, he could see she was horrified and angry that she had been the reason he was captured.

In that moment, she got a determined look on her face, and that was his only warning as she stomped on the boot of the man holding her, grabbed the weapon from the rebel, and shot him, then her captor. The three rebels who had frozen with him, fumbled for their weapons. Blue dispatched two and Elena shot the third man. He rushed toward Elena, grabbing her arm. They raced to the barn, then through the interior to the back. Bursting through the back door, Blue could hear the shouts and angry feet in pursuit.

They ran across the field at a breakneck pace. Elena stumbled, but Blue caught her arm. They headed for the hills to hide themselves, but Elena tripped again and went down hard. Their pursuers caught up, and when he turned to face them, one of their weapons discharged and the bullet hit his arm. He dropped the gun out of nerveless fingers. Before he could recover, the leading rebel hit him in the jaw with the butt of his rifle and he went down.

The rebels bound their hands roughly, hauled them back to the road, and threw them in the back of one of the trucks. Elena snarled at one of the men, but he just laughed and backed out.

She turned to Blue. "I'm so sorry," she said.

"We'll get through this. Just stick with me. We'll get through this."

Wearily, she leaned her head against his shoulder as the truck lurched into gear. From the back they had a perfect view of her burning and demolished farm, now completely engulfed. A few miles away he could still see it. They'd destroyed her life—again. The bastards had taken so much from her.

But most of all, she'd risked it all for him.

He couldn't let her down.

TANK SAW the fire and smoke ahead of them, anxious and eager to get there. "Stop driving like an old man, Wicked. Step on it."

"I have it all the way down," Wicked growled. They sped up the driveway to an ominous sight as they piled out of the vehicle, but there was no one left standing. What had once been a structure was completely burning to the ground; dead animals and men littered the area.

Hollywood ran up the road a bit and shouted back. "Tire tracks, LT!"

"Back in the vehicles!" They followed the tire tracks, Wicked driving just as fast, his face determined. They were so close to Blue and they weren't giving up.

Finally they came around a bend to a contingent of rebels who had blocked the road. Everyone piled out of the vehicles and took cover behind the doors. Returning automatic gunfire with the rebels, Ruckus sent Dragon into the small ravine next to the road to belly crawl and get a bead on the shooters.

Suddenly, the door erupted with bullets and Tank ducked. Bronte remained close to his body.

It was clear when Dragon was in place. Rebels started to drop. Distracted from the fire to their right flank, the rebels started firing on Dragon's position. Hollywood rushed forward and threw a grenade and it blew the hell out of the remaining rebels. One more shot from Dragon's weapon and everything was quiet.

He took Bronte in to make sure nothing was booby trapped, and with the Humvee, they punched through the line. After driving like a complete maniac, Tank holding on to the side as they bumped over the rutted road, Tank spied a truck ahead of them. He shouted, "Vehicle!"

They were now right on their asses and gaining. The Humvee was much faster than the truck. But unexpectedly the truck veered off the road into a field, and in the distance Tank saw a chopper approaching.

"They're taking him out by helicopter." The Humvee reached the cut off just as the chopper landed. Two people where hustled out of the vehicle. *Blue!*

The Humvee came to a halt, and all of the SEALs piled out, running for the truck. Several rebels returned fire as Blue fought against his captors, dragging his feet. But two burly men had him and a woman by the arms and they were almost to the chopper.

Dragon sighted and took out one of the rebels holding the woman, but it was too late. They were to the chopper. Suddenly, the woman broke away.

They could hear Blue shout from across the field. "Elena!"

The woman never slowed. She bravely kept running, her long blonde hair a stream of sunshine in the dark. One of the rebels put his gun to his shoulder a split second before Dragon got his shot off. It was too late; the woman fell to the ground and didn't move.

Now Blue was struggling fiercely, his face ravaged, contorted in pain, shouting "Elena!" over and over again as he fought like a madman to get to her. But he was hit, then forced into the chopper.

The SEALs were halfway to them when it lifted off. Together they stared helplessly as the engine gunned, the rotors spun, and it banked and then sped off into the distance. Scarecrow erupted into a rage, screaming at the top of his lungs, going to his knees. Wicked walked over there, knelt down and grabbed him by the back of the neck, speaking in soft tones to him.

For a minute they just stood there, unbelieving that they had been so close to their teammate but lost him. Blue was gone, this time in enemy hands. The Golovkins had taken him. A sick, hollow feeling welling up inside, he watched as the speck disappeared.

Hood was kneeling beside the woman when they all approached. She was breathing hard, blood at her mouth, a wound to her chest. Hood was working fast and efficiently as blood soaked through her coat.

She gasped, her voice hitching with the effort to get the words out from her bloody lips. "Blue," she whispered.

He knelt beside her and took her hand as she reached out to him, clasping it firmly. Tears welled in her eyes. "He's gone. They have him," Tank said hollowly.

"No, those monsters will do unspeakable things to him. I couldn't let them use me against him. Save him. Please. Save him," she rasped, tears flowing freely down her face. "I tried to keep him safe, but I couldn't. He can't remember who he is, and I made a mistake. I shouldn't have trusted him."

Tank got the immediate sense that last sentence didn't refer to Blue. "Who?"

She closed her eyes, her breaths going shallow.

"Hood!"

"I'm losing her!"

Her grip weakened in Tank's hand, her blue eyes imploring him. Then she closed them as if garnering all her strength. "I had a government contact. He must have betrayed us. Working with the rebels. There was no other way for them to know." She took a deep, labored breath. She stared up into Tank's face. Instead of telling him the vital information on who her contact was, she whispered, "Tell him I love him."

Her breath expelled, and her eyes went glassy as life left her.

15

THE C-130 WAS UTTERLY quiet as they sat numb from the terrible loss of Blue, now in the rebels' hands. Bronte made a soft, distressed whine and Tank dug his hand into her fur. Losing Blue was a bitter pill to swallow. He stared at the body bag, his eyes moist. She had decided that it was more important to tell him that she loved Blue than it was to give up the name of her contact.

Still, she had confirmed what they already knew. Even now LT was on the line with the brass and he was telling them there was a confirmed leak in the Kirikhanistan government. The very same government they had been working with. Every mission had been compromised, and whoever had given out that information was going to pay.

He leaned forward and covered his face with his hands. He could sure use some of Blue's philosophy right now.

Be like the fish.

Tank hadn't understood that during the masquerade ball, and he didn't understand it now.

A hand descended on his shoulder and squeezed. He looked up into Ruckus's stern face.

"We did everything humanly possible. Don't beat your-self up." Ruckus looked at the other men on the plane. "None of you should feel one ounce of remorse about this op. We almost had him. The good news is we rescued the NATO and Green Berets and the three SEALs from Bravo. That's a victory."

"Hoo-yah," they responded.

He rose and said, his voice reverberating through the metal aircraft, "We're going to find him and Speed and we're going to bring them home.

"No matter the cost," Scarecrow said to Wicked.

Wicked looked at him, and when Scarecrow raised his arm, they fist bumped. "Hoo-yah," Wicked said, then again, louder, "Hoo-yah!"

"Hoo-yah," sounded in a chorus of men's voices.

Ruckus sat down next to Tank.

"She deserves a hero's burial," Tank said. "I'll pay for it."

Ruckus nodded. "Her name was Elena Sokolov. She was a naturalized American citizen, translator at the UN. We'll make sure she's buried with honors," he said.

"I intend to deliver her message to Blue."

Ruckus smiled. "I have no doubt. We'll find him, Tank."

He took out his cell and texted Alyssa that he was coming home and his ETA. He needed her right now. Needed her arms around him.

The rest of the trip was quiet as each of the men gave in to their exhaustion, both body and soul. When they touched down, Tank headed to base and took care of Bronte. Before he left her, he hugged the dog. "You did good out there, girl." She licked his face, effectively saying he also had kicked ass. He ruffled her fur and slipped out of her enclosure.

He closed the kennel and drove over to Alyssa's apartment. When she opened the door, she could tell something was wrong right away. She threw her arms around his neck and hugged him. "Oh, Thorn," she said softly. He could see that her dad was still there, and Alyssa seemed subdued and on edge.

"Come with me?" she said. "Unless you're hungry."

He shook his head. "I'm not hungry, at least not for food," he whispered. "I just need to hold you."

She drew him into her bedroom, not seeming at all concerned by her father's presence. She started a bath and he just stood there as she removed his uniform. When he was naked, she brought him into the bathroom and the tub of steaming water. He got in, and she stripped down and settled in behind him.

"Lean back," she whispered tenderly, and she washed his hair, her gentle but firm fingers massaging his scalp. He sighed as she finished. Then she got a soapy washcloth and washed him.

"Tell me what happened."

He couldn't go into details, but told her about rescuing all the hostages, then going after Blue.

When he said, "The rebels have him." she sagged weakly into his embrace.

"I'm so scared for him," she whispered, her voice shaking.

She wrapped her arms around him and held him for a long, long time. Tightening her arms around him, Alyssa ran her hand over his hair and kissed him on the temple.

"I know," he said softly. "It's been one hell of a six weeks."

She rubbed his back, cupping his head with her other hand, trembling with reaction. Adjusting his head on her shoulder, he curled his arm around her waist. He hadn't realized how strung out he was until the terrible tension let go. The pressure in his chest finally abated, and he was able to take a deep, relieved breath as Alyssa pressed him more tightly to her.

Her voice unsteady, she whispered, "When are you leaving again?"

He rubbed her thigh beneath the water. "I don't know. Soon."

She held him for several more moments, then brushed another light kiss against his temple. Her tone still quiet, she said, "After Thanksgiving?"

Tank turned his face into the soft skin of her neck, swallowing hard against the sudden cramp in his throat. He fought back the emotion. He looked up at her, an exhausted kind of numbness settling in. "Probably. I could get the call any time."

Maybe he had to rethink his plan to fight for her. They were both serving their country, and he was going to be caught up with finding Blue. As soon as the brass decided what course of action to take, they would be going back. To build a strong relationship, proximity was important. Maybe he should keep his opinions about what she should do to himself. It would free her to make her own decision about taking the job at Lackland.

The thought of losing her, of not having her here when he came off deployment was like a kick to the groin, but he refused to pressure her like her dad. He'd learned too much from her in the past weeks about being there for her and how important it was. He would support her in any decision she made, even if it meant that he would lose her.

No more his way or the highway.

He was no longer that man.

"Let's get you to bed," she murmured as she rose out of the tub.

"I like the sound of that," he said, stepping out, water sluicing off him. She stared at him for a moment, her eyes going glassy. Reaching out, she ran her hand over his biceps, then let her breath go with a soft, dreamy sigh. He caught her by the back of the neck and drew her head against him. "You drive me crazy. I couldn't stop thinking about you when I wasn't dodging bullets."

Her face went serious. "Not something I want to hear," she said. She wrapped a towel around him, hugging him briefly before drying him off. He grabbed her chin and kissed her long and slow.

Once they were on the bed, he pulled her on top of him. "Ride me hard, Alyssa."

And she did, taking him to a new height of passion and pleasure. Afterwards, he dragged her close, so tired he could barely put together a coherent sentence. His last conscious thought was how fucked up everything was right now; then the gray fog of sleep pulled him under.

It was three in the afternoon when he woke up, a little surprised at how long he'd slept. He dressed in his running clothes. Exiting the bedroom, he walked into the kitchen. A piece of paper on the counter caught his eye. He read the short sentences. Alyssa had gone to work. He stood in the kitchen and looked up from the note to find Kyle St. James standing in the entrance to the kitchen.

"Hello," he said, looking distinguished in a pair of jeans, a black pullover, and cowboy boots on his feet. Tank wondered if he had a cowboy hat like his teammate. Cowboy wore it every chance he got. After spending several weeks with him and Kia in Reddick, Texas, he wasn't really keen to go back there. At least not to the small town. But he wouldn't really have any need as Kia had moved here and she and Cowboy were getting married as soon as they set the date. It was easy to see that his teammate was besotted.

"Mr. St. James."

"Oh, I don't stand on formality. Call me Kyle." His good ol' boy drawl put Tank on edge. "Had a tough·go of it?"

Tank opened the fridge and grabbed a bottle of water.

"It was a tough deployment, but I can't really talk about it." That hollow feeling hadn't diminished. After his run, he needed to make arrangements for Elena Sokolov's funeral. Blue would want her to be taken care of, even in death. His heart broke for him, and he tried to block the images of his teammate, his brother, being tortured. He knew all too well what the enemy did to captured US military.

"Of course," he murmured.

Tank went to go past Alyssa's father, but he grabbed Tank's arm, stopping him. Her dad was an opposing man, but taller where Tank was broader.

"I'm suspecting you don't want to hold my daughter back. She's wanted this job for a long time. It's what she had been working toward before she let that ex-husband derail her. I've told her before, emotion has no place in business."

Tank stopped and stared the older man down. He let go of Tank and stepped back. "I have no intentions of telling Alyssa what to do. It seems she's already had enough of that."

"What is that supposed to mean?" her father growled. He glared at Tank.

Unaffected, Tank walked toward the door and opened it. "If the boot fits, Kyle... Have a great day." He shut the door behind him and broke into a run. He'd have to burn off the energy of holding back from socking her father right in the kisser. His disapproval could go to hell. Tank was determined he wasn't going to be that kind of asshole.

After his run, he went home, showered, and changed, then went out to the base to check on Bronte. He walked her, played tug with her for a bit, then put her back in her kennel. He couldn't help thinking about Echo.

He headed over to the clinic and walked inside. The receptionist looked up and smiled. "How can I help you?"

"I'm here to see Dr. St. James."

"If you'd like to take a seat, I'll buzz her."

He waited for five minutes before Alyssa came out. "Hey," she said, looking like she wanted to kiss him, but they kept it platonic in public while in uniform. She did squeeze his hand, her warm gaze connecting with his. "What's up?"

"Lunch?" he asked hopefully.

Her eyes twinkled. "Ooh, at the delicious mess hall?"

He laughed. "Yeah, if you're pressed for time."

"I am. Let me grab my purse."

At the Mess, they took their trays to a table. "How are you doing?"

He shrugged. "Keeping it together. Ready to go look for Blue."

"I can imagine. Do you have any leads?"

"A contact in the Kirikhanistan government." He explained about Elena, and Alyssa reached out and covered his hand.

"That is so tragic and awful. But it's good of you to handle her burial. So sad she lost her parents and her life over there. What a brutal way to live."

"Yeah, after seeing that shit, protecting our freedom takes on a whole new meaning."

"It does." She toyed with her food. "Tank, I'm thinking

about going back to active duty, leaving San Diego and moving back to San Antonio."

Feeling as if his lungs were closing up on him, he didn't say anything for a moment, and she filled the gap.

"I know. We just met, and it's been so wonderful, but I keep thinking about Echo, about how I can make a difference there for those dogs who come in severely wounded. I want to be an advocate for them; that's why I started the charity."

"Only you can make that decision, Alyssa. I support whatever you decide to do."

Her lips tightened, and she sat back as if she'd expected something more. She rose. "I need to get back."

He dropped her off, not understanding her obvious anger toward him. There was no good way to discuss this while she was working. Potentially heated arguments were better saved for privacy. He had a funeral to manage, and that required him to be at the morgue in half an hour.

He left the base feeling as if he was losing the one thing in his life that made sense. He wasn't quite sure what he was going to do if she followed through.

ALYSSA WALKED BACK into the clinic and opened her desk, chucking in her purse and slamming the drawer. She'd held it together because she didn't want to look like a fool in front of Tank. *Only you can make that decision, Alyssa. I support whatever you decide to do.*

She pressed her fingers to her eyes, refusing to cry. What had she expected? Him to declare that he loved her? That he didn't want her to go? God, she was such a fool. Just because she was in love with him didn't mean that he was as invested. They hadn't talked about that at all.

She was torn between her desire to be here for Tank and moving on to Lackland, taking what she had been offered and proudly serving her country. But, the feelings of wanting to run the clinic she loved and continue to raise money for her charity wouldn't go away. Her father had pointed out that she was a skilled surgeon and the Army needed dedicated professionals like her. Part of her knew he was being manipulative, but that didn't diminish the argument. The thought of leaving Tank almost wrenched her in two. He had to be feeling the same way.

But maybe he was being practical. She sat down, glad she had a few minutes to compose herself before she needed to see her next client.

They were caught between serving and their own personal needs. Which one took precedence? He certainly wasn't going to leave the SEALs for her, and she didn't want him to do that, make that kind of sacrifice. But she also had the opportunity to continue to serve her country and this was more about compromise. Was she willing to relinquish her commission? Was she ready to go down a different path? She stayed late and caught up on some paperwork, unable to face either her father or Tank. It lightened her load so that she could enjoy Thanksgiving on Thursday. She still had a million things to do for that.

When she got home that night, she sighed when she saw Tank's truck. That was Tank. The man who didn't give a damn that her dad was still here. Didn't worry about the awkwardness. Did he want to talk? She expected him to be up, but when she tiptoed into her room, he was in her bed.

It had been such a bad night for him last night. She'd never seen him so quiet and withdrawn, his expression grim, and Alyssa wondered if he needed space to come to terms with his teammate's capture. Feeling too raw to wake him, she was careful, an empty ache unfolding in her. She understood his mood; she didn't want to talk, either.

He had left the bathroom light on, and she paused by the bed, her heart contracting as she watched him sleep. He was lying on his stomach, one arm tucked under his head, his face turned away from her. He had shoved the pillow aside, the position of his arms drawing his muscle structure into deep definition, revealing the even rise and fall of his rib cage. She gazed down at him, an ache forming in her throat, remorse finding a hold among all the other emotions that clogged her chest. He didn't deserve this. None of them deserved it.

A deep weariness settled on her, and she went into the bathroom and got ready for bed, suddenly so tired she could barely move. Two more days until Thanksgiving, and she was cooking for a crowd. Tank, his two brothers, Dan was bringing a date, Holly and her dad. She slipped into bed beside Tank, relieved she didn't wake him up.

Tank was up already when Alyssa woke the next morning, the empty space beside her resurrecting the same feeling of aloneness she'd experienced the night before. And her spirits sank even lower when she found out he'd already left.

At some gut level, she knew that something had happened to make him close up the way he had. It hurt to realize he had withdrawn behind that wall of reserve he'd had the first time they'd met, that he had shut her out. The one good thing that had come out of this mess was the new intimacy they had discovered over the short relationship, and she desperately didn't want to lose that. If that happened, it would be, in some ways, the greatest loss of all.

The next two days were full of getting prepared for the meal she was going to cook. Trips to grocery shop, buying fresh flowers, cleaning her apartment. Tank was absent. He texted her a couple of times and said he was caught up on base, but she couldn't be sure he wasn't avoiding her.

She'd be glad when it was over because by then she would make her decision, but the accumulated stress and strain left her almost numb. When Thanksgiving morning dawned, she woke up and got out of bed. It was early, and when she went into the kitchen to start her stuffing, she halted. Tank was standing there drinking coffee.

"Hey," she croaked, then cleared her voice. "How long have you been here?"

"I just got here. I didn't want to wake you. You sounded so exhausted on the phone last night. Sorry I've been absent."

"I understand," she said softly, and she did. He was part of a gun slinging team that kept the US safe. She couldn't be petty about some time away from her.

He stepped close to her. "I've missed you," he murmured. As a reconciling gesture, it was a good one.

She leaned up and kissed him, her voice uneven as she whispered, "I missed you, too."

He nodded. When she went to go past him, he caught her arm. Startled, she looked at him. "That stuffing and turkey aren't going to make themselves," she said.

His mouth curved. "Do you know how much I want to drag you into your room and have my way with you, babe?"

She blushed, still not used to the way he made her body sing with declarations like that.

"Have I ever told you I fucking love it when you blush?"

"No."

"Now you know."

Her throat cramping painfully, she slipped her hand into his and gave it a squeeze, wishing they could just spend the day together alone. He brushed a kiss against the back of her hand, then released her. "Can I help?"

"No, you can relax. My stuffing is a one woman show."

"I'll get my run done, then."

That one brief exchange eased the awful heaviness inside her, and she faced the dinner with a renewed energy. She put everything together, greeting Jordan with warmth when he knocked at her door, a bottle of wine in his hands. He joined Tank and her father on the couch for the endless hours of football.

Was it her imagination or had she detected tension between her dad and Tank? They were cordial, but there was some underlying animosity there.

She wasn't sure she should even ask Tank about it. Their relationship was a bit shaky now. At the next knock, she opened the door to Dan and the woman she'd seen at Tank's house. For a moment, she was confused and blinked a couple of times.

"Hello, Alyssa," Becca (or Tinkerbell) said as she flounced inside in the most gorgeous pink outfit, a fluffy pink, three-quarter sleeved sweater over a white chiffon blouse, the sleeves flouncy and a slim pair of white designer jeans. Her shoes were also pink with little pompoms on them.

Tank rose and looked from Dan to Becca. He cocked his head. "What's going on?"

"Becca and I are together," he said

Tank's brows rose, and Alyssa said, "Well, that's nice," to break the tension. Jordan looked from Tank to Dan, then exchanged a wry look with her.

Jordan took that moment to say, "I have to go to the hospital to have exploratory surgery."

They all looked at him startled, which, she realized, was his way of breaking up the tension by focusing on him. "I'm sorry, Jordan," Alyssa said, looking at Tank who reached out and squeezed his brother's shoulder.

Holly took that moment to arrive. When she walked in she was all smiles, toting a pumpkin pie. She stopped short for a moment and looked at everyone's faces. "Happy Thanksgiving," she said, but it was more a question than declaration.

The tension was mounting with Tank and Dan seeming at odds. It overpowered the festive spirit that should be present in the room. Family dynamics were always interesting, but this took that to a new high.

Finally, after dinner, Tank grabbed Dan and dragged him out to the patio. Alyssa could only hear the muffled conversation while she cleaned up.

"Hearing anything good?" Becca said.

Alyssa jumped and whirled around. "No...I wasn't...you caught me."

Becca smiled. "I don't have any siblings, so this has all been really interesting. It's true that Thorn and I fooled around." She nudged Alyssa. "He's great in bed, right? Can I say that and not have it be weird?" She smiled.

"You're definitely right," Alyssa said. "But that might still be a bit awkward."

"Of course, but we can be friends. I hope so." She peered out again. "He loves you."

She said it off the cuff while she was staring out the window. But Alyssa's heart jumped in her chest at the sound of those words.

"Anyhoo, at the time, I didn't know why he stopped call-ing, but after I met you, the mystery was solved." She looked out the window, her eyes focusing on Dan, her face going soft. "It's no secret that all three of them are pretty amazing catches: Thorn, a Navy SEAL protecting his country, Dan a firefighter protecting us all, and Jordan as sweet and smart —" her voice caught. "I can't believe the unfairness of him getting sick. I intend to pay for his treatments. Dan argued with me at first, but I told him it was futile. I'm rich, but I don't want that to be what defines me anymore. I understand you have a charity. I'm wondering if you'd let me participate. I need to learn the ropes to prove to my dad I've changed." She squeezed Alyssa's arm and smiled. "I thought I wanted more from Thorn, but after I met Dan, anything I felt for him withered into friendship. We're both pretty damned lucky."

Alyssa smiled, any wariness or worry she had about Becca dissolved.

"Hey, do you have any more of that delicious pumpkin pie?" Then she leaned forward and said with a mischievous, infectious grin, "I bet if we opened the window, we could hear what they were saying."

Later that night, Alyssa waited for Tank to join her in bed, but as it got later and later, she went back out to the living room. He wasn't there, and for a moment she thought he had left without saying goodbye.

But then she saw him outside staring up at the sky. Grabbing her throw off the back of the couch, she wrapped it around herself and opened the patio door and stepped outside.

"You all right?"

"Just thrown with the news about Dan and Becca. He told me he was in love with her and she'd already explained about me and us sleeping together."

Alyssa laughed. "Yeah, it's awkward."

Tank laughed, too, and slung his arm around her shoulder. "Who am I to stand in anyone's way?"

"Including me?"

He straightened and turned to face her. "Including you."

"If I go active duty and take the Lackland job, it will make it very difficult to see you."

"It's going to make it impossible," he said. "I'm not leaving the SEALs, Alyssa. I'm based out of San Diego. I want to be with you, but I'm not going to be that selfish jerk I was before I met you. I'm not going to demand you change for me. You have to make your own decisions about what you want to do. It's not my way or the highway anymore. I care about the decision you're going to make. I just won't influence it or make it for you."

Her breath caught in her throat. "That's exactly what I need to hear. I just don't know what I'm going to do. I'm needed at Lackland. Stephen is a good example of what can go wrong. It keeps me up at night."

"You want me to stay?"

"Yes," she whispered. "Please."

"I'm going to hang out here for a bit. You do have some thinking to do. I'm here for you if you need to talk some more."

She nodded and left. An hour had passed since she'd left him on the patio. The luminous numerals showed 1:32 when she heard the telltale squeak of the door. She stopped breathing, every nerve in her body on alert, a flutter breaking loose in her chest. There was a soft click as the door closed, a brief silence, then a rasp of a zipper. Her heart pounding so hard she was sure it could be heard halfway across the room, Alyssa stared into the darkness, a hope-riddled anxiety immobilizing her. She felt the covers being pulled back, then the mattress shift as Tank slipped into bed.

More than anything, she wanted to turn into his arms, to close the physical and emotional distance between them, but fear that she would just lose it kept her still.

Feeling the warmth of him only inches away from her back, she opened her eyes and stared into the blackness, wondering if she would risk breaking the tenuous intimacy if she said something. Expelling a long sigh, he slipped one arm under her head and the other around her midriff, drawing her securely into the curve of his body. Thrown into emotional overload, she tried to turn in his arms, but he held her fast, the arm around her middle locking her against him.

Could she really give this up? What was more important? Her personal needs or her vow to serve her country?

16

THE NEXT DAY, when she woke up, Tank was gone. She decided it was better this way. Easier.

Shortly after that, she got a call from her commander. "I'm just calling to find out if you've made up your mind, Alyssa. You need to make a decision about active duty and taking that plumb job at Lackland."

She hadn't been able to get what happened to Echo off her mind. If she was there at Lackland, she could make a difference. Her personal needs would have to take a back seat to serving her country, no matter how much that hurt. "I'm going to transition to active duty and take the job. Thank you for the opportunity."

"I'm so glad to hear that." He started to talk about going to Lackland, interviewing with the director, moving, paperwork and a million other things, but Alyssa had just effectively ended her relationship with Tank. Everything else was just semantics.

As soon as she hung up with her commander, she was called into an emergency at her clinic. A dog had been hit by a car and needed immediate surgery. She spent hours repairing the damage, and it was touch and go a couple of times, but when she closed, the black lab was going to have a chance to make it.

When she went to leave the operating room, Jordan said, "I'm so impressed by you, Doc. You have a gift." That's exactly what the anesthesiologist had said to her at Lackland.

She had to close herself into the bathroom as the combined emotion hit her at once—losing Tank, then having to give up her clinic when these people needed her sent her into a tailspin.

Over the next few days, she went through the motions. She and her dad left San Diego and flew to San Antonio. After landing, they drove to his house and she settled in her old room. She'd have to look for a place, move, sell her practice, and leave all her friends behind. Feeling shaky, she kept pushing her emotions away.

She went through the motions of eating, making conversation, washing, sleeping. Then when she woke up, she went to dress in her uniform. She pulled it from the hanger and simply stared at it. She backed up and sat on the edge of the bed.

Then with a shaky sigh, she got dressed, made sure she was polished and spit shined, her hair ruthlessly pulled back into her customary bun. Her dad waved from the table where he was having his breakfast and said, "We can have lunch after you're done."

She nodded and got into her rental car and drove to Lackland like an automaton. She entered through the doors and headed for the director's office. But as she rounded a corner, she ran right into Stephen.

For a startled moment, she stared up at him, then she said, "Why didn't you adjust for my job?"

His chin went up and his eyes flashed. "Why couldn't you adjust for mine?" he shot back at her, his mouth flattening out, his resentment clear in every word. "I was offered a once in a lifetime opportunity. I couldn't turn it down, but you were caught up in your own selfish goals, Alyssa, as if you thought you were better than me. You could never seem to see mine."

"You wanted me to compromise because you're the man and that's what is expected of women. Your desperation to outdo me is what the problem was, not my awesomeness. Fuck you, Stephen. We never really had anything. It was built on a foundation of nothing in the first place. I know I'm better off."

"You're such a know-it-all cold bitch. Have a good life, Alyssa. I hope you choke on it."

He brushed past her, and she had to place her hand on the wall to steady herself. To face the ugly fact about their marriage. She hadn't seen his goals because she was too focused on proving to her dad that she was as tough as a man. But her marriage to Stephen had many more problems than her unwillingness to compromise. It was his resentment every time she excelled. He was never really there for her and she told herself that was okay, but emotions didn't rule her. It was more about her not realizing that she and her husband weren't compatible. He wasn't supportive. If she hadn't been so worried about giving into her emotions, she would have been more in touch with who she was and what she needed. He was never going to be that man, not in her heart, not in her bed. Not wanting to come to a compromise with Stephen was her deep-seated way of telling herself she wanted out of the marriage. It wasn't the distance that killed it. It was Stephen's narrow-minded expectations.

Her breath caught, and she came alive again. The numbness disappeared. Instead of going to her appointment, she went to the front desk and filled out a very important piece of paper. She was ten minutes late for her meeting.

She walked into the director's office. "Hello, Dr. St. James. Thank you for taking the time to meet with me. I feel that face to face interviews are much better than talking through a computer." He indicated a chair.

She didn't move. Instead she said, "Forgive me for keeping you waiting, but I've decided to leave the Army altogether. I won't be taking this post. I'm sorry I wasted your time."

With that done, she reached back and pulled her hair out of its bun, and as it came unraveled, so did she. She turned and exited the office, the director sputtering in surprise.

What had she done?

Pressing her fingers to her trembling lips, she ran, feeling freer than she ever had in her life. She'd convinced herself that this was exactly like what had happened between her and Stephen, but Tank wasn't Stephen. The situation wasn't the same at all. She'd let her fear of the distance Tank's service to his country would take on her. But this wasn't about distance, it wasn't about love. This wasn't a compromise at all. She realized that's exactly what she wanted to do. She loved her practice. She loved what she did for the community. Loved the charity and making MWDs more comfortable and safer in their service.

But most of all, she loved Thorn Hunt and she couldn't live without him.

When she got home her dad was dressed and sitting in the living room listing to NPR. He rose when she came in.

"I can't go to lunch and I can't be what you want me to be."

He walked toward her. "What? Are you all right?"

"No, Dad. I'm not Robbie. I'll never be him. Your son, my wonderful brother, died, and I could never fill his shoes."

He looked at her, a shocked expression on his face. "Alyssa—"

"This is me, Dad. I work hard, but I love harder. I'm messy and emotional and complicated. I'm a woman! I'm not a man and I don't think like one and that doesn't diminish me at all. My femininity defines me, and I love high heels, pretty dresses, letting my hair down and makeup. I can't be the son you wanted, but I'll be the daughter I know you love."

He stiffened. "Why are you bringing your brother into this?"

"Because his death devastated you, Dad. You wanted me to take up his mantle as some way to assuage your grief. Holding onto his potential through me."

He looked away, his eyes fluttering. "I didn't...I couldn't..."

She touched his arm. "You did, Dad. I felt it and I won't let you diminish my emotions. I know what I feel, and I know how it's affected me. Be strong so that our relationship can move past this. It's time for you to embrace your own emotions."

He rubbed absently at his face. She'd never seen her father cry, not once. Not even at the funeral, but his moist eyes showed her that she should have had this talk with him long before now. "I'm going to put the past in the past. I'm going back to San Diego to run my practice and be with Thorn. That's my decision and I'm so happy about it." She turned to go, and he stopped her with a soft touch to her arm.

"Give me some time, Alyssa." He paused and rubbed his hands over his face. "I guess I was so devastated by your brother's death, I just pushed everything I had hoped for him onto you. Over time it got lost in the mix and I started to believe that you wanted the same things."

"You take your time. We both need that. We'll talk again," she said.

"Oh, Alyssa." He embraced her, squeezing her tight. "I'm so proud of you for all your accomplishments. I think you've proven your brother's shoes never really fit you. They were too small." He cupped her chin and said. "Go find your tattooed hunk.

Six hours later, she was back home. Home where she belonged. She resigned her commission and went to the clinic to find Jordan. Tank hadn't answered any of her calls. When she spied Jordan, she rushed at him, and he stepped back at her enthusiasm.

"Where's Tank?"

"He's deployed. He's due back in an hour."

She kissed him on the cheek and laughed. "Thank you."

She made the airfield in record time and paced until the C-130 carrying her man landed. With other family members, she went onto the tarmac. She recognized Ruckus's wife Dana and Kid's wife Paige. Cowboy's fiancée was also there.

The sound of hydraulics filled the air, drowning out the zoom of planes landing and taking off and the general chatter of the people waiting for their husband, dad, significant other. The rest of world fell away when she saw him deplane and walk toward her on the tarmac.

Thorn "Tank" Hunt. Her future.

~

ANOTHER DEAD END in the ever-vigilant search for Blue. Even the careful inquiries to the Kirikhanistan government were frustrating. He hated diplomacy. He did his politics from the business end of his weapon.

The tarmac was crowded, and it parted as he made his way toward his truck. Again, he hadn't been able to get Alyssa off his mind. He'd second-guessed himself so many times, he was giving himself a headache and a complex. Maybe he should have told her how he felt. Maybe in this instance being an obstinate jerk and telling her he didn't want her to leave was what she needed to hear.

But it was too late. She'd made her decision and sealed it up by now, was all ready to pack up and move—

His thoughts abruptly cut off when he saw her. Dressed to perfection in a pretty dress and coat, her hair blowing in the wind, her face enhanced by the subtle application of makeup, she was stunning, but she was always stunning being her plain Jane self. His heart stalled. He dropped his pack and surged forward. Reaching her, he grabbed her and swung her around and she laughed with glee.

Setting her on her feet, he cupped her face. "I don't want you to leave. It killed me to let you go. I want you in my life. Forever, Alyssa. Tell me it's not too late."

She wrapped her arms around his neck.

"Damn, Alyssa...I hoped you'd change your mind—" He got choked up, his voice strangled. "I was afraid."

She stared at him, then she closed her eyes, and said, holding on to him with desperate strength, "Shut the hell up and kiss me." Closing his own eyes, Tank roughly turned his face against her neck, locking his arms around her. Inhaling raggedly, he tightened his hold on her, an agony of relief rushing through him. She gave a soft sob and he picked her up in his arms.

"Hey, Hunt, you dropped your pack," Hollywood said with amusement in his voice.

"Take care of that, would you? I'm busy."

"You got it, bro."

Tank walked off the tarmac to his vehicle. He took her back to his house and straight up to his bedroom. He pulled her onto the bed with him and faced her, fully clothed. He was hard as a rock for her, but he wasn't done talking. "I want to explain."

"You don't have to, Thorn." She reached for his buttons, but he covered her hands.

"I want to, babe."

She pressed her forehead to his. "Talk fast, then. I have to take my turn, too."

"I had to work hard to keep everything together growing up. To survive. There were so many things that could kill us, least of all my father. He killed my little sister and he walked away from it. I've been protecting the people in my life instead of supporting them. Jordan's illness opened my eyes to how separate I was from them. Dan, too. He does a dangerous job and I am so proud of both of them. We made it together. Fuck everything else." She moved, and he clenched his teeth against the powerful surge of sensation. "But I got here because of you, Alyssa."

He met her eyes, his face contorting with raw emotion as she came fully into his arms, fusing herself flush against him. His face pressed against her neck, he hung on to her, grateful—God, so grateful—for her. "No one else could get me there."

Making a choked sound, she tightened her arms around him and turned her face into the curve of his neck, her voice watery. "All I want is to be with you, Thorn. I came here to tell you that I turned down the position and I'm resigning my commission and leaving the Army completely."

He held her with all the love and strength he could muster. Finally she drew a hard breath.

"I'm doing this for us," she whispered brokenly. "I want to be there for you when you come home, handle things so you don't have to worry about anything and can focus on saving the world. She cupped his face, caressing his face, her heart in her eyes. "Because there is no doubt in my heart that I love you more than life itself." He hugged her hard, holding her so tightly, so grateful. "That's the way I can continue to serve my country. I'm doing it for me, too. I thought I had to somehow fill my brother's shoes. Do what he would have done, to make his death mean something."

"You are enough exactly as you are, babe. It doesn't matter what your dad thinks."

"I know that now." She smiled and it was the most beautiful thing to him. "All my life my father's been dictating to me who I should be. I couldn't be the son he lost because I am the daughter he has left. He is the one who has to reconcile that, not me. I've done the work and I don't need commissions and a uniform to seek my own path. All I need is you, our charity and my clinic. I love you, Thorn Hunt, so goddamned much that the thought of not being with you brings me physical pain. You're my one and only, my warrior, my man, and I pledge to support you and protect you forever."

His chest was so full of her and he'd never been this happy in his life. "Then move in with me, Alyssa. I love you more than I could ever express. I need you in my life." He didn't know how he would have gotten through the loss of

Echo if it hadn't been for Alyssa and her pushy, know-it-all attitude. He'd needed a swift kick and she'd given him one.

She gave a soft, shaky laugh, caressing his face.

Shifting her so that she was on her back, he braced his weight on his elbows on either side of her head, holding her face between his hands. He stroked her cheek with his thumb. "Is that a yes?"

"Um...yes, that's a yes..." She swallowed hard and smoothed her hands up his back, her eyes filling with tears. "...on one condition."

"Name it," he said, brushing his mouth over hers. He wasn't sure how much longer he could keep his hands off her.

"You and Bronte be my spokesperson and spokesdog."

He threw his head back and laughed.

"Spokesdog? I can one hundred percent say I'm your man, but I'll have to ask Bronte about that."

As he dropped his mouth to hers, he was always aware that they were missing a team member. *We're coming for you, Blue. Don't give up.*

Tank had surrendered to Alyssa and let control go. Blue knew what he was talking about. *Be the fish* was his cryptic message, and Tank finally got it. A fish swims in a sea he cannot control, but has no illusion of control. He just swims with the flow, dealing with it as it comes. He would do exactly that. He'd immerse himself in the experience, live each moment and try not to control the outcome, but deal with the flow as it came.

BLUE STARED at the space between his feet, watching water drip off his hands and puddle between his bare feet. The soles of his feet were raw from being forced to walk the length of the cell for half the day. They were either dunking his head under water or prodding him through the cell bars with a baseball bat to walk and keep moving. His body hurt from all the jabs, and once he'd grabbed the wood and yanked hard, smacking his tormentor's face against the bars. The guy now had a broken nose.

That got him no food or water, and he was running out of stamina to fight back. Which is what they wanted. He hadn't slept in at least forty hours. Or was it thirty? Time meant nothing except a string of minutes stretched with pain. His clothing was soaked, but nothing mattered right now.

The anguish at seeing Elena gunned down was balled up and shoved into a place he refused to open. He called it his guilt box.

He barely found the strength to keep his head upright. It thumped against the wall.

His brain was fuzzy, time and day lost in his disorientation, and his stomach rolled loosely. No light came into this dark place. The light that had beautiful blonde hair had been snuffed out.

He tried to use his sleeve to wipe off the dirt on his hands. In the dark it looked like blood, and even in the back of his mind where sanity still existed, he knew he was in a state of delirium.

They'd taken everything.

The tall doors opened and some light penetrated the darkness. Men came in and dragged him out of the cell. They sat him in a chair, tied his hands, and his head lolled. Fear ripped down his spine. There was a syringe and the needle pricked his arm.

He barely registered it.

"Tell me your government's plans."

He laughed softly. He had no memories for them to access.

He blacked out, and when he woke up, he was being dragged between two men. He was in a different location and he shivered with the cold. They hauled him through ornate doors that closed behind him with a great, terrible boom.

Many people thought hell was hot.

But they were wrong.

It was cold. Very, very cold.

EPILOGUE

Tank paced in Jordan's hospital room, waiting for them to take him into the operating room for exploratory surgery. Alyssa grabbed his hand and forced him to sit.

"That's not going to make them move any faster."

Tank scowled at her.

"That's not going to help either."

Jordan crunched on ice and played his handheld video game. He looked up. "She's right," he said.

As if on cue, the doctor walked into the room, and she looked grimmer than she'd ever had. Tank's gut churned. What now?

"Mr. Hunt. You don't have cancer."

There was complete silence in the room. Tank's anxiety deflated like a balloon. "What did you just say?"

"It seems that when you went in for your stomach distress, and had your blood test, there was an unfortunate incident. Your records were mixed up with someone else's. You don't need any more tests or any kind of treatment... well, except for an antacid."

"What?" Jordan said again.

"Antacid. You had heartburn the day you came into the ER. Bad heartburn, but not terminal."

"It was a mix up. I don't have cancer?"

"No, you're very healthy."

"Thank you. Can I go home now?"

"Yes, you'll be discharged and there won't be any charges for today. I'm sorry about all the tests," she said. "I can't waive those, but I can waive my fees. Take care, Mr. Hunt, and I apologize once again for the mix-up."

Tank got up and leaned across the bed and hugged his brother hard.

IT WAS a typical Southern California day: sunny, mild, perfect for a charity softball game.

"Batter up," Alyssa shouted. Two teams. Nine players each. Ruckus was one team captain and Wicked was the other. The stands were full of patrons who had paid to see them play. All the proceeds would go to her MWDF charity.

Alyssa was up to bat first with Ruckus pitching. He had a mean fastball, but she'd grown up with all kinds of sports under her belt. She wasn't intimidated. Dana, his wife, was at first base, Dan on second, with Cowboy holding tight at third. Dragon was right field, Hollywood left field with plenty of ribbing, and Scarecrow center. Tank was catching, and Paige was at shortstop.

Alyssa's team was up by one run.

Ruckus put one over the plate. Becca made chicken noises and called it foul.

Ruckus shook his head. "Ump, you need glasses."

"Don't make me throw you out of the game, mister," she said, looking cute in her mask.

"You tell him, honey," Dan called from second.

"Whose side you on?" Ruckus groused.

"I don't have to go home with you." Dan grinned.

There had been plenty of trash talking and shenanigans, like Tank lifting people off base so they could be tagged. The second inning was not exactly pro ball. The opposition team was made up of Kid on first, Alyssa pitching, Jordan hugging second, Kia on third. Wicked in right field, Pirate in center and Hemingway, Paige's little brother, at left. Sara Campbell, Dana's boss, was at shortstop, and she'd proved to be quite the baseball player. Alyssa hadn't missed how hard it was for Jordan to keep his eyes on the ball and off the beautiful reporter.

She got another sheer wash of joy knowing that Jordan was not only going to become a vet, but when he graduated, he was going to partner with Alyssa.

The afternoon progressed, and the two teams battled it out. In the final inning, the score tied with two down, Tank hit a clean line drive to right field. Deciding they had to use any tactic at their disposal to stop him, the outfield swept in and brought him down in a gang tackle as he rounded second base, then tried to hold him down so he could be tagged. The outcome was an infield brawl, with Tank finally making it to third with Alyssa on his back.

Hollywood came to bat, pointing with an obvious warning to the backfield fence with his bat. Grinning at Alyssa with an open dare, looking so damn handsome it should be outlawed, he told her she'd better deliver the best she had. She suckered him on the first pitch, but he suckered the whole team on the second. They expected a hit deep in center field. He delivered a perfectly placed bunt that brought in the winning run.

Back at his...their house, Tank flipped burgers and guys drank beers calling out their orders. A volleyball net had been set up, and a group of people had started a game.

There was squealing, and someone held up Becca's hand. Dan called out, "Becca and I are engaged." There were hoots and congratulations in a raucous chorus. He shook his head. "Pretty crazy, right?" Jordan said as he hooked Tank around the neck.

"I never saw that relationship coming. But what the hell...they love each other." He wasn't going to let the fact that he'd boffed his brother's soon to be wife bother him...much.

"I know we've had our differences, but you were here for me every step of the way." Jordan glanced a Dan and Becca holding each other and smiling and talking. "Here for both of us. We're brothers. That's all that matters."

Tank grinned when he saw Sarah looking at Jordan. With his acceptance into the University of San Diego, he was on his way and maybe something was brewing for him with Dana's pretty boss. "Someone has her eye on you, little man."

He squeezed Tank's neck and said, "Who you calling little?"

Tank laughed as Jordan let him go and headed for Sarah. Tank walked over to the two lovebirds. "Congratulations you two," he said, hugging them both.

Alyssa showed up beside him and grabbed Tank's hand, her eyes sparkling. "Could you excuse us," she said to Dan and Becca." She looked up at him, giving him a soft kiss. "I have something for you."

He looked at her quizzically but allowed her to draw

him down the driveway to the front of the house. Ruckus got out of the car, a huge grin on his face.

He went to the back door and opened it.

Echo, who had been lying down on the back seat, sat up. Tank's throat closed up when he saw his buddy. A tremor coursed through him, the rush of emotion so intense it was almost unbearable, and he clenched his jaw against it, his eyes growing moist.

There was a collective sound of surprise from everyone who was riveted by Tank's reaction. He stared at Echo, then turned to Alyssa. God, but he loved her. So much. So very much. Tank drew a deep, painful breath as he grabbed her and hugged her hard. She slid her hand up the back of his neck with infinite tenderness. Pressing his forehead to hers, he whispered. "Thank you."

"He's yours. I put in for adoption and I'll care for him when you're deployed. He'll have the home you always wished for him."

Moved beyond words, he blinked away his tears.

Echo made a half bark, half whine as he jumped down from the vehicle. He recognized Tank, and there wasn't a dry eye in the group as he started to run/limp across the lawn to get to Tank.

He rushed forward and went to his knees as the joyous dog danced around him. Other than Blue home safe and sound, he had everything he could ever want.

Later that night as they lay together in bed, Echo taking up the end, Tank said, "You're going to regret letting him sleep with us. He's a bed hog."

Her eyes twinkled. "I think the first night it's not going to hurt."

Echo might move a little slower, but he still got around pretty damn well, a testament to his determination and to

Alyssa's skill in patching him up. And better yet, he was home to stay.

In the days that followed, they went on with their routine until Tank was summoned officially to Washington where he and Echo received their medals, their family, friends, and teammates proudly watching. Tank told the President that he was just the handler. His partner had saved all those lives, including Tank's. Echo was the true hero.

As they were drifting off, Tank's cell phone buzzed. He grabbed it and looked at the display. This was the alert he was waiting for. Alyssa woke, her voice groggy. "Blue?"

"Yes. We're going after him."

"Call me when you can. We'll be here when you get back."

As he drove to the base, gathered what he needed, got Bronte, and headed for the airfield, Tank had no doubt that they were going to find him and rescue him. Then he would come home, too. To Echo and his growing family. To his beautiful, warm, and giving Alyssa.

Look for *Blue*, the next book in the SEAL Team Alpha series. Blue's in the enemy's hands and SEAL Team Alpha will have to pull out all the stops to rescue him. What will Blue have to endure? Will he lose himself in his trauma and grief? And will his healing get a boost from the most exotic and forbidden woman he's ever met?

GLOSSARY

- BUD/S - Basic Underwater Demolitions/SEAL training
- Comm - The equipment that SEALs use to communicate with each other in the field.
- CO - Commanding Officer
- DoD - Department of Defense
- DZ - Drop zone, the targeted area for parachutists.
- HALO - High altitude, low opening jump from an aircraft.
- HVT - High value target
- IED - Improvised Incendiary Device
- Klicks - Shortened word for kilometers.
- LRRP - Long-range reconnaissance patrol.
- LT - Nickname for lieutenant.
- LZ - Landing Zone where aircraft can land.
- Merc - Mercenary - guns for hire.
- MWD - Military Working Dog
- MRE - Meals, Ready-to-Eat, portable in pouches

and packed with calories, these packaged meals are used in the field.

- NATO - North Atlantic Treaty Organization
- NCIS - Naval Criminal Investigative Service
- NWU - Navy Working Uniform
- RIB - Rigid Inflatable Boat
- RPG - Rocket Propelled Grenade
- R&R - Rest and Relaxation
- Tango -Hostile combatants.
- SERE -Stands for survival, evasion, resistance, escape. The principles of avoiding the enemy in the field.
- Six - Military speak for watching a man's back.

ABOUT THE AUTHOR

Zoe Dawson lives in North Carolina, one of the friendliest states in the US. She discovered romance in her teens and has been spinning stories in her head ever since. Her heroes are sexy males with a disregard for danger and whether reluctant, gung-ho, or caught up in the action, show their hearts of gold.

Her imagination runs wild with romances from sensual to scorching including romantic comedy, new adult, romantic suspense, small town, and urban fantasy. Look below to explore the many avenues to her writing. She believes it's all about the happily ever afters and always will.

Sign up so that you don't miss any new releases from Zoe: Newsletter.

You can find out more about Zoe here:
www.zoedawson.com
zoe@zoedawson.com

OTHER TITLES BY ZOE DAWSON

Romantic Comedy

Going to the Dogs series

Leashed #1, Groomed #2

Hounded #3, Collared #4

Piggy Bank Blues #5, Holding Still #6

Louder Than Words #7 What Matters Most #8

Going to the Dogs Wedding Novellas

Fetched #1, Tangled #2

Handled #3, Captured #4

Novellas (the complete series)

Romantic Suspense

SEAL Team Alpha

Ruckus #1, Kid Chaos #2

Cowboy #3

New Adult

Hope Parish Novels

A Perfect Mess #1, A Perfect Mistake #2

A Perfect Dilemma #3, Resisting Samantha #4

Handling Skylar #5, Sheltering Lawson #6

Hope Parish Novellas

Finally Again #1, Beauty Shot #2

Mark Me #3, Novellas 1-3 (the complete series)

A Perfect Wedding #4, A Perfect Holiday #5

A Perfect Question #6, Novellas 4-6 (the complete series)

Maverick Allstars series

Ramping Up #1

Small Town Romance

Laurel Falls series

Leaving Yesterday #1

Urban Fantasy

The Starbuck Chronicles

AfterLife #1

Erotica

Forbidden Plays series

Playing Rough #1, Hard Pass #2, Illegal Motions #3

Made in the USA
Monee, IL
08 June 2022